GW00536609

The Househusband

Also by Christine Park

JOINING THE GROWN-UPS

CHRISTINE PARK

The Househusband

HEINEMANN · LONDON

William Heinemann Ltd
Michelin House, 81 Fulham Road, London SW3 6RB
LONDON MELBOURNE AUCKLAND

First published 1989

British Library Cataloguing in Publication Data

Park, Christine, 1942–
The househusband
I. Title
[illegible]

ISBN 0–434–57742–1

Photoset and printed in Great Britain by
Redwood Burn Limited, Trowbridge, Wiltshire

To dear friends:

Gundy, Andrew, and Freddy

Acknowledgements

I'd like to thank Jim Pye for his valuable help at a crucial point in the book's development, and my daughter Nira – for just being herself.

Late Summer and Autumn

TONY TURNS to the girl who is abreast of him on the path.

'All she does is weep,' he says. 'Weep, weep, weep, it drives me crazy.'

Alex laughs her special laugh, half embarrassed, as if she cannot quite understand why the world is pulling her in, half friendly. Then she walks on, ahead of him, out of hearing of the little girl's sobs.

Her pace is a fast one. She moves with a limpid grace, holding her lithe body upright and subtle, her legs making long and determined strides, a movement which is as unhalted in its execution as the man's she has just passed, struggling with his children, is jerky. She is dressed in an orange T-shirt – showing still on this October day the summer's tan on her arms and neck – and in faded blue jeans with a number of patches and other worn places which haven't been darned. On her feet are orange suede boots way up her calves, unsuitable for striding over the Heath, but in such bad state are they it is apparent that it isn't the first time she has used them for this purpose.

Moving his attention from the crying child in her push-chair, and after having turned around to locate her elder brother, who is lagging behind, Tony enjoys one last glimpse of the girl as she disappears down a densely wooded path. A good sight, he thinks. It momentarily cheers his spirit. Seconds later she has passed out of his mind.

She too carries the image of the man with her for a moment or two. Walking on the Heath on a sunny day, and indeed how sunny it is today, is like that: the whole world seems to be out and about. Every type and kind you could imagine. Families, lovers, kids, weirdos, picnickers, sunbathers, joggers, acrobats, a trumpeter, the kite flyers, fishermen, boat sailers, any and every kind – God, the conversations you catch wisps of. It's something, it really is. Miseries, solitaries, cranks, the lot. If they're striking or say something funny or interesting you concentrate on them for a time, then you pass on. All the world here on the Heath today.

And why not? Why not indeed. What kind of a crazy day is it to be inside?

A brilliant day. A-mazing. Hot, so hot. Not hot like Greece, but hot enough. Hot enough to lie down in the grass and get mesmerised by the colour of the leaves as the sun drains down on you, and just give yourself up to it. She remembers the advert: when the leaves turn golden, so can you. And a picture of Greece. But here on the Heath today – you don't have to get on a plane. Or spend any amount of money. You can just lie down and give yourself up to it.

Despite this, she keeps walking. And walking fast so that she's like a brand new sports car in the outside lane. She will not lie down on the grassy ridge above a pond that she has come to, with its water-lilies and red-brick viaduct at the far end – such a serious bridge for a small pond. She will not lie down because she is eighteen, and alone: self-conscious, even vulnerable. Though she will not admit any of this to herself. She tells herself that she prefers to keep on the move. She looks at other people lying down, lapping up the sun, and even pauses for half a second; but no, on she moves.

As she looks at others, they of course look at her. She is accustomed to being stared at, has strengthened herself against cat-calls and wolf-whistles which two years before had taken her by surprise and left her feeling invaded and exposed. Now she has adopted a way of raising her chin ever so slightly and holding her eyes level. Keeping them composed, dead, not showing fear. A certain appearance of coolness which allows her to move on her way, unimpeded, with the cat-calls receding behind her.

Strange then that she has not reacted in that way to the man with his weeping child. He'd looked directly at her as she passed him, wide pale-blue eyes, so personal, as if he knew her. It wasn't at all a pick-up kind of thing, more as if it was born out of an impulse, a kind of 'help me', like other people she knew projected; that's usually when she gave that smile, half friendly half as if – even with her family – 'what's it got to do with me?' Fuck, not a good line of thought. Move off, move off on to something else.

Tony and his children make altogether a more leisurely path. The thicket which they enter (and out of which many moments before Alex has passed) entails the ups and downs of a switchback at a fair to the little girl who sits huddled up in her canvas seat, sucking one corner of the faded pink blanket which covers her bare untanned knees. And to her brother, Timothy Martin (Moth), who trails behind collecting sticks and saying every now and again to his apparently unhearing Daddy, 'We've come an *awful* long way, haven't we Daddy,' each ridge seems like a mountain: it is fun running down but not climbing up.

'Moth, what are you doing?'

'Stopping.'

'Don't stop there, you silly, you're blocking the path.'

'You carry me.'

'I can't do that and push, you know that.'
'Leave the push-chair, then.'
'Don't be a silly.'
'I'm not a silly.'
'Moth, please . . .' Tony holds out his hand to his son. Somewhere along the line he is aware that he shouldn't be pleading with him. He sighs, looking back along the path to where the boy is sitting in a hollow. Yellow leaves sailing down from the trees fall on him and around him. A potential magical sight, his small son in dappled sunlight on a golden autumn day. But for Tony the day could be the colour of the snot running out of the child's nose. Meanwhile, beside him, she keeps up with her noise, the constant backgroup, weep, weep weep.
'Moth, climb as far as here, then I'll pull you up the rest of the way.' He stretches out his arm to his son, hoping there is sufficient authority in his tone to overcome the child's obstinacy. Miraculously, Moth gets up and makes his way towards his father.
'That's better. Now, you hold my hand tight and I'll pull you up this last bit.' The push-chair in front, manoeuvred with one hand, the little boy behind, they proceed. Once they reach the level, he suggests they find a bench and sit down for a while. Moth doesn't want to.
'But if you're tired, we should rest.'
'I'm tired 'cause I want to go home.'
'You're right, perhaps we'll all feel better when we get home.'
'Ellen won't.'
'She won't?'
'She wants her Mummy.'
'Come on Moth, this path is much smoother. Look, it's downhill all the way to the ponds, then flat after that. We'll be home in no time at all. Tell you what, we'll get a bus when we leave the Heath, how would you like that?'
'We'll have to wait,' says the boy flatly.
'Yes, but . . .'
'We'll have to wait.' It's said with finality. Why do the grown-ups pretend? Who are they kidding? When you're a schoolboy and it's been like this for some time, you know what the score is. And, after all, six is very big compared to Ellen. But I wish she'd shut up.
The trio walk along without more communication for a while.

Alex speeds round the lower parameters of Kenwood. She sees the house in the distance. Today the intensity of the light makes it even more brilliantly white than usual. Shall she cross the lawn and go up onto its terraces? No, today she will stay in the wooded area, by the ponds, perhaps cross the small bridge to the place where the concerts are held in summer, then out again into the wilder open spaces. The lawns in front of Kenwood look too formal for a day such as this. And too crowded, though it's a weekday. You do call Friday a weekday, don't you? Or perhaps not, in Hampstead. Think of her mother and her . . . her . . . well for God's sake call him her step-father, it's so much easier. What would one have her say? She's tried them all: 'My mother's common-law husband,' what a mouthful. 'My mother's C.L.H.' 'Your what!' 'My mother's partner.' 'Sounds like some kind of business deal to me.' 'My mother's lover.' 'She's a one, isn't she!' 'Oh look, can't we just discuss something else, please?'

All that crowd, the hours they work, you'd hardly know if it was weekdays or weekends or what it was. But they're pretty weird. Most people, unless they're on the dole, or studying, or looking after kids or something, they're at work. You wouldn't think so here. I like it, it's good – though the lawns look boring. Backtrack then, out of Kenwood, find that wide path again if I can, and then off it onto the one where I found those mushrooms?

Doing a loop inside Kenwood she leaves it by the same gate that she'd entered. It is about four-thirty. In the density of the woods the light loses some of its brightness. When she veers off the main path she finds herself quite alone. Fuck, it doesn't really matter. Just keep walking determinedly. Now *he* looks a bit crazy. But then one's bound to think that. It's never the ones you suspect, anyway. You can't tell. They're going to look normal, those people, I suppose. They're not going to look crazy. I could turn left here. That would get me back onto the main path. On the other hand, then I'll miss the mushroom tree. On the other hand they've probably all been picked anyway, or ruined; that's life.

'Go on, run ahead,' says Tony to his son. 'Why don't you run to where those boats are being sailed? It's downhill all the way so your legs will just carry you if you get going.'

Instead, Moth dawdles behind. Some grown-ups always have the wrong ideas. Mummy on the other hand . . . The moment he says it he feels disloyal. But however hard he tries, one thought prompts another. She said she'd be back early tonight; she promised. On the other hand, how early is early? That it would be when they got back from the walk, he doubts; she's never got back that early. Not even when he had measles, or when he fell off the climbing frame at nursery school and bonked his head and Dad took him to hospital, she'd still had to stay at work, because so many important people needed her, she'd said. And he had thought but how could anyone be more important to her than him? Still, he hadn't minded as much then. Though he had minded. Everyone else seemed to have a mummy who picked them up after school. Miles and miles of mummies, of all different shapes and colours and things and all smelling good and smiling and he had a dad who didn't smell – well, didn't smell so comforting. But he had smelt more comforting those times with the measles and him going to hospital. He'd kept holding his hand all the way in the ambulance and saying nice things. But now he never seems to say anything nice, he never seems to notice. It just isn't the same.

He'd asked Mummy, 'Is Dad sad 'cause I'm more bad now?'

'No, it's not that at all. You're not bad, are you?'

'Is he sad 'cause Ellen cries?'

'All babies cry.'

She was so bright, making a joke of it all, tickling him so that he wriggled off her lap, and she said, 'You just pop upstairs and into that bath I've run and I'll be up in five minutes to scrub your back. Then afterwards we'll make a big surprise for the others, eh?'

'Just you and me?'

'Just you and me, my little man.'

How could he spoil it all by asking her *why* is Daddy sad? And instinct told him that even if he asked, his question would go unanswered.

Now he is thinking, perhaps if he can while away the time for hours and hours, then perhaps, by some magic, Mummy will be at home when they get there. From his position at an angle to the path he stares at the profile of his father's face, at the droop of his moustache, the large pale-blue eyes looking vacantly, then he darts away into the trees thinking to find the largest one he can to hide behind.

As Alex rounds the corner and into sight of the tree where the mushrooms grow, Tony, having walked some way deep in thought, suddenly becomes aware that his son is neither with him nor trailing behind anywhere in sight. Moth, meanwhile, bored of counting the moments hiding behind the tree, squatting down, begins to concentrate on the bracken, the long grasses, the feathery ferns growing beneath its roots. Separating them, he discovers three mushrooms, so red they look like a colour from his paintbox, but enormous, the size of a night-light. He imagines them lit up; red for danger, red in traffic-lights stop, they are doing road safety at school, red flags, red rag at a bull, blood is red, but red is a nice colour too, the best, red buses, red pyjamas, red sunsets, Mummy always gets excited then, she loves the sky like that, his friend Seth's red setter, red deer, no, reindeer. Father Christmas's gown, that was this kind of red, soon it would be Christmas. Quite soon. Mummy said, 'Every year people talk about it earlier: spare *me*.' But Moth had laughed, he thought she was teasing, he didn't think she'd be spared. 'We will have stockings, won't we, we will have presents?'

'What do you think, Tony, shall they have presents?'

'You're the boss.'

'Of course there'll be presents, Moth, and maybe we'll go and see Father Christmas at Selfridges.'

'When? Next week?'

'It's only October, you chump.'

Both of them had started calling him a chump, a silly. 'When then?'

'December. The Christmas month . . . if I'm not too busy. Otherwise Daddy can take you.'

Moth had looked across at Daddy and known that that would be it. The two of them in Selfridges like before, except that this year there would be Ellen in her push-chair crying and crying, and it wouldn't be the same as going with Mummy, not one bit. Why couldn't she see that? Yet he wouldn't say that he didn't want to go because he did, even with all those people there and Daddy's long face. He wanted to go because he wanted to touch Father Christmas's robe, to look at his white beard and into his eyes and make up his mind once and for all whether he was or he wasn't Father Christmas. Because Seth had recently told him something unbelievable. He wasn't going to ask Mummy or Daddy. And Ellen was just a baby. There was no one to ask, he was going to make up his own mind. In . . . December, whenever that was.

In the meantime, there are these mushrooms and whether it is just the colour or what, there is a strong connection with Father Christmas's robe, that red, that magic, which compels him suddenly to wet two fingers and stretch them out towards the shiny domes.

As he is about to put the fingers into his mouth someone dives towards him and catches his arm.

'Stop . . . Daddeee! Get off! Let go!'

'If you promise not to touch them and not to put your hand in your mouth. They're very, very dangerous.'

'I don't believe you.'

'It's the truth. You'd be sick and it would be horrid. You might even have to go to hospital to have it all pumped out with a stomach pump.'

'Let go of my arm.'

'Will you promise then?'

He nods. Alex lets go of his hand. In order to pin his arm down she has thrown herself awkwardly on the ground and now takes a moment to adjust her position and brush a number of thistle-heads off her jeans. Where are his parents, she wonders? Moth, meanwhile, is tantalised by her words. From a place which isn't a place of reason but of instinct he sees a way in which he can draw attention back to himself. He grabs the mushrooms and darts off up the hill.

Damn! She jumps to her feet. Her fashionable suede boots aren't made for running in. She believes him even at this minute to be biting into the mushrooms, why should she care but she does. He is streaking ahead. She can see she won't catch him. She looks round wildly for anyone who might claim responsibility for the kid. No one. But there is a guy with a dog . . . 'Look that kid has got some poisonous mushrooms, could you . . ., quick, I can't . . .?' The man and the dog set off obligingly after Moth. Alex trails behind, watching the gap being closed. She doesn't even know why she is running any more but keeps on over the grass and up the hill in the wake of the others. She hasn't any idea what she's going to do when she catches up with them.

Meanwhile, Tony, having left Ellen (shrieking now at being so abandoned) with a family by the boat pond, is retracing his steps up the path, calling for his son as he does so. He is cursing, calling and muttering, I thought he said he wanted to get home quickly, what is he playing at? If anything happens to Moth today, I don't think I could cope, I have had it up to here. I just. No one knows what it's like. And all these bloody women, they do it so simply. Or do they? And some men do, of course. And I used to. I used to think. Christ, I just don't know what's happening to me. 'Moth, Moth, where are you?'

As he climbs higher up the path, other people seem to be gazing towards the top of the hill. So he looks too, shading his eyes against the brightness of the setting sun. And blinks. For there is that girl again, and others, chasing, it appears, his son. Too far away to tell but it looks like his son. He stands stock-still for a moment. And all of a sudden energy returns. He sets off at a run to catch up with the girl.

As she sees him coming up beside her she recognises him, and again that half smile, not unfriendly, as if she doesn't like to be involved but apparently is.

'The boy . . .' she says, panting as she runs, '. . . poisonous mushrooms.'

'Moth, oh no!'

'Ah, *your* son?'

'Yes, of course.'

Moth has been caught and surrounded. Alex and Tony draw up to the outer circle of the group that has been attracted by the commotion. Tony pushes his way through. 'What are you thinking of?' He grabs Moth's shoulder and shakes him.

'I didn't know, I didn't know,' lies Moth. He tries not to cry, crying is for Ellen. On the other hand, so many people, he wishes they would go away. His father is talking to the tall man with the dog. 'Thank you so much, you managed to get hold of the mushrooms, he didn't put any in his mouth, did he?'

'No, he handed them over.'

'All of them, Moth?' Tony asks.

Moth looks at him solemnly and nods.

From the edge of the circle Alex says, 'Are you absolutely sure you didn't keep just one in your pocket?'

'Dad, I just kept one very little one to show Seth, that's okay, isn't it?'

'No, Christ, it isn't. Here, I'd better take it.'

Moth gingerly puts his hand in his pocket and brings out the bright-red mushroom. Some of the crowd peer forward to see what the fuss has been about.

'*Agaricus muscaria*,' says Alex. Then she laughs as if she shouldn't have spoken. She turns on her orange heels and begins to stride away across the grass. Following her example, the crowd starts to disperse. Tony, grabbing Moth's hand, sets off at a run after Alex.

'Wait a moment . . .' He catches up with her. She stops and looks from one to the other, from father to son. He cannot think what it is he wants to say to her. 'Thanks.'

'No, it was nothing, I just noticed . . .' She shrugs her shoulders, diffident, uncertain. 'Well then, got to go . . .' Yet again that half laugh.

How do people make contact? What are you doing by yourself on the Heath? What am I doing? What are any of us doing? What is it about? How old are you? Do you know that your orange boots are now caked with mud at the heels? Do you mind? What are you going back to? What am I going back to? you ask. A tip on the Kentish Town Road, it needn't be a tip, it wasn't a tip once upon a time, it's just that we let it get that way, with the kids and no money and she says she hasn't the energy to do anything about it, neither of us have the energy though for different reasons. You'd have the energy, I'm sure of that. I'd like you to come back there, despite it being a tip, and give the kids their tea with me until she comes home. It would be so much less cheerless. Yes crazy isn't it but that's what I'd like, your orange boots even with the mud on them – for that wouldn't make a darn bit of difference – in our front room.

'Have you really got to go?'

'Yeah, I have. Why?'

'Well, frankly, I'm desperate.'

Zoonks! His large pale-blue eyes look directly into hers, it's the same look that he gave her when she first passed him and he said about the baby weeping. Where was the baby incidentally? Hope he hasn't forgotten about the other one now, left *her* somewhere. The same look, an uncannily direct contact, and yet somewhere in the core of that look, despite its appeal, despite the words he was using, desperation and all that, she senses that he isn't desperate mad, she senses, trusts to a kind of normality. Eighteen. She trusts herself and her assessments. Just beginning. Budding, needing adventures, able to take up a kind of challenge that someone more world-weary, more cautious, would recoil from. Eighteen, in the peak of health, resounding with a kind of physical energy that it doesn't take much perception on his part to note. It is there in the speed of her walk, the vitality of her hair, the gleam beneath her make-up, or maybe she has none on at all, maybe that is the colour of her skin, the colour of her cheeks. At a stage when from wounds the body will heal, almost certainly, a cut will not be visible a second day, a broken bone will mend with speed, a cough or cold hardly worth remarking on, an upset stomach, a matter only of half an hour's violent retching followed by hours of deep sleep. So too with the emotions. And as far as her own go, in the way that body and spirit are tied together, her energy, her life line, whatever one likes to call it, propels her forward, encourages her not to be cautious as if she can afford something, where perhaps an older person might be more unwilling. And especially on the Heath.

'I dunno. Where's the baby, by the way?'

'Ellen? Oh God, I left her with people over there – they must be wondering.'

'You'd better collect her.'

'Yes. Won't you . . .'

'What?'

'Walk with me, just as far as the boat pond. Or is it, I expect it is, in quite the wrong direction?'

She is on the part of the Heath she calls the crown. From there down to the ponds is open land. The light already suggests the onset of early evening. People in all directions are turning homewards but there are still plenty around. She will walk with him as requested, what the hell.

'C'mon then.' She turns to the boy. 'With all that running you must be out of breath. You're so fast; I bet you win all the races at school.'

'Some.'

'What school do you go to?'

'Elliot.'

'I babysit for kids from there. I wonder if you're in the same class. How old are you – about six?'

Moth nods.

They are getting along famously.

Meanwhile, Tony has time to collect himself. To get this far, to get her to walk down the hill with him, has demanded something enormous. He is still reeling from its effects. He is aware of his own escalating and debilitating loss of confidence this last twelve months. To a point where it has almost seemed no longer possible to ask anything for himself, lest it should be refused. He doesn't hear what the girl is saying. The state of his need rattling around inside him is too noisy to allow him to concentrate fully on what is going on. He is only aware that between him and his son is the girl. That the two are talking and the conversation appears to be flowing naturally. That he is no longer alone with Moth's impossibly inexplicit demands. That he is buffeted by this second adult presence. Though as yet she has hardly said a word to him.

*

Carole is winding down at the office. She has told her secretary that she wants to leave at five-thirty prompt, that she has made a promise to that effect to her son. But the secretary, though she smiles at Carole, agreeing with her, knows better. She has worked for Carole for six months and wonders what her family life is like. Because it doesn't take a particularly observant eye to be aware that Carole is one of those who usually puts off departing for home. Oh yes, she is full of good intentions, but somehow she seems to hang around the office asking for these intentions to be ambushed. Like tonight.

Tonight Sarah and her boyfriend are going to a film and, since the office is near the cinema, Sarah's boyfriend will pick her up here at seven o'clock. Meanwhile, she goes to the Ladies and takes ages with her make-up, then comes back and toys with the papers on her desk. Today's letters are franked and ready to go. There is just the one to the Italian publisher; she reads it off her pad, but cannot make head or tail of what Carole has dictated. She could ask her tomorrow, or now when there isn't any kind of rush on. Sure as hell Carole would oblige. She has that kind of a reputation. Good with her staff. Fair. Encourages you to work off your own bat and doesn't try to keep you down, like some.

Carole is Rights Manager. Sarah had written to the firm on spec specifying editorial. Hot out of an English department, with all sorts of ideas about the developing shape of literature, Rights sounded more like business than anything else. But once she met Carole and heard about the imminent shift in Carole's own career – the editorial director was leaving and Carole was to take over the job – Sarah felt comforted.

However, with the change-over came all number of complications. The outgoing editorial director, a major figure in the British publishing scene, left, taking with her not only a number of authors about whom she and the MD had come to an agreement, but many others about whom they had not. The drain on the firm was much greater than had been anticipated. Every week another one or two authors left. One never knew who would be next.

Was the magnetic personality of the departing editor such a strong lure? Or was it that the authors lacked confidence in the situation at A&P? For, mysteriously, Carole was no longer going to step into the outgoing editor's shoes. The staff were told that someone was coming in from outside. The identity of this person was kept quiet, though naturally all number of rumours circulated.

Meanwhile, in the period between the outgoing editor's departure and the arrival of the new incumbent, Carole has taken on a dual role. And Sarah, despite initial feelings of keen disappointment, has thrown herself into supporting the older woman as best she can.

From Carole's point of view the greatest challenge has been the editorless authors, who need constant reassurance. Today has been typical. Johanna Cohen, whose first novel they'd published last year, just wanting to come in to make contact. The phrase is beginning to sound ominous. Carole has been held up over lunch and by the time she returns to the office she is met by an anxious Sarah who tells her that Johanna has been waiting twenty minutes.

Carole sails into her office and when she sees Johanna's hurt – why aren't I important to you? – look, apologizes for being late; but she does not think it comes across sufficiently graciously.

'Look, I need a cup of tea, can I get you – ?'

'I've already had.'

Johanna scowls at her, tense, complex, waiting. Carole knows that what she has to do is say, look, I think you're a brilliant writer, we can't wait for your next book, and other words to the same effect; she can't somehow bring herself to do it.

She buzzes Sarah. 'Sarah, love, I'll have a cup of tea if you've got a moment.' And to Johanna, 'You're sure we can't give you a second cup?'

Apparently not.

Then the phone rings and it is the call from France she has been waiting for. Putting her hand on the receiver she apologizes to Johanna and promises it will only take a moment. It doesn't. Johanna sits on, sighing from time to time. She gets up from the dinky sofa that would hardly fit two people unless they snuggled together, and wanders around the room picking up books, gazing at dustjackets, then she sits down again and crosses and uncrosses her legs. All the time her face looks more closed and unhappy.

Sarah comes back with Carole's tea. The telephone conversation comes to an end. Finally Carole turns to Johanna.

'Sorry about that, now let's get on to you.'

Who is Johanna's agent? For an awful moment it slips her mind, is it Giles or Peter? Peter, yes surely.

'Peter's been telling me about *Anarchy in the Cupboards*. I love the idea; you must tell me all about it.'

'I'd prefer not to.'

'No?'

'When you're writing, you know . . .' She is still very tense.

'I quite understand.'

Carole sips her tea. Where to next? Is there something Johanna wants to say to her, after all she's made the appointment to come in? Christ, this isn't a cocktail party. It isn't as if she hasn't enough to do. Anger begins its danger signals, she feels the arteries above her eyes pulsing ominously.

'Excuse me a moment.' She forces herself to avoid the look on Johanna's face. She heads for the toilet. Has a pee. Sitting on the seat she shuts her eyes and tries to let the tension go.

When she gets back she tells Johanna that the rough of the jacket for the paperback edition of her first novel is ready and she'll see if she can get the design department to send it up.

The jacket arrives. Johanna smiles for the first time. 'I've been so worried.'

They talk about the scheduling of the next book and that leads into how Carole feels about the change-over at A&P. She is cautious, but can feel that she is winning Johanna over. Eventually Johanna opens up and says how difficult it is to lose an editor, especially one you have been close to, how hard a shift of trust is, and Carole finds it easier to like her. She senses that Johanna is prepared to hang on, wants at least to believe that she is going to be left in good hands. At the end of the meeting the atmosphere is decidedly more upbeat than when it started.

Then there are more letters to be dictated. So Carole calls Sarah back in and that is when she dictates the letter to Italy which Sarah cannot make head or tail of.

Sarah would like to ask Carole about the letter now. The office is quiet. There is not the pandemonium of the mornings. She knows Carole will explain in full. Will have time. There is less chance of being interrupted. The work might lead to jokes, to more personal things, to a run-down on the day. All this Sarah treasures. What she would really like is to ask Carole to come across the road for a drink. And she knows that it is as likely as not that in half an hour Carole will be in the pub, persuaded by someone, even if she's said she is determined to leave at five-thirty, a deadline already past. But no, if she wants to go home, I shouldn't be the one to.

Carole is on the phone. The wind from the open window causes the door between the two offices to bang shut. Sarah pulls out of her basket the first manuscript she has induced one of the editors to let her read – outside work hours and unpaid, still, a step forwards – and looks at *The History of the Humming Bird* with awe and greed: let me get my hands on this. She is halfway down the first page when Ian Steer, the Sales Manager, bursts through the door. In the corridor she can hear the voice of the MD.

'Carole still here?'

'Yes, but she's on her way out.'

Ian, disregarding that, moves across Sarah's room.

'She has to leave, she's late already, couldn't it wait . . .?'

Ian has entered Carole's room and a moment later Charles Bruneski, the MD, follows.

At seven, when Nick calls for her, the trio of voices can be heard buzzing in the inner office. This could go on for hours, she thinks, picking up her basket and grabbing her coat, poor kid whoever he is, he doesn't see much of his mother. Glad it's not me. Then she makes a concerted attempt to turn her thoughts to Nick and the evening ahead. After all, as Nick says, you can't take it home with you, it's her burden, her life.

*

Alex sits on the bench with a scowl on her face. The pond is full of sodden leaves. The poplars reflect their tall shapes in the water. The day is overcast, so much colder than a week ago that she huddles into her blue jacket and blows on her hands. Now what the hell has she done with last year's gloves? Has she taken them downstairs or not? She cannot visualise them anywhere around the place. Shit. But the 'shit' is more directly to do with Angelica's letter. 'Angelica'! Why should she change things so artificially? Just because Alex has chosen to move into the self-contained basement of their house, to shut the door and be treated 'like any other lodger' (except of course to pay a lower rent) why should her mother suddenly stop signing herself 'Mum'? As if she was trying to make a point. It was so goddam unnecessary.

She looks through the letter again, '. . . *by the time you turned on the telly last night no doubt you hit the most boring bit and turned it off again. But do you know that Aids is increasingly becoming a heterosexual disease; and that anyone having sex with people who have had or are having* . . .' On and on and on. Two neatly typed pages. She closes her cold narrow hands – the blood showing purple through the skin – tightly round the pages and tears them swiftly into tiny bits, then throws them into the pond. Fuck, why not? There's enough litter here for more to make no difference. 'But look around you, darling, there's sure to be a litter-bin. You're never far from a litter-bin in England now. If people like us don't take a more reasonable stand then how can you expect . . .?'

It will sink; paper does. She looks at her watch: 3:45. Anyway, she never intended to sit down in the first place. She gets up and begins to walk. She is in white wellingtons, for it has rained all morning and the ground, she reckons, will be muddy. She has lain in bed in the basement, and listened to the rain. Tania had left at two, Chris later. She'd woken with a sense of having drunk too much, the smell of the others' cigarettes, the butts cold in the ashtrays, out hours ago, but the smell staler now, lingering. Upstairs, hoovering, activity. The two cats pawing at her door, but she wouldn't let them in; they were part of something she was separating herself from.

Great. A whole day with nothing particular to do.

By midday, the rain ceased. If I got up I suppose I could . . . what could I do?

White wellington boots, a blue padded jacket, the same jeans as last week, through which in the two open places the wind whistles and catches at her bare flesh. Next time, tomorrow, she'll wear tights as well. Or darn her jeans. The wind will be a plus for the kite flyers and the kids sailing their boats. It will, though, be bloody cold up there. But good to see them flying wildly, crazily. Needn't stop, can just take the path up. And then see.

She stands at the top of the hill on the level, opposite the new bronze plaque which maps visible landmarks. The speed of some of the kites makes her want to laugh aloud. A whole orchestra of kites up today. Racing, swooping, diving. Dying. Not a kid holding one. It's a day for professionals, a difficult day. A day with grit in it.

A bloke is manoeuvring two. She watches the fiery dragons do a succession of swallow dives; it looks as if the higher one will eat up the lower one. Now another, a skull and crossbones, comes crashing down at her feet. With her apologetic laugh she jumps out of the way, moving to stand near a cluster of women and children. She does not want to be talked to, only to be part of this scene. Head back she follows the path of a silver snake, released higher and higher into the sky.

The sky is beginning to make subtle changes, darkening, filling out, lowering. Will it rain again? The sounds are louder, the leaves rustling in the trees. The wind makes smacking noises with someone's scarf. The kites burr and crackle and zizz. The two held by the same owner are heading for a collision. Wait for it. They are coming down fast. The first drops of rain. All of a sudden a huge roar of wind, in which one, two, three kites come dashing down and land on the ground, quivering, then still. Spent.

If it's going to rain I don't have any kind of decision to make. Nobody sails boats in the rain. Not even crazy men.

Yet she proceeds down the hill.

It is Moth who is first aware of Alex coming towards them. They are at the far end of the pond, where he is crouching over the water. His father is deeply involved with the boat whose sailing pattern is proving erratic. He has been issuing instructions to the boy but somehow cannot give over the control of the boat and Moth is growing impatient. He looks up out of the water. First at his sister, then at the sky to see if the rain would blow away. Will the sun come out? Will they stay for a long time? Will there be a rainbow? Mummy says when the sun comes out after rain there is always a rainbow. But where is it? Or isn't the sun, a white blob behind clouds, strong enough? Then he looks over to the far side of the pond and up, up the hill. Suddenly his body is alert and bristling, his nose twitching involuntarily. Surely that is the pretty lady who . . . who . . . 'Daddy, Daddy . . .' But Tony has just moved off round the pond in order to be there when the boat sails in, and is out of earshot.

Moth thinks of running over to tell him, but doesn't. He shoves his cold hands in his pockets and looks back up the hill. The rain is getting in his eyes, making it difficult for him to see far. A moment ago it seemed to be stopping but now it's blowing across the grass in sheets. Oh, don't let it come on any worse, then she'll turn back. She might. He strains his eyes to watch her progress. Looks like her, but is it?

It is. He's sure of it now. 'Dad . . .' Still something holds him back from saying. Instead he turns to his sister and tickles her under the ribs through her pink padded coat. 'We've got a friend coming to see us today, Elly. A real friend, who held you last week, remember, and you didn't mind, did you?'

Ellen is munching a crust of stale bread, which was meant for the ducks. As Moth tickles her, her hand releases the crust, which falls to the ground. She opens her mouth to object but quick as a flash Moth returns the bread to her. There is mud on it. He doesn't notice. Her face is quite smiley. The rain is making rivers down her face which mix with the mud at the edges of her mouth.

He skips up and down. 'Maybe she'll sail my boat with me, Ellen. Maybe she'll let you sail it too.' He bends down so that his face is on a level with hers. 'Would you like that?'

Tony, at the far end of the pond, curses the rain drops. Not because they will keep the girl away. Other factors will do that. No, it is simply going to be one more of a seemingly endless run of afternoons with the children and on and on into the years ahead. There is no possible end. He tries to accept, he tries not to shout out, 'I can't, can't bear it any longer.' Or to fix someone else with the look he gave Alex and to say again 'I am desperate.' That is what his heart is saying. 'I am desperate, I am desperate.' A moan, a shout, something inhuman, persistent, more and more so.

He does not expect the girl to come and relieve the potential of the remaining part of the afternoon. Nor is he even sure that he would like it if she did. What had she been, after all, other than a more than averagely pretty female, with time on her hands – despite her protestations to the contrary. No, as he watches the toy boat's erratic progress what he thinks about is his own situation. Seven years unemployed to the day. What had seemed as if it must surely be endured for a matter of weeks before something else came up, quickly became a matter of months, then years. And now there seems no hope. 'No', is the word he wants to scream. He has a brief vision of Carole deep in conference with errant writer Tudor Balfour, 'Think of me,' she'd said; he'd mumbled something which was no longer support. She no longer expected it, he suspects. For what is between them seems increasingly mechanical. Like the kids. 'You wipe her bottom, I'll find his school book.' 'You give them their bath, I'll put on the soup.' 'You. You.'

Rage swells inexpressible, inarticulate; he grabs the boat and swings round. 'No,' he hits out, the arteries showing purple in his blotched red and white face.

'No what? It's only me. But if you don't want . . . ?'

She looks so disconcerted, so embarrassed and angry, the rain now pouring down so that she puts out her tongue and catches the raindrops off her lips, at the same time hunching her shoulders as if she would fight if she had to. Such a kid. He has to laugh.

'Well, hello there. I didn't expect you to come.'

'But you asked me, didn't you?'

Belligerently, he laughs again, this time out aloud. 'Yes, I asked you. I'm pleased you've come.' He has a desire to put his hands on her shoulders to reassure, but resists.

Moth sees Alex talking to his father and runs over, now hopping from one foot to the other, 'Alex, have you come to sail my boat?'

'What else do you think I've come for, Charlie?' She ruffles his hair.

'Oh, goody. Daddy, can we do it now . . . ?'

'Where's Ellen?' asks Alex.

'Damn it, Moth, didn't I tell you to stay right beside her?'

'You are a family for losing one another,' Alex states, calmer now. Feeling wanted.

'But she's not lost, she's over there.' They walk round the pond together, Moth taking Alex's hand. Alex is pleased, more pleased by the minute. So is Moth. Perhaps now he really will get to sail his boat.

Tony pushes Ellen's push-chair backwards and forwards. He has put up the plastic shield and, snug inside, the little girl, finished with the bread and now chewing her teddy-bear's ear, coos to herself. She is unusually contented today. Does she sense the better vibrations that Tony emanates as he pushes her back and forward, back and forward? He himself is getting wetter by the moment. He's wearing a skiing jacket (he has never ski'd but Moth's school jumble sale, plus army surplus stores and the like, are useful for clothes nowadays). The hood is not flattering. He is aware of being conscious of the girl and of deliberating. He likes his dark curly hair, though it has grown too long. Usually Carole cuts it. But feeling how he does, he has not wanted that kind of contact these last weeks, her hands on his head. In the world in which he has entrenched himself, what does it matter anyway? So he grumbled when she suggested, and she has stopped suggesting. True about many things. Still, take away the hair, encase it in the hood, and what are you left with? Whatever you're left with, I'm getting too bloody wet to go on like this any more. It's just damn stupid, can they really be enjoying this? He looks around. Of course all the other boaters have departed. Everyone else is hurrying off the Heath.

Alex, crouching by the pond with Moth, sees what is left when Tony's ski hood frames his face. A round heavy face, sharp nose, fleshy lips. The rain collects on his limp moustache and on the dark hairs that protrude from his nostrils. There are a number of what appear to be broken arteries along the lines of his cheek giving an unnaturally white and red look. His mouth is set. The whole face is drawn downwards to the jowl. God, what am I doing?

Tony watches the people scurrying off the Heath, the boat's bobbing progress, listens to his son's joyful laugh and to the instructions that every now and again Alex gives, which the boy seems to be taking so much better than if they had come from him. She is bending low, stretching out for the boat as it comes in towards the rim of the pond. Suddenly he is aware of how wet she is, her jeans sodden through. Hell, what am I doing letting her.

'Right, kids,' a jocular voice which he has put on, is saying, 'time to go, *fini*. Fun over.'

'Oh Daddy, why? We're not cold, we love the rain, don't we, Alex?'

'Nonsense.'

'You're such a spoilsport. You want to go on, don't you, Alex?'

'Well.' She stands up and makes a gesture with her back and shoulders which is non-committal. She looks at Tony, then back at Moth. 'I think your Dad's probably right. Enough is enough.'

Minutes later they are running.

I want to talk to him but it's absolutely crazy, but I've got to talk to him. I want this to go on. I don't want them to go away. I wonder if he'll ask me to his place. If he does, I'll go. No, I won't.

Running. The rain dripping down their necks, from their wrists into their jackets, through the holes in Alex's jeans down her legs, making her socks damp and her feet wet. Ellen in her push-chair is the warmest. Next, Moth in his new jacket from the hood of which his face peeps out, inquisitive, delighted. One warm wet hand is clasped in Alex's, the other holds tight to his father's free hand. This is how he likes to be, a knot of family, for that's what it feels like, running.

Alex likes it too. Wet and cold and running. Running off the Heath. I'll go with them, it's okay with the kids. Nothing will happen. It's probably okay even without the kids. She looks at the man sideways as they run, the chain of hands connecting her to him through the boy.

'Where are we going?' She manages to make him hear through the wind and rain.

'Any ideas?'

'Leave it to you.'

This too will change. Angelica's recent phrase. So many times she has taken up an intense interest in some new fad, movement or philosophy. This time it's meditation. In the last year she's been away on a number of retreats, taken lessons at Swiss Cottage library and talks about setting aside time to meditate daily, though Alex is sceptical. 'This too will change' is her recent response to any complaint of Jerry's or Alex's, as she sails through the house. Now, as Alex runs, the saying comes to her like a chant.

The wet and the cold and the hands that are hard to cling to because they keep slipping. That is why we feel so exhilarated, the pleasure of knowing we are going somewhere else, we are running to warmth, outside to inside, silence to talk, to a different space, bright, hot, intimate. Suddenly she wants crumpets. She sees herself toasting them over a fire and handing them to Tony.

The rain comes on even harder, the noise tremendous as it crashes onto the leaves and through the trees.

'This too will change,' she says to Tony.

'Come again?'

'As my mother would say.'

He can't hear, or make out. 'This is something! Do you want to try sheltering under a tree maybe?'

'Not unless you do.'

'I think it's fun,' says Moth, squeezing their hands hard.

The place is a tip, thinks Tony.

He remembers Carole saying this morning, 'Tony, I know you don't like cleaning any more than I do but just this once I . . .' She had put out her hand to him. 'There's nothing unusual about it,' he'd replied, 'you're always . . .' Their eyes met, telling each other danger signals. They had been down this avenue many times before. And Carole had to leave the house in two minutes or she'd miss her bus. That is if you believed that the bus would be on time, which Carole chose to do. So she'd stayed with her hand on his inner arm, physical contact was always the best, cooled things, diluted them, mysterious though it was, and after ten years and with all the difficulties, and him not even sleeping with her this past fortnight, yet it was still there. And the anger, the readiness for a fight went out of his eyes and he said, okay, okay, and she doubted that he would but at least she calculated he wouldn't start another day angry and take it out on the children, and off she went to work to her other world, and thank God for it, even now, even when.

Their running seems so purposeful, that is what Tony likes about it. But where are they heading? Soon they'll be at the road. He wouldn't take her back to their place. Not today. The implication of 'not today' shocks him. Anyway, he'll have to clean it up sometime, whether she comes or not, that isn't the point. But apart from it being a dump, it is too far. The point is to get out of the rain as soon as possible. As they run he takes his left hand off the push-chair and with his right, with Moth's fingers still enclasped, bends over so that his arm keeps hold of the bar. With his free hand he digs down into his coat pocket. It is the end of the week. She 'pays' him on Friday night, or, as she puts it, hands over the money for the use of the family. He won't take it from her hand. Too humiliating. It didn't start that way. When it was for only a few months it was almost a joke. He who had once been her boss. But the longer it has gone on the more difficult it has become. So now she simply sets it down in an empty tobacco tin in a mahogany cupboard that houses everything, groceries, booze – if there is any – books, documents, his precious collection of records, the lot, in the tin on the top shelf and sometime later he takes it out and neither of them talk about it unless they have to, not any more.

He feels down into his pocket and in an effort to count the coins sends the push-chair skidding this way and that. Moth is cross, 'What are you doing, Daddy?'

One fifty pence and that little fucker must be a twenty and a couple of other coins. Enough for drinks with luck but no buns for the kids. He looks at Alex. And you can't even offer her a bun, he growls to himself. It is almost enough to make him give up the whole idea.

'I've got to stop,' she says, 'I've got a stitch. Oh.' She takes her hand away from Moth's, folds her arms around herself, and bending down touches the gravel. Once, twice, three times. It is then that Tony becomes aware of the ridiculous holes in her jeans, just below her bum on the right and over her knee on the left. The skin glistening with drops of rain. 'Oh,' she says, 'phew, oh.' She stands up straight, blows her hair out of her mouth, tosses it off her cheek. 'Well?' she says. It strikes him that he is completely in charge. If not he then no one.

'Do you know Mel's cafe in Highfield Rise?'

'Is it a bakery?'

'That's right.'

'We've stopped for bread. Mum has this thing about . . .' She stops herself. Now why bring her into it? 'Why, what were you thinking?'

'That we'd get a cup of tea, or hot chocolate, or whatever you'd like.'

'Great,' she says.

Sitting drinking hot chocolate. Moth happy with a large currant bun. He had of course demanded one. Tony had said no, no money for it, and Alex had said, quick as a flash, I'm paying for my own chocolate, I wouldn't expect, anyway I don't believe, oh shit I just think that everyone should pay for themselves always, it's easier that way. So he gave in, with a growl, and Moth had his bun and was asked to give a piece to Ellen and after some prevarication did so.

Now there is silence between them. It is much more intimate than on the Heath. They are the only people in Mel's. Sitting at the fourth table, the one furthest into the interior, away from the draughts and the gusts of rain that attack the small room every time the door opens and another wet person comes in, shutting it against the wind and saying to Mel, 'Ghastly day, isn't it? What can you do with weather like this?' 'Bleedin' awful,' she'd agree, standing square behind the counter with her hands on her hips, her fair hair drawn up in a roll, her face still young, like a Swiss milkmaid though she must be over fifty. 'Bleedin' awful,' but she doesn't seem distressed. 'A day to take cakes home,' she says. When no customers are there save themselves she observes them. As she fiddles with the cakes, changes things around on the shelves, they feel themselves being observed.

Into the silence – the silence is too much for Alex but she doesn't know how to break it, wills Tony to do so – into the silence he asks suddenly, 'What was that phrase you used when we were running?'

'I've forgotten.' She quickly bends over her hot chocolate. And then up again looking him full in the face when he doesn't expect it. 'This too will change, it's something my Mum's been saying recently over and over. She's a writer, she writes – um – a column, a weekly column in one of the papers. She's like that, she picks up phrases then uses them over and over till we pick them up too. It's annoying, like, you know, like a tune you can't get rid of.'

'What paper does she write for?'

'That would be telling.' She blushes and laughs and he wonders why she withholds this information.

'Would I know her?'

She drinks more chocolate, regretting that she has given away so much. The usual mixture, proud of her mother, furious, uncertain. Where am I in all of this? She looks at Tony again, sideways, as she drinks; she thinks that he is nearer in age to Angelica than herself. He too bends over his drink. As he does she again notices the dark hair in his nostrils. Laughter starts inside her then quickly dies. Of course Angelica wouldn't approve. And with that thought comes a spurt of power.

'My wife's in publishing. As crazy as you like, most writers, however much the publicity machine tries to persuade the public otherwise. The stories Carole comes home with . . .'

'Crazy and you've said it,' acknowledges Alex, glowing. At the same time it's disappointing. Him with his wife in publishing. Maybe despite his clothes, and him not being at work and everything, he's not such a downbeat after all . . . oh f. She sighs.

'What's that sigh for?'

'Nothing. Just some days I get so. Everything seems wrong. Actually I've just got a pissing hangover, if you want to know.'

He doesn't believe it. He thinks she thinks this sounds grown-up.

'What do you do?'

'Do?'

'Well, do you go to school, or college, or what?'

'Nothing.' Her face is blank, immobile, shut away from him. But still it moves him, the way the muscles in her smooth translucent eyelids are working, the way her eyelashes are fluttering, hovering on her still wet cheeks.

'What do your parents think about you doing nothing?'

'Please,' she says. 'The less I think about them the better.'

'Why?'

'Because they go on and on. And look, if you don't mind me saying so, you're going on a bit with all these questions.'

'I'm sorry.'

More silence. Tony could do with an interruption from Moth or Ellen. But Ellen has fallen asleep and Moth is strangely peaceful, nibbling at the last quarter of his bun, his body twisted around on his chair so that he can watch Mel reorganise the cakes.

Why do I need this? Tony thinks. What's the point of making an effort anyway? It's time we went on our way.

She, meanwhile, wants to retrace, to keep things going. She hasn't meant to sound so edgy; after all, it isn't his fault her parents. Her mother. Her father. She seeks a way.

'At least you've got a job,' out of the silence.

'Oh yes and what's that?'

'You're a househusband,' she tells him.

His laughter is not pleasant. It goes on for a long time.

She walks home across the Heath with the ugly sound of it booming in her ears.

*

As Tony walks towards the bus stop his thoughts are inevitably taken back to the first time that someone had called him a househusband. A lot has happened since. Besides, you try to submerge old hurts. But on an off day it still grabs you by the throat.

He'd been a prize idiot undoubtedly, had not got the qualifications that he might have. But then he'd been involved in his own complicated growing experience, the adopted son of a solicitor who was implicated in an unpleasant scandal, went bust, lost professional status and took to drink. Tony was the youngest. They had intended to give him a 'proper' education but there was no money for it at the time. He went to the local secondary modern. Mucked around and couldn't wait to leave and make some money of his own, to support his adopted mother. Opportunities passed him by and, well, one made the wrong decisions. There were times when he might have done this or that. But he'd had a hell of a lot of experience of one kind or another. He'd bummed around America, Australia, India, and in Spain for a while he'd helped his adopted father who had turned to real estate. Eventually Tony missed London. He'd been on the move for five years. He wanted to come back, get work, achieve some kind of stability.

When he saw the ad. for the job in the record shop, it was great. He'd been interested in music ever since he was a kid. He found he was good with the customers. Enjoyed all the types that came in. Within six months he was Assistant Manager, and a year later Manager. He had a staff of eight when they bought the shop next door and extended. Carole was one of them, it was her first job. She'd grown up on a sheep farm outside Melbourne and was determined to spend a couple of years working in Europe before returning to settle down in Australia.

Tony had worked in Sydney. They had Australia in common, and music and sex and good looks. And the world ahead of them. For Carole the job was just the springboard. She was having trouble with her permit and Tony was able to fix something. But she had her sights on something more literary. She who'd been a grade A student all the way through school. Soon she left the shop for a job in music publishing. The money was less but what the hell, she was living with Tony and he was earning very nicely. The opportunities seemed infinite. She moved again, this time into book publishing as Rights Assistant. Then, when the Rights Manager left, thinking she wouldn't stand a chance, she nevertheless put in for the job. It was advertised outside, of course, but a decision had already been taken. Carole had such a wonderful way with her, everyone liked her. It was said that she could sell anything. Of course she didn't have much experience overall and might consider the post offered an honour; she would not be expecting the same salary as the outgoing manager had got. This was tempting to the firm, they'd be saving on money, making it so much easier to swing the decision with the Chairman, who had a little tiny thing against Australians. So Carole accepted, for what else could she do?

Then, on the morning of Tony's thirty-first birthday, he had gone to work to be cursorily told that the firm he was working for had been taken over. He could hear the cold wind blowing at that moment. New faces appeared. Of course he would be staying on as Manager. Well, wouldn't he? It was generally let about that the sales figures for the last year were not what the company was looking for. Of course it wasn't Tony's fault exactly. But there was some question. Wasn't he buying in too much jazz? Besides, with no management or other qualifications, they implied, he didn't really have what it takes. 'Look here, I worked my way up, there's not much you can tell me about the record business.' But the young guy from MIT thought otherwise.

Carole became pregnant. They had been living in one room off Tavistock Square. The months were miserable ones. Day after day Tony's confidence took another knock. Day after day new indignities. 'They're trying to squeeze me out, Carole.' 'Hang in there, honey.' For her things were looking better and better. Except what a time to have a baby. The MD of a publishing company she had a particular respect for had mentioned that they should get together for a little lunch.

'Tony, I think I'm being head-hunted.'

'Well, you must know, woman, for Christ's sake.'

It wasn't that easy, there had been flowers and innuendoes. It seemed that each was sussing the other out. But what about the baby, then? Previous to this she'd been talking about taking six months off and then finding something more flexible.

Tony was finally pushed out. It was bloody and damaging.

'Keep your pecker up,' Carole urged. 'You've got lots of contacts. Besides you're bloody good at what you do.'

'I'm not so sure of that.'

'Oh, none of that defeatist talk.'

Seven years ago, the first time the phrase was brought up between them. Didn't it just seem a cheek then, coming from her, several years his junior!

Carole's mind those days was working like a cash register. And not only in relation to the books she was selling, no, she was calculating how they were going to live until Tony sorted himself out. Say it took another six months. That would be over the time of the birth of the baby. They had to move before then. She waited for a firm offer to come through. But it didn't. And a fortnight later it was she who was negotiating another lunch with the MD. Now she let him know, if he could see his way. Could the resident Rights Manager be about to leave?

'No.'

'What then?'

'Ducky, she could always be . . . shifted.' There was something he needed to bring up which was always a delicate matter. 'But I'd be blind if I wasn't aware that', he looked at her stomach, 'you'll soon be having another role to play.'

She raised her face and looked at him, eyebrows raised.

'Motherhood.'

'Oh, that. Yes, well, luckily enough I'm about to marry, well, the father of the baby . . .'

'That is lucky,' murmured the MD.

'What I mean is so lucky, is that Tony, Tony Davis, is one of these modern men, who believes in being a househusband for a couple of years. You know . . . giving me a chance to keep working.'

'Well, I must say, you are very lucky,' said the MD, resting his hand momentarily on her wrist.

'But the pay would have to be good. In the circumstances. You can see that?'

He could.

She insisted to Tony later she had never until that moment thought of him as a househusband; for a time didn't even tell him what had transpired. The offer came. She changed jobs and the pay was substantially increased. Tony was given redundancy compensation which, although it seemed paltry compared to all he'd put into the business, ought to tide them over the six months until he found something else. They moved into a two-bedroom flat in Kentish Town and Tony put down some of his redundancy pay as key money on a long-term lease.

Timothy Martin was born. Tony was overjoyed. His pride had taken a terrible knock but this was a good one for the books. People said he looked just like Tony.

Carole was at home for six weeks exactly after the birth. And even then it seemed to Tony that her mind was at work and not with them in the Kentish Town Road. She talked only of how soon she could get back and the arrangements she would make. From the start Tony felt sorry for Timothy Martin. Identifying with him, he wanted him to have more love than he had done as a child, wanted him to have a real mother who cared for him. When he saw this was not to be forthcoming in the way he had envisaged, he started doing more and more for his son to make up for what was lacking. Of course, despite Tony's protestations, the little chap was bottle-fed. So it could as soon be the one that fed him as the other. Then Carole was pointing out that Tony changed a nappy more efficiently, and as to getting him to feed or stop crying, why, he was the master.

Carole went to see the social services about putting the baby into daytime care. Then she talked it over with Tony.

'We'd have to lie, say you're definitely working,' she told him. 'What do you reckon?'

'While I'm at home it seems pretty daft,' said Tony. 'I'll look after him for the moment, and when I get another job we'll sort something out.'

Carole went back to work. 'Isn't it awfully hard to be away from the baby all day long?' the other women asked, especially those of Carole's age or older, not married, those who would give anything for marriage and having babies of their own. No, she told them, she was lucky to have a husband who was so good with the baby, it was not like farming him out and feeling guilty in consequence. She surprised herself – she told them – but it is only in these circumstances that you really come to know yourself – I actually prefer work.

Though Carole called Tony her 'husband', because it was more convenient, they were not in fact yet married. Before the advent of Timothy Martin there had been no expectation that they would take that particular step. Tony had been against marriage, he'd told Carole so the moment she started to become serious about him. He remembered only too clearly the unhappy and apparently undissolvable knot of his adopted parents' marriage, as well as having had sufficient experience of divorce amongst acquaintances, to believe that saying 'for keeps' was no longer any guarantee. Far better, he believed, to keep away from that whole scene. Live for the day, he'd told Carole, just enjoy it while we can. But Carole, at the point of thinking about permanency, thinking about pregnancy, had asked him – this a year before – 'Do you reckon we're for keeps, even if we don't get married?'

'Why?'

'I was thinking of little Tonys.'

'Would you like one, then?'

They had been lying in bed on a Sunday morning. It had given him a hard-on just to think about it. The way she said it.

'Come here, woman.'

And afterwards. 'Seriously, Tony, what do you reckon, you reckon we might?'

'I reckon we might.'

This was apparently enough for Carole. Two years in his bed and the need to make a nest was strong. Besides she loved the man, they were immensely compatible, easy together. They had fun. She wouldn't find better. So she'd gone ahead and become pregnant. And marriage, what the hell, luckily with her parents in Australia and his in Spain there was little family pressure from either side.

But in the months after Timothy was born it was Tony, as he walked his son in his carrycot, down Kentish Town Road, into shops, to the library, to the job centre, who began to reconsider the question. He had been adopted. Had suffered a great deal of uncertainty. He did not want the same for his son. Before Timothy's birth he'd thought about it only from his own point of view. But now, spending so much time with him every day, he began to have the curious and slightly disturbing experience of looking at life from Timothy's point of view. And from his point of view it would probably be better if they married.

It was something that needed some thought. He wouldn't mention it to Carole until he was quite certain.

In his fourth month of staying at home looking after his son, the possibility of a job did raise its head. Not through the job centre but through former work contacts of Tony's. It would mean that he would not be manager in his own shop; he would be assistant to someone he thought was a right old woman. He had grave doubts. The last six months when his own place had been under new management and he was being squeezed out had been bloody painful. He wondered if he could go back to being an assistant, whether he could work to anyone else's tune. And if the job turned out to be a bummer then he would simply be compounding his mistakes. He asked Carole what she thought. 'You could try, at least to keep your hand in. What have you got to lose?' Yet when he responded, 'Yeah, but what you don't understand is that when you've had one blow to your confidence, matey, you don't want to walk into another,' she seemed to agree. A moment ago it hadn't been a sure thing, only a possibility. Now Tony was increasingly becoming sure of the negative side of the prospective job. When he finally decided to say no and hang on for something where he'd be the manager, he sensed that she was secretly relieved. He even wondered whether she had manipulated him. But no, she couldn't have. It had been his own decision.

A month or two went by. Financially it was beginning to be a pull.

He was often in his pyjamas when she left home. He would hear her padding around making Timothy's breakfast, and from their bed he would shout, 'Get us a cup of tea, love.'

Sometimes she showed that it niggled her. She was over the honeymoon period at her new job. A number of new situations had presented themselves, each more difficult to cope with. At that point she still shared the frustrations and problems of her work life with him and every evening expected a helpful response.

Then, one evening when she'd had a particularly daunting day, when she wondered if she would ever be on top of the job, would ever have the balls to be as pushy as some of her American (or now even her English) counterparts, she walked into the flat tired, dispirited, and got upset by what a dump it was. They had been there for seven months and hadn't even done the most basic redecoration. On top of which Timothy's paraphernalia was everywhere. There were unwashed mugs and bowls and plates on every surface and a cold kitchen in which no food preparation had taken place. She said that she needed to sit down for ten minutes with a beer, and then to eat. It was another day on which she'd gone to work on black coffee and not had time for lunch. Tony had not exactly been feeling great himself that day.

'I thought being Rights Manager meant a row of sumptuous lunches. You can't expect me to cook for you after that.'

'Christ, it's not like that every day! Where have you been, you can't have been listening to a word I've been telling you these last months.'

'Steady on, steady on, woman.'

'You said you'd cook in the week, there's not even any food here by the looks of things, and the place is the pits.'

She burst into tears. Timothy at eight months and quick to move, was already in her arms. She hardly had one foot in the door these days when he would start off towards it.

They had taken to calling him Moth. His way of approaching the door at Carole's step only to collide with her briefcase reminded them of a moth moving towards the light.

With Moth now in her arms, crouching on the floor, Carole cried and cried, she didn't quite know why, she said, just the last seven months, just everything since Moth was born; it hadn't been what she'd envisaged somehow, not quite how she'd intended her life to go. And Tony was surly, that made it worse. He told her again how pissed off he felt with life in England and the job scene. Maybe they should think of taking off for the Costa del Sol where Tony's brother was apparently doing well and had written that he might fix Tony up with a job, on commission, no fixed income but for someone who was prepared to work there was a hell of a lot of money to be made in property in Spain, he reckoned, so what did Carole think?

Eventually they got Moth to sleep, then Tony went out for fish and chips and a pack of beers while Carole did something about straightening up the flat and washing the many mugs. They ate together in front of the gas fire, she sitting on the floor, he on the only comfortable chair. While they ate they watched telly. He put out his arm and she came to sit near him so that the warmth in the full extent of his leg was against her backside. With a full stomach and a couple of beers she seemed to feel better. Even to crack jokes about the inane cops and robbers thing they were watching.

'Well, shall we go?' Tony asked. 'Me, I'm for quitting. England's all the way down hill, nothing much of a future. Can't be worse in Spain, and at least it will be warm. Of course, for you, it's a different kettle of fish. I know how much you wanted that job.'

'Did I?'

'Yeah, and you're good at it. I'm not dragging you away if you want to stay. It's your decision, got to be.'

'My decision, why does everything have to be *my* decision?'

He was shocked and hurt at the way she'd said it. And when he thought he was genuinely trying to be considerate. How can you win? You bend over backwards, and look what you get.

'Right, well there's one decision I've made. We're going to get married.'

'Married! Christ, Tony, what's that got to do with the price of eggs?'

'A lot. It'll be better in the long run for Moth. Besides I think we should. We're for keeps, aren't we? Or have you changed your mind, now the old man's out of work, eh?'

He was saying, he knew, did she love him less? He was actually feeling insecure about her, when it had always been the other way round. Jesus! He waited. Was there a split second before she responded? 'Yes, we're for keeps. Nothing's changed, Tony.'

And so, at Tony's instigation, one Saturday a few weeks later they found themselves at the registry office getting married. It was a quiet affair, a couple of Carole's friends turned up from work (she asked them to keep the matter quiet) to act as witnesses and to hold Moth during the service. Then they all went off to lunch.

Carole's mates, though, did not keep it quiet. They thought she was just being modest and decided they couldn't let something like this go by without at least a glass of bubbly. Charles B., when told, was of the same opinion and a surprise party was arranged. Carole's home number was rung and Tony contacted. Later, he understood that an author was coming over from America whom the firm wanted to fête but not be seen to fête. This offered an excellent opportunity. It could be subtly suggested that the two occasions nicely tied in. Such a thought led the MD to be generous with the champagne, if they got this particular author there would be enough money in it for crates of the stuff.

At the time, Tony wasn't aware of any of this. When the girls from the office phoned him he took it as a gesture of genuine goodwill on the part of the company towards Carole and was pleased for her. The last weeks had been going better for her. She had expressed to Tony her preference to stay in England and hang on at work. She was sure he would find himself a job. After all, he was only thirty-one. They were both optimistic.

Up till now there had been little mingling of Carole's private and work life. She seemed to prefer it that way. He too. But a wedding celebration was different. He was in the mood to celebrate. After all, you only take this step once.

When Carole went off to work that morning she still didn't know it was happening. They were planning to tell her only in the course of the afternoon. He'd washed his hair the night before, and got her to cut it. 'Anything special?' she'd teased. 'You're not going out on the town without me, now that you're an old married man, are you?'

'Nothing like that.'

He'd sorted out his most decent clothes and polished his shoes.

'So you've been in on the secret?' she challenged him when he arrived.

'Just for a few days, yes.' Kissing her, he sensed her tension. He wanted to say, 'Christ, Carole, I'm not going to embarrass you.' But he knew she'd say, 'It's not that.'

The boardroom was thronging with people.

'What about Moth? What have you done with him?' she wanted to know. He told her not to worry, he'd left him with a neighbour. Soon Carole was taken off to be introduced to the American author and Tony had a few seconds of wondering who he should talk to until Charles B. bustled over and introduced himself.

'So you're the lucky man.'

'I do think I'm lucky, yes.'

His second glass of bubbly was going down a treat. He'd imagined he'd feel self-conscious. 'What do you do, Tony? What's your profession?' It could still be tough, especially in a gathering like this where work was often the easiest passport into conversation. But no need to worry, Charles was carrying him along with stories about how he'd left Hungary in the fifties with nothing much more than the clothes he was wearing, and about the difficult early years trying to make a go of things here. Now this was something that Tony could readily lock into. Once or twice he saw Carole looking at him with concern, but he tried to indicate to her, don't worry, I'm having a great time. Finally she moved to join them. He put his arm round her waist.

'I must say I admire you,' Charles B. was saying.

'Me. Why?'

'Your attitudes certainly aren't mine but they're admirable, after all. Especially when they allow us to have the advantage of Carole's full-time commitment.'

'My attitudes, what do you mean?'

'Your desire to be a househusband. I remember when Carole first spoke to me about the job, and of course your young nipper was on the way then, when Carole explained that it was your intention to be a househusband, that you'd decided it was time to give women the opportunity to work, I thought not for me, of course, but that is certainly a turn-around for the books. I'd like to meet the man who . . .'

The rest of the evening passed in a blur of anger and a sense of having been deeply let down by the woman he'd just married. God, was he angry! Angrier than he'd ever been in his life. He had only a vague recollection of the speeches that now seemed empty and tasteless, of the drive home, except that he knew he had driven at a reckless speed (he still had the car then), of the things he'd said to Carole when finally the brakes jerked the car to a stop and the smell of rubber died in the night air.

She would not cry. She sat there letting his words rain over her. When at last he'd finished, she tried to make peace, to get him to listen. She didn't mean to do him down, when she said it, it didn't mean that she wanted him never to work again. Couldn't he have sufficient faith in her to see that it was something she'd said on the spur of the moment to get herself out of a spot? Mightn't he have done the same in a similar situation? She put out a hand to him, hoping for reconciliation.

That night, the night of their wedding party, Tony was beyond any such thoughts.

But somehow a reconciliation was reached after all. Tony couldn't exactly remember how it had happened. Nothing huge or noteworthy. More that they both got on with their lives, she making all sorts of small gestures towards him, careful to show, it seemed to Tony, how much she did need him. And then there was Moth, who needed them both. And then they were married. And then sex was a great healer. And then that was the choice he'd made. How can you say about these things; it seemed to Tony that that was how it was and he had no option but to take her as she was.

Maybe she was the stronger of the two. This incident had revealed something in her character, her deeply ambitious side, perhaps even her ability to be ruthless. But as time went by, he had come to tell himself that this had some advantages too. The less he saw her as someone who needed to be protected, the more he was free not to do so. And thank heavens she was so competent, for otherwise what would have happened to them both?

From that time onwards, there had been an unspoken shift in their relationship. Maybe it had been happening all along, even since he had first employed her in his shop, her first job after leaving Australia, and had helped her to get her work permit. As she became stronger, so he, in a sense, became more dependent. As she grew into her role at work and found herself able to do more each day, took on new challenges and succeeded in them, so it seemed he gave over to her more and more realms of dominance in their relationship until only sex was left unchanged.

There she was still the girl he had first known, pliant, dependent, as if all her defences melted away. There they healed and renewed the marriage, almost nightly since the beginning of their relationship a decade before. And perhaps because it expressed another side to her, and now to the marriage, it seemed to be of vital importance to her. However tired she was when she returned home, she was never too tired for that. Indeed, it occurred to Tony that her prodigious energy was something that highlighted the differences between them. Energy is only an effort of will, she would say, of feeling good about yourself. Besides, Tony, you know how tired I get. Yes, but she always kept going.

Almost always showered last thing at night and then arrived out of the bathroom, smelling sweetly, another person, ready, gentle, deeply female. Ready, almost however tired she was.

Why? She had once indicated to him that it was not so much that Tony was a brilliantly imaginative lover but more that early on he had found just the right place, the way of entering her and finding the angle that, by moving his body up and down in slow rhythmical movements, excited her clitoris internally and gradually sent messages all the way to her uterus. It was in one sense incredibly simple and as reliable as a sure-shot camera. She came virtually every time. There was little need for foreplay. They could come in a matter of minutes if neither had abundant energy or drive, or he could hold off, taking a much longer time, bringing her perhaps in a series of waves and himself to a larger, longer, more satisfying and complete ejaculation. As some people have a bath or shower at night and others a glass of brandy or Ovaltine, so they had sex. A routine. And this release night after night was an essential part of what had held them together through the rocky days of their far-from-easy marriage.

But now, either because these last six months had been the hardest yet, or because it was the only power she left him, he felt his desire freeze up. A relationship had to have more to it.

The first years of staying around the house had in some ways been easier than the last. Moth was one thing, a basically good, easy-going little boy. Ellen was another. She came into the world at a time in which their relationship was going through a more difficult period. And then she was such a pain. All that crying, all that female needing. Without more support from Carole, who appeared even more cut off from her daughter than from her son, Tony just didn't know if he could handle it.

But finding a way out had become more and more difficult. There was something about being long-term unemployed, he reckoned, that was difficult to pull back from. You begin to wonder if anyone ever again will employ you. You begin to lose any sense of your own worth. A lot of things happen. Not all at once, but gradually.

Certain things that were uncomfortable in year one, no longer felt like any kind of trouble. The loss of ready money, oh, that first year, how it hurt, gradually stripping himself of those things he enjoyed: the car, the weekends away, the meals out, the booze, the football matches, and the music. No longer going to concerts, no longer buying new records and tapes, no longer keeping up with all the latest equipment.

But gradually these things fall away, along with old friends, and if you're Tony you settle down to a life with simple boundaries. Your horizons close in. That way it's possible to live. But that way too separated the life he led from the life Carole led. It hurt less but it was increasingly isolating. Until this last six months a voice inside had said, no, I can't go on with this. Something must happen. I can't.

Alex. Just a girl on the Heath. A pretty youngster. Hundreds of them around. Still, she'd been good with the kids. Moth had talked about her all the way home, his eyes big with worry, why had they quarrelled like that, why had she gone off angry? Wouldn't they ever see her again? Why? why? why?

'It really doesn't matter, Moth.' He'd tried to distract his son's attention, and his own, from something so incidental.

But Moth was not to be distracted. 'It does matter, Daddy. I like Alex, she's my friend.'

'You don't make friends as quickly as that.' He ruffled his son's hair.

'I do.'

They said no more about it but it was a strange feeling Tony went home with, as if a window had briefly opened and then blown shut again. In his laughter at Mel's cafe he saw the edge of his anger and was ashamed. Carole was so strong, it was his way of getting at her, to sound cutting like that. And of course she would ignore it, let it rise over her head. So that he ceased to see it as a weapon, but still persisted. With Alex today, it was as if he no longer realised the power he had to hurt. But what a fuss over nothing. Still, if he'd had the opportunity again he would have been careful to play it differently. Though it's unlikely to happen again. The chances of bumping into her again are one in a million. Another window shut, and what can one expect?

Their stop. With Ellen in his arms and Moth holding firmly onto his hand, he negotiates himself off the bus. Expecting the usual black despair to attack him the moment they open the door of their cold, unloved, unlovely flat.

But, strangely, it doesn't. It is as if a gear has shifted. However small. He turns on the gas fire, for the rain has made the place damp. He turns on the bath water for the kids. He washes the dishes from lunch, then starts to prepare the supper.

*

'I must go,' says Carole, 'I really must.'

'You might as well help us finish the last of this bottle, then we'll all make a move together.'

With some part of her she idly watches Charles tip the head of the bottle into her wine glass. What the hell, what is an extra quarter of an hour here or there? The interaction between the three of them has been intense. Much ground has been covered. The firm is suffering many changes in fast succession, it is like a rocking boat. In the new situation people are pulling in different directions. Ian has some radical new ideas and Charles is uncertain, hating to be dominated, feeling his age, putting on a brave front but continually cursing the ulcer in his stomach. Knowing risks must always be taken. Less ready to take them. Uncertain of the calibre of all his staff because in this new ball-game uncertain of himself. And the staff feel that uncertainty and react in different ways. So that difficult decisions are more difficult to make because each knows he or she will be questioned in a way they haven't been for some years.

She had felt that she had earned Charles's trust and friendship. She knew about his ulcer, over which, very much like her with her headaches, he kept up a brave front. She knew about his wife's growing alcoholism, she had always known about his philandering, and there was a time when he would have liked her. But she had kept walking the tightrope, guiding the relationship into friendship, where it steadily rested.

Now, all of a sudden, things were haywire. Her own reaction was a drop in confidence. Ian's was to make him more belligerent, losing all subtlety, goading Charles into rows, pushing his point, overstepping given boundaries. Yet he was bright, irritating, infuriating, but often at Charles' elbow he pushed where Charles knew he needed to be pushed. Now they have been arguing for the last three days, bickering about this and that, the row affecting the office and subsiding only to blow up again. To both, Carole is a calming influence. It is not so much what she says but more her presence.

At the end of the day, she sits in the wine bar between these men she has worked with for almost a decade, from her twenties through into her mid-thirties, with whom there has been increasingly a way of being, when the tension is over, when there is just nothing more to dispute, when they can relax easily together, she needing to talk less than the men but knowing that her presence is important.

Maybe it will be okay, maybe we'll come through all this. I don't like this kind of turmoil, but was it too smooth before? You wouldn't think so. It'll all settle down in a couple of months. I'll get on top of it.

She looks at Charles. He sees her look and winks. I've got to read that Macdonald manuscript tonight, he's in tomorrow and I've hardly. Even if I only read half. Christ, what am I doing sitting here? She pushes both hands onto the table and stands up. 'There's a bus in five minutes,' she says, 'I'm going to grab it.' She might have said, I promised Timothy, but that promise was already broken hours ago, which inevitably, as so often, she felt sorry about. Felt sorry and let it pass because there were only so many emotions you could keep going. And this was one she could expend with. To Sarah she might mention her son but not to the men. This she had learnt over the years, by observation and political sense. The men did not want to know about her domestic situation, it was almost as if that was the deal. More and more this got to her, but there it was. She was not one of those who believed it would easily change.

Now she doesn't mention Timothy – or Tony, who would be. Shut it out. She puts on her jacket, kisses them both lightly on the cheek and makes for the bus.

Of course it isn't on time. Silly of her to think it would be. She stands now feeling how tired she is, at five past eight in Tottenham Court Road outside a sex shop whose window sports a curious display of wear and gear. Sex, turn your mind off from it. Can this go on for months? Years? Christ, that's our way to one another, without that. Stop thinking about it. Tired, a long day. A longer one tomorrow. Why is there always a wind in Tottenham Court Road, even when there's a wind nowhere else in London? 24 and another and another. Oh come on bus, is this one? Wait, the only one in the queue, Tottenham Court Road is not full at this hour. At last. Thank heaven.

On she gets, pays her money and sits at the top in the front, a compact small woman with blue eyes and soft fair hair turned up in a duck's tail at the nape of her neck. A face pale a tinge of grey, very tired now feeling it on the bus. She shuts her eyes over rims that are pink and throbbing. She feels the lurch and movement of the bus. This route twice a day ten times a week for the same number of years.

As the bus nears Camden Town she visualises what will greet her. It is past their supper time. Ellen ought to be asleep, Moth ready for bed. Oh God or whoever you are for once let it be like that, the flat clean, let him have cleaned the flat, quiet, calm. The toys neatly picked up. Ellen asleep in her cot on her tummy, her face washed, her hair brushed. Moth bathed, in his dressing-gown, being read to, even watching TV, I don't mind, so that I can just hug him and sing to him. And Tony with a meal ready. No, that's going too far. I don't expect. I'm not even hungry any more. Just.

But she knows it will not be like this. She knows what to expect and as they pull out of Camden Town and along Kentish Town High Street her shoulders begin to tense, her neck pushes her head up in an awkward position, as she clenches her hand round the strap of her briefcase inside which is the heavy Macdonald manuscript which must be started tonight. She braces her whole body for what is to come, for it is a pattern now, and she does not know the way out of it.

*

All morning while Alex is trying to apply her mind to the history of the Second World War she is aware of the brilliant sunshine outside. The voice of her teacher comes and goes. Her teacher would say the same about Alex's concentration, and her attendance. It might be the policy of the school to encourage those who had failed their exams to retake, but sometimes it simply seems a waste of time. She wonders why Alex bothers to turn up at all, when she comes so rarely. Having nagged, cajoled and pleaded over the last year, written letters to her parents, done everything she could, and all for a negative result, she is disinclined now to do more. Indeed she tells herself there is nothing she can do except get on and teach her class, notice Alex's pattern, her comings and goings, hanging on by a thread but not turned away, and just possibly something will happen to give her the impetus she needs. She is there, in class today rather than in bed or somewhere else; that is surely something.

So Alex listens to Mrs Morrow's words and takes some down – but of course she already has notes from last year so really no need. Then, after another interval, five minutes but to Alex it seems like half an hour, she looks again out of the window at the brilliance of the light, at the leaves of the walnut tree in the courtyard which seem alive with colour.

'Oh Christ, it's you,' says Alex to Tony later, standing between two of her school mates on her way to lunch at a Greek cafe they frequent in Kentish Town. Well she has to say something. At first she'd looked away and hoped he'd have the sense to pass by, but he'd stood squarely before her and addressed her by name. You could sense the interest of the other two. There was no way she could slip by, however much she wanted to.

'Look, I'm sorry, I didn't mean to be as rude as I was,' he tells her.

'You was bloody rude.' The bad grammar all part of the pose.

Oh Christ, how to convince her? And why bother? She seems so separate. Watching her standing there, her hair flicked back on her shoulders, her eyes flat, half a head taller than her companions, her neck floating gracefully out of her shoulder sockets, her weight so evenly distributed, so light, brings an extraordinary buoyancy to Tony. Since chance has again delivered her across his path, he has to somehow.

'You took offence so dramatically. I wasn't expecting you to.'

'You wanted me to take offence. You bloody aimed it that way,' she flares, 'but it really doesn't matter. I . . . We've got to be going. Busy lives and all that,' she snickers. Deena at her side begins to giggle too.

He focuses his eyes directly on Alex, with enormous effort, and speaks in another tone. Calmer. 'You're right, of course. I did half intend to. But that's my hang-up. Nothing to do with you. Ridiculous. Please?'

'Please what?' Now she too is calmer. Relenting.

'Please, three-thirty today. At the ponds, with Moth and Ellen. They want you so much to.' He doesn't finish the sentence. He just looks at her again, willing her to agree.

'Maybe.'

She makes a movement forwards and he recognises that he can do no more. 'Hope to see you there then.' He steps off the pavement to let them pass.

'Who was he?' *He* was hardly out of earshot.

'Just someone whose kids I babysit for.'
'What did he do, what was he talking about?'
'Nothing. Nothing really. Just a misunderstanding.'
'But . . .'
'Deena don't be boring.'

Boaring to soaring – though God knows why – thinks Alex as she sips her Coke and plays with her baklava, her choice of lunch. She's only eaten two mouthfuls and already she is full. Three-thirty. She'll just have time if she steps on it to leave the ten pounds she owes Chris at his Dad's garage first. The day is taking on quite a different shape. A glow spreads over her face. Her friends notice it but say nothing.

I'd thought, I'd thought. Hell then, he did want. Huh!

What is the sun doing leaving the Heath before she gets there? Not quite leaving it either, just diluting itself behind the thinnest of white screens. And yet isn't this in its own way more spectacular, she is thinking, as she slams the door of her basement flat, making her mother and Jerry both at home working in their separate offices jump and curse, tears across the busy road, saunters across the bridge, turns right and then runs up the hill – for she is late.

It seems to her as she runs that everything, herself included, is lit with an extraordinary light. Because the light around, on grass and sky, is duller than earlier, the trees are sharper, they seem to have caught and held the earlier light, so that each one is shimmering, highlighted, glowing.

She runs down the hill towards the tennis courts. She is in trainers. Her jeans have been darned. She wears a boldly striped long-sleeved T-shirt and carries a sweater. She is running, running, aware of the time, oh don't let them not be there, don't let them have gone. Please, please.

But they are there. Tony is kicking a football to Moth. 'I'm late,' she pants, 'I'm so sorry, I, well I got delayed. Glad you waited.'

Tony throws her the ball, 'Catch,' he says. She catches it and throws it to Moth. Ellen parked in her push-chair is today clutching a golliwog. While the ball is between Tony and Moth, Alex darts over and gives her a kiss. Well I don't know what all this is about, her always weeping, she thinks.

Throwing the ball is just what Alex needs. She is so alive after all that dry, sad and stupid stuff in the class room. What idiots politicians are. It is almost unbearable to think about the Second World War because impossible not to turn one's mind then to the possibility of a third. And if people like that . . .

'Gosh, that was a hard one,' calls Tony.

'Sorry, didn't mean it to be.' They are moving fast, throwing fast. Moth occasionally drops the ball and gets angry with himself. Alex and Tony are careful to run nearer to him than to each other, giving him more chance. On and on they go. Alex doesn't want to stop. It is something like a dance. They throw the ball high, low, Tony throws it under his legs, over Moth's head to Alex. Then she misses the ball and does her little laugh and he realises that that is what he has been waiting for.

'Daddy, Daddy, let's stop, I'm so tired.' Moth flings himself down on the ground next to the push-chair, then Alex, then Tony. Alex, after a moment's consideration, gets up and tentatively releases the safety straps and lifts Ellen out of the push-chair. Tony doesn't comment. Alex wonders if she will cry. It just doesn't seem fair to exclude her from all the fun. She does cry.

'Don't. Put her back,' orders Moth. 'She doesn't like it, she only likes Mummy to hold her.'

Alex is uncertain. She looks at Tony who gives no indication. She half gets up. But then Ellen stops. 'I think she'll be okay. She is getting used to me,' she tells Moth. 'You don't mind if I hold her, do you?'

'Not if she doesn't cry.' Moth likes it that Alex considers his opinion, that she never says 'silly'. He likes her. In some ways she is like Mummy. He will tell Mummy that, this evening. Why can't Mummy come on the Heath too and then they will all be friends.

'Daddy, now I'm hungry,' says Moth, making big eyes and hoping for a sticky bun. Tony looks at Alex. They are sitting on the grass, lying back, resting on their elbows. Alex has Ellen in her lap. Alex's hand is near Tony's. Some years ago when Moth was a baby, Ellen's age, Carole used to come out with him like this. It was Regent's Park then, and Hyde Park. They would listen to the bands, they would play on the grass, relaxed, a young couple much in love. He is tempted to put out a hand towards Alex, to touch her hand, but declines. 'Well, what do you think? Tea and sticky buns?' he asks.

Alex looks up at the sky and the tips of the trees. 'It's too good to go inside now, don't you think?'

'But I'm hungry,' protests Moth.

'Tell you what,' Alex suggests, 'we'll go and find some blackberries.'

'Too late in the season for that,' says Tony.

'Do you want to bet?' She looks mischievous. 'Come on, follow me, you lot.'

They get to their feet. This time Alex continues to carry Ellen. Moth pushes the empty chair; Tony hangs on to the golliwog.

Out onto Millfield Lane, then they branch off to take a path past allotments and cottages that look as if they could be situated anywhere in the English countryside. Then into a field curved round the side of a hill. 'Now, wait for it,' Alex says. 'In a moment we'll come to them.'

'There won't be a blackberry left. I'll bet you anything you like.'

'I wouldn't bet if I were you.'

For a few more moments they walk on. Then she slows down. 'In here, you see it's the way they face, and something to do with them getting little sunlight, yet being protected, it's the autumn light when the leaves are already falling, that finally hits them giving them the last spurt they need. Wait. Any moment now.' Like a cat she creeps round the bushes and then pounces. 'Here,' she points. 'I just knew it, now what do you think of that, Tony? Moth?'

'Pick some for me. They're too high. *I* want some.' Moth is jumping up and down.

Alex lowers Ellen onto the grass, pops a couple of blackberries into her mouth, gathers a whole handful and passes them first to Moth, then, her hands cupped, to Tony. He holds the tips of her narrow fingers steadying them as he scoops some out. She looks him straight in the eye.

'I'm glad we bumped into one another. I thought about it after . . . after, you know, last time and wondered why . . .'

'You hit a raw nerve.'

'Oh?'

'The word is a kind of family joke of a bad kind. But you weren't to know and besides it was churlish of me, as I said this morning.'

'I didn't mean to.'

'We've apologised enough, don't you think?' He is smiling at her.

'Yes I do.' She can't think what she wants to say next. 'Anyway,' she tries tentatively, 'we're both . . . not working, we're both sort of in the same boat.'

'My boat?' asks Moth, pricking up his ears.

Which makes Tony chuckle. It is a good low sound, thinks Alex, quite different from that in the cafe. Then she sneaks a look at the curly hairs appearing from his nostrils and wants to chuckle a good deal more.

'I went to school this morning, a rare event,' she tells him.

Christ, a schoolgirl!

'Sometimes I think I'm retaking either one or two A-levels. But it's very marginal. And then I babysit a bit. And – see friends. That's about it. Not very interesting, is it?'

He could have said, 'You interest me,' but checked himself, he didn't want her to think it was a pass, pretty girl like her. Besides he didn't know why she did interest him.

'What do you, I mean how do you fill the time?'

'Get up, dress Ellen, Moth dresses himself. Wash up the breakfast stuff. Carole, my wife, has usually fed them before she leaves. Take Moth to school. Pick up any groceries we need. Find something to do with Ellen, while the time away somehow. Then home, give her lunch, then she'll usually nap, pick up Moth, come on the Heath or take them home to watch TV. Supper, bath, bed, and on and on, most days pretty much the same. Interesting eh?' He is grinning at her.

'*Touché*.' She feels it out of place as she says it. She can hear Angelica gaily saying it at a dinner party in Hampstead. She regrets that she has said it here.

She pushes the hair angrily from her cheek and as she does so stains her face with the blackberry juice from her hands. Moth is quick to point it out. A number of diversions from the children. Then they start to make their way back. She has been thinking about what he's said. His day is in a sense packed so full except for that narrow gap when Ellen sleeps. His time.

'What do you do in the time when Ellen sleeps?'

He looks at her surprised, not displeased.

'Oh, why have you stopped, Daddy? Keep walking,' insists Moth, now eager to get home.

'I'm compiling a discography. But it's rather like your schoolwork from your account. Done occasionally.'

She nods, 'When Ellen's not . . .'

And just at that moment Ellen starts to cry, and she raises her eyebrows to him in amusement and his droopy moustache at the edges flickers and he feels the corners of his mouth in a strange new position, as if they haven't been there for a long time.

The following Friday Alex is waiting for them. He knows it in his bones as he buses to the Heath from Moth's school with the two children. He has not needed this time to say, will you? The week has been a better one as a result – such a small thing. And yet even Carole has noticed the change. With the vague anticipation of inviting Alex back, he has cleaned up the flat. For days he has managed not to be exasperated with Ellen. He is still not sleeping with Carole. But will soon, perhaps this weekend, Sunday morning if. Yes, his footsteps are lighter altogether as he makes his way with the children onto the Heath. Just a small respite, but so vital.

Moth is already running to her with news that he is desperate to impart. He is going to act a part in the Christmas play. Ellen is clamouring to be let out of the push-chair. Alex and Tony greet each other with more ease. It seems perfectly natural this time.

'What shall we do?' she asks.

'Have you any ideas?'

'Some, but what about Moth?'

'The swings, please, the swings.'

So to the swings they go.

Setting Ellen in Moth's arms on the roundabout, and pushing it, running with it, one of a quartet of parents all similarly running and pushing, watching and participating in the pleasure of those they are responsible for, the ugliness Alex has brought with her onto the Heath evaporates. Tony and she balance the see-saw, she behind Moth, Tony putting his strength on Ellen's lighter side. Together they rock the seats so that the children bob up and down. Alex sits on a swing with Ellen in her lap. Tony pushes. Moth, on the adjacent swing, pushes himself. 'Look, I can go higher than you, Alex.' Tony pushes Alex higher and higher. She clasps Ellen tight. She is as light as a child, Tony thinks, she doesn't feel like a woman at all. Go on, take me up into the sky, Alex thinks, clutching the warmth of the trusting little girl. 'Stop, stop I can't go as high as that,' says an indignant Moth. For a moment they have forgotten him. They slow down.

He is bored, jumps off his swing. 'Look, the sandpit!' He runs to it.

'Better take off your socks and shoes, Moth,' Alex calls.

'Don't need to.'

'Oh yes you do, they'll be sandy afterwards and then you won't be able to walk back in them.'

Moth considers for a moment, then he walks back towards Alex and lets her take them off.

'You seem to have such a way with the children,' Tony tells her, while they sit watching the two playing with others in the sandpit. 'Where does it come from? Do you have younger brothers and sisters or what?'

She is awkward. It is easier with the children than with him. Because she's got this urge to speak to him, to say things she doesn't to anyone else, crazy really, why him, for heaven's sake, such an oddball, such a weirdo to look at and never mind that wife of his in publishing and that. She looks at his socks. One brown, one aquamarine, and at the pale-blue v-neck sweater he is wearing which is much too small for him so that his ribs stick out. He is, she sees, thin, wiry, although his clothes have up till now made him look quite bulky. How old is he, early thirties? Probably older.

'I'm an only child. My father's dead. My mother – well, you know about her. We live with this man called Jerry who sets my teeth on edge. But she's crazy about him so I suppose that's all right.'

She waits for a response. When he doesn't give one she goes on, 'I've got lots of younger cousins. Mum comes from a huge family. I did a community project from my secondary school at my old primary school, helping out and that with the first-year kids. I've always liked kids. Actually it was meant to be helping out but when the teacher found I could cope she often just left me to get on with it, when she wanted to do other things. I suppose she knew I was okay with them and didn't have to worry.'

'She was lucky to have you.'

The blush comes up on Alex's face. 'She said that,' she acknowledges quietly. Tony notices how animated she's become, whereas when she speaks about her home situation it's with a flat bored voice.

Gently she swings her legs under the bench. Tony appears to be watching the children, or thinking his own thoughts.

'I feel a fool for asking, but what is a discography?'

'It's a list of all the discs brought out by any one company. Who played, who contributed. That kind of thing.'

'Oh, you like music?'

'Yes, I do. I used to be in the record business. It used to be even what they call a consuming passion' (he laughs at himself and she hears the tone, the dangerous negative tone, even the cruelty in it, or the anger, but it is not directed at her this time) 'but it all seems a long time ago now.'

'Do you like pop or was it all . . . ?'

'Classical music?' He laughs at her, making her blush again, catching her out for the thought that he is of another generation. 'I enjoy most kinds,' he says, 'but my real love is jazz.'

'Bet you've got some . . .'

'One day you must come back and hear my . . .'

Both thoughts, overlapping one another, are drowned by the noise of the uproar from the sandpit. Ellen, who has grabbed someone else's bucket and will not let go, is being punched by the little boy who is determined to retrieve it.

There was a fallen oak deep into the Heath. Alex had noticed it a couple of days ago when she was walking alone. It was hard to imagine the weight of it crashing. Or the circumstances. In a way she wished she had been there. In another she didn't. She looked at the trunk of the tree for a long time, helpless and soft. Defeated, where once it had been so strong, so *for ever*. She thought of her father. Tears came to her eyes. She brushed them away, pleased that she was alone, that no one could see.

Now, two days later, she is saying, 'Come quickly, follow me, I've got the perfect place for you to play, Moth. Oh, you're going to like this so much.' Tony looks at her bright enthusiastic face. Her hair has been newly washed and bounces on her shoulders. She walks so swiftly, leading the way, sure that they will follow. The day is coolish and she is wearing her jacket. So straight is her back that the jacket hangs from her shoulders like a cloak. Moth follows at a half run. Tony brings up the rear with Ellen in the push-chair.

'I want to stop now,' says Moth, 'I'm tired, we did too much running to get here. Daddy made us run all the way.'

'I did not! What a lie, Moth.'

'You did so.'

'Anyway we're nearly there, you can't stop now,' says Alex, slowing her pace. She turns to put out a hand to him. 'Come on, Moth. You won't regret it when we get there. Trust me.'

So he ran all the way here, did he? He's quite. I don't know what it is. I feel the same. I actually managed to concentrate on History this morning, telling myself.

Tony moves alongside her.

'They're going to love it.'

'I believe you.'

'It's the best trunk for playing on. How's it been going?'

'What?'

A vague gesture with her hands. 'Anything, everything. Nothing particular, just, well, you know, it's good to see you.'

'It's good to see you,' he is careful. After what Moth has said about running he has all the more reason to be careful. It's for the children he wants to remind her. He's not. In all the years since he's been with Carole, ten in January, he's never.

'The kids count the days till Fridays. You're such a hit. I think it's become their favourite day of the week.'

'Well, here's the tree trunk, Moth.'

'Phew.'

'Out, out,' screeches Ellen.

'Do you know you can fly from that log?' says Alex to Moth.

'No?'

'Try it, climb on and flap your wings like this.'

Tony watches, amused.

'It takes all four of us for it to work,' she tells him.

'Come on, Daddy.'

Half an hour later the children are still scrabbling over the trunk and between the roots of the giant fallen tree. Tony has taken off his jacket and he and Alex sit in the grass watching. He is wearing the same pale-blue, too-tight sweater, she longs to give him a new one.

She asks, 'How is the discography going, then?'

'Disastrous.'

'Oh, why's that?'

'Ellen's been teething all week, which is another way of saying impossible. And then a lead who I just got hold of in the US and was likely to be source of all sorts of useful information, went and died on me before he had time to reply to my letter.'

'Bad luck. And did you face it with equanimity?'

'Come again?'

'That's Mum's latest. It's a pain in the neck. All of a sudden everything's got to be faced with equanimity. Something I must say she's hardly equipped to do.'

'Carole comes out with remarks like that, particularly after her yoga . . . "Grow into your pain."'

'God, she's not into it too? Grow into your pain!' Alex rolls around on the ground, laughing. 'Grow into your pain!' There are tears in her eyes.

Looking at her Tony begins to laugh too. The weight that has been so heavy on him throughout the winter has begun to lighten with each new meeting. He thinks again of Sam Schmidt, eighty-three, dying in Los Angeles just as Tony makes contact, then back to the way they squeezed him out. The way that bastard. Even that becomes funny. He laughs and laughs till Moth, amazed at his father, and angry, comes and punches him on the chest. 'What are you laughing at, Daddy?' All of a sudden Ellen is on his chest too. He wrestles and tickles them with Alex beside him, released, youthful. Then the moment passes and they start to walk back towards the tennis courts, more peaceful, Moth again swinging his arms between Tony and Alex.

Alex says little, she is looking at the clouds, she is looking at the darkening sky, aware of the months passing. Soon there will be an end to these warm sunny days, but please let it go on just a bit longer. I don't think I'll go back to his flat. It's too good here on the Heath. It's better this way. Why did Chris just say 'cool' when I told him about Tony last night? He's an idiot. What does cool mean. No, he's not an idiot, but he could do with a larger vocabulary. Then why go around with him? Because. Oh stop this questioning, Alex. Moth's a great little boy, the best. Ellen's not bad too. They just need. Just need.

'You won't stop coming?' says Tony to her at the tennis courts.

She keeps coming. First once a week, Fridays, then comes the point when Tuesdays get added. They adjust to one another, feel their way. She knows particular things about the Heath: where the best conkers can be found, where there is an oak with a hollowed trunk, where the green green leaves interweave with the red and the yellow making a huge beech tree into a speckled eiderdown, the trees in which birds have made their nests.

As she gets to know the children better she becomes more and more a source of games, arriving with her pockets full of raisins, apples, carrots, wire figures, matchbox games, clues for mini treasure hunts. There are days in between their meetings when Tony thinks to himself, thank heaven tomorrow is Friday, or Tuesday, then I can simply give them over to Alex.

Yet to Alex it does not seem that way. On the bright days, the days when the Heath is brimming with colour and sunlight, making her feel young and strong and pleased to be alive, on those days she does take the lead. He appears willing to give over, to be passive. It seems then that she must blow energy into him as through a pair of bellows. And up onto the Heath she runs, from her basement flat, with the bellows inside her.

But on darker days, wetter days, and as October draws into November there are more of them, then the swings of mood work the other way. Hers quickly spirals down. The basement flat is a pain it is so cold. When she can't feel her own vitality then what can she feel? Sometimes it seems to her that she is nothing more than a blown leaf. Despite all protestations to Angelica and Jerry that it is not so. Where is she going, what is she doing? What should she be doing? Then she is as glad as on the good days to meet Tony and the children on the Heath, but for different reasons.

On the blown-leaf days, she stays in bed often all morning, snuggled under the duvet, and nobody and nothing would get her up.

Someone earlier today has knocked at her window but she's pretended not to be in. She has missed three lessons in a row. She has received a note from Mrs Morrow, '*Where are you? We do hope nothing is wrong*.' Sometimes everything makes her feel so on edge. She doesn't want to be asked questions at home which sound innocent but aren't. She feels, however cleverly they disguise it, that they need her reassurance that they have done her no harm, so they can sit back pleased with themselves and get on with their own lives, so they can say, 'Alex is at college . . . doing . . . ,' when they talk about her to their friends. Is that all they want? No, they love her, they worry for her. But when she goads them into saying so, it's even worse.

'If it goes on like this, I'll have to stop coming up, or move out or something.'

'And what would that solve? Anyway, where would you go?' Jerry is implying she couldn't pay for anywhere decent.

'I could always squat.'

'I can't really see you doing that, Alex.'

'Why not? Lots of my friends do.'

She is repeating this conversation to Tony on a dull day when a grey lid seems to cover the Heath, and though it isn't yet cold there are few people around, trying to enjoy the drizzle.

So far she has done more talking, he listening. That she confides in him puts him in a position that he hasn't experienced for some years, and he realises how much he enjoys it. Since he has little to say at the moment, this suits him well. He finds it an easy and strangely comforting interaction. Sometimes she asks him direct questions.

'Any more people dropping dead on you?'

'Not a peep in the post. I'm only good for bills and circulars, it seems.'

She actually likes his negativeness because it cuts across her own. They are beginning to share jokes, find dry, ironic connections. Sometimes she asks questions about Carole. But only occasionally: she doesn't want or need to be too inquisitive on that score. It's just. What is it? A good way of spending time on the Heath. He's becoming – Christ! – a kind of father confessor. She likes more and more to tell him things and relies on him being completely non-judgemental, almost uninterested, that is the trick of it. And yet he's got to like me, and it's not just because of the kids, I know it's not.

When Alex asks about Carole, Tony answers her as honestly as he can. But then the questions she asks are not deep and complex ones. He does not think he is being disloyal to Carole.

They are gaining a certain body of knowledge about one another. Alex knows about Tony's earliest years, moving between a number of uncaring relatives, then eventually being fostered. About his step-father going bust and the bout of drinking that followed. She knows about his fondness for his adopted mother, who died some years back. She knows about Tony's itinerant life after he left school, the countries he travelled to and worked in. She knows something of the years leading up to his becoming manager of a large record shop in Oxford Street. The years of stability, he says, when he met up with Carole and things were going relatively well. She doesn't know what went wrong. She doesn't ask. She doesn't think it is simple. These things aren't. She has established that Carole is a Rights Manager for A&P and is going through a tough time at work, and copes with this, or doesn't, by yoga and running in her lunch hour, when she gets the time, which is less and less frequently. And shares less and less with Tony. But he speaks well of her, he obviously likes her, even admires her, I guess he loves her, I guess, you can't really tell about these things, I know enough to know *that*.

I've told him about Chris, but that's different. That's really difficult. I don't know if he'll understand. It's different for our generation. I had to tell him Mum's name in the end, it seemed bloody silly not to. Carole is a great admirer of her articles, apparently, but what's new? At least he doesn't read them, which is something. We reckon Angelica and she must know one another because it was A&P that published that collection of her essays a few years ago. I've told him a bit about Jerry but again not much really, so difficult to give the flavour of that. I've told him a bit about the A-level. All right, I suppose I could actually do the two. I have been thinking about it occasionally. Still, I'm not making any promises. I'll just see. Just coast. When the clocks go back things will be different. No more Heath, I expect. Just coast.

*

'Clocks go back tomorrow night.'

'A whole hour more to sleep.'
'But darker afternoons.'
'Do you mind?'
'Suppose I do.'
'When it gets too dark to make it worth coming on the Heath we'll have to persuade you to come back to the flat.'
'I suppose so, yes.'
It seems nevertheless such a long, long way off on a day such as this. They are running through the leaves. She can feel them as crunchy as cornflakes under her feet. She has Ellen on her shoulders, the little girl is whooping with delight. Tony, keeping abreast with a heavier burden, has his son on his shoulders. 'Good horse, giddee-up, giddee-up,' shouts Moth to his father. Tony, running, turns to say something to Alex and is transfixed watching a shower of yellow leaves fall onto his daughter's pink bonnet, and then, dislodged, tumble down Alex's shoulder and onto the ground.

At Kenwood in The Olde Kitchen.
'What a long way we've come! I don't like my orange juice, it's too sweet.'
'Here, Moth, do you like tea?'
'No.'
'Not even with sugar in it?'
'Don't know, never tried.'
'Have a try. But blow on it first.' Alex passes over her mug.
'Now you're without,' says Tony to Alex. 'Finish mine.' He passes it over.
'But look, you haven't even started it. And besides,' she peers down into the cup, 'it doesn't look like tea at all to me. I think they've given you chocolate. How odd.'
'I want chocolate, I want chocolate,' says Moth.
Alex pushes the cup round the table till it is facing Moth. At the same time Tony leans over and draws Alex's now-sugared tea towards his place. Alex turns to the high chair beside her and helps Ellen's hands to clasp the mug and steady it as she sips her milk. 'It's like musical chairs,' says Moth, delighted.
'We could play properly,' suggests Alex. 'One sip and then pass on.'
'Yes, let's.' He is already pushing the chocolate to his father. The chocolate, the tea, the orange juice go whizzing, it seems to Moth, round and round the table. 'I can have a sip quicker than any of you.' He looks from one to the other, excited, laughing.
'That first time, Tony,' Alex is more confident now; she is beginning to

judge that what they have, whatever it is, will not just disappear, 'when we were having tea at Mel's, and you know I said about you being a house-husband, would you like to . . . could you tell me why it made you so angry?'

He looks at her thoughtfully and pulls at his moustache.

'Not if you don't want to, though.'

But Moth, inevitably, has started to talk.

'One of these days,' Tony says to Alex, 'one of these days when I lure you back to the flat and the kids are watching TV.'

'Sure,' she says, 'okay.' She knows that she will not go back to his flat. Strange. The more she is drawn to him – and the kids – the less she desires to leave the Heath with them. Keeping boundaries seems to her important. Then she can tell herself, and others if need be, it is only.

'Do you ever think about Aids?' she asks him suddenly. 'Well, no, I suppose you never need to, not personally, you being married and that.'

'Marriage in itself is no reassurance.'

'S'pose not.'

'What about you?'

'Well it makes a difference.'

'To you and Chris?'

'Yes.'

He wonders: her face has that adolescent, shut-tight look. She is right, he does find it hard to put himself in her place and imagine her morality, her frame of reference.

He shifts the direction of the conversation to the subject of her supposed second A-level, Politics. At first she denies all interest; with her face still closed she says she hasn't the faintest idea what they are being taught, really, she doesn't listen at all. He's got to believe her. She starts fussing with Ellen, making a boat out of her paper napkin for Moth. But Tony stubbornly persists. Probing, throwing out opinions, waiting for Alex to take the bait. Eventually she does and her own voice comes out ringing clearly, suddenly saying words she didn't know she could string together like that, didn't know she had in her. She is amazed at herself. Then suspicious.

'You led me on.'

'And look what happened,' he laughs.

She's flushed. It is all very strange. Did she really say those things? She considers. They don't sound like anyone else she knows. And yet? Usually she envies people of her age who are really articulate. Her mum is so like that, you'd have thought she'd have got it off her. At school she sometimes thinks the teachers are only nice to her because they've read Angelica's articles. 'Not me,' she'd said, when Jerry had one time asked why daughter wasn't more like mother, 'Not me, I don't believe that much in the value of words, it's overrated.' Well, they'd certainly have been amazed to have heard this little discourse!

She considers Tony. A bead of chocolate is hanging on his moustache. It disturbs her. She says, 'There probably isn't a teacher at any comprehensive pro Maggie right now, you're right about that. And with all those that teach Politics – it certainly makes you think.' Go on, put up your hand and wipe your moustache, it's driving me crazy, that drop.

'Would you go back to work yourself, if you could, if there was a job?'

And then he gets up from the table, 'Time to go, everyone.' They are becoming adept at ducking issues they find difficult to deal with. Yet it seems, thinks Alex, that there are always plenty of avenues open. That's what I like. It's not like. It's just different.

And to Tony, perhaps a little dishonestly, as long as she keeps coming, as long as she continues to be so good with the children, I don't mind what the hell she talks about.

*

'Come on. What are you waiting for, Daddy?' Sometimes Moth notices Daddy looking at Alex, or them looking at each other, and feels left out. And uncomfortable. He can't explain why. Still it is such a little thing. He loves Alex and feels just like his daddy does. Daddy is not always so sad any more and that must be nice, mustn't it? Mummy even said to him one day, one Saturday when they had gone out shopping together, just he and she, 'Daddy is much happier now, isn't he Moth?' She'd talked to him about Daddy being so nice. When was it? Just a while ago. A day that wasn't a school day. It had started out by something happening that wasn't nice at all.

Crash bang. He was in the bedroom he shared with Ellen. Mummy and Daddy were still in their bedroom, in bed. They just wouldn't get up that day and it was so so annoying. They said he was old enough to get himself his own cereal on some days, like not school days. And Ellen had been left a rusk and bottle of juice by the cot that was once Moth's and now was hers.

But this morning it seemed they were never coming out of their bedroom. He'd looked at the pictures in the books near his bed and had played with his soft toys and now what more was there to do? He didn't really want breakfast, he wanted them to get *up*. He wanted to talk to Mummy. He loved it on the days she didn't have to go to work and why did she have to spend any of that special time in bed with Daddy? He looked at the clock on the wall in his room. He was just beginning to make out the time. He thought it was nine o'clock. If it was, Mummy and Daddy ought to be up by now. Why were they taking so long?

Then it was annoying him that Ellen was awake and just as fed up as he. She was banging against the sides of her cot wanting to get out. He hated that noise. 'Stop it, Ellen. Stop it, do you hear?'

But Ellen wouldn't stop. So Moth decided that if he was big enough to get his own cereal he was big enough to get her out. He'd seen Mummy and Daddy do it many times before. He got a chair, put it beside the cot, scrambled up on it and undid the two latches. The side was easy to pull down. Ellen was so eager to get out she fell on the floor. He said to her sternly, 'You're not to cry, do you hear? If you do, I'll get into trouble. If you do I'll never do anything for you ever again.' Ellen puckered up her face but she didn't cry. So Moth felt tenderly towards her and offered to make her some cereal.

Afterwards, he'd gone back to his bedroom to play with his toys, and he'd stopped thinking about Ellen.

Bang crash bang. He ran out of his bedroom towards the noise. Mummy and Daddy came out of the other bedroom and ran towards the sitting room. He squeezed in the door between them. All three stood looking at Ellen, who'd broken one of Daddy's records.

'Oh Tony, please, please don't go at her the way you did before,' Mummy says. Daddy is looking absolutely heartbroken. Moth runs towards him and puts his arms around Daddy's legs and starts to cry. These are Daddy's specially best things. Mummy has said when Ellen broke the last one, 'These are very very rare, which means you can never buy them any more. Only Daddy and a few other people have these records now.'

Mummy grabs Ellen. 'What are you doing, Ellen? How did you come to . . .?'

Then Moth realises. It's he who's going to be in for it. He who let. Daddy seems to be counting to ten like he's taught Moth to do when he had an 'ow'. 'Count to twenty, Daddy,' says Moth. It's frightening, but only for a minute. Daddy suddenly says, 'Well, there's no point crying over spilt milk or broken records. There doesn't seem to be anywhere in this flat that imp can't get to now. You wouldn't have thought . . . And by the way, Moth, why *is* she out of her cot?'

Mummy put her arms around Daddy. 'I'm so sorry, Tony, I really am. But you've taken it like a man.'

'And how else did you expect me to take it?' He ruffles her hair. 'I could do with a pot of strong coffee, I don't know about anyone else.' They all troop into the kitchen.

Sometimes Daddy does all the food shopping in the week. Sometimes he does it on Saturday when Mummy looks after Moth and Ellen. Sometimes, rarely because Mummy doesn't like doing it she says, but sometimes she does it and sometimes Moth goes along. Those days are special treats.

Today Mummy says to Daddy, 'You stay here, I'll do the shopping.'

They have an arrangement with their neighbours; if they get through with their shopping by eleven o'clock then Mr and Mrs Stewart will put their stuff into the car with their own. So they have to get going quick. Mummy says, 'Can you be ready and dressed in five minutes, my little soldier? If not, I'll have to leave you here with Daddy.' Moth swears that he can.

They leave the house and run for the bus. Moth loves this, running with Mummy. He jumps on the bus beside her. This is their special time together. There are some things he wants to tell her about what Mrs Harrison has said this week at school.

Carole listens. His voice is a high one and the very precise nature of his pronunciation sometimes grates. She finds it much harder to enter his world than Tony does. Her own world presses in on her. She cannot any longer leave work at work and there are a number of things she wants to turn over in her mind this weekend, if she ever gets any peace. At the same time there is something with Tony niggling at the back of her mind.

They were making love again, and she ought to be relieved, and is. But there was something different in the way he'd been with her this morning. Something new. How to explain it? He'd fucked her long and hard. On and on and on. After such drought, each time now it was intense relief, as if they'd got back to where they were. And she'd come but at the last moment she'd almost not wanted to because. There was something about his will. Something she couldn't put her finger on. Just something different. No, it was more that it was as if he was holding something back, some new piece of himself. Is that what it was?

And then afterwards, the way he was about that 'Brooklyn Bridge' that Ellen broke, so different to. And God, even she would have made more of a fuss. Of course she was pleased but it was as if. It was strange.

'Moth,' she cuts across his chat, 'Daddy is much happier now, just as I told you he would be.'

'Yes he is,' says Moth, happy himself.

Then she surprises him.

'And why do you think that is?'

'I know why it is, it's because of . . .' All of a sudden he can't say it. Then Mummy might be sad, because Mummy had to go to work to make lots and lots of money to feed them all and she might want to be on the Heath too playing like he and Alex and Daddy and Ellen did.

'. . . because for the reason that Ellen doesn't cry any more.'

Mummy looks at him. It seems to be a funny look she's giving him. Then she tousles his hair, just as she sometimes does Daddy's. 'There, didn't I tell you that Ellen's crying is only natural? She's growing up now. But you mustn't let her out of her cot in the mornings unless we give you permission. Not ever again. In another few months, though, we'll have to find her a bed. She's growing up. And so are you.'

But again she looks at him. There's something in the way she's said it, in the way she looks at him, which makes him not sure that he wants to grow up if it is like that.

He holds her hand tight and says, 'I love you, Mummy.'

'And I love you.'

'And I love Daddy and Ellen.'

'We all love each other, Moth, that's how it is in families. Now come on, let's get into Sainsbury's before the queues are too awful.'

*

'But Daddy,' Moth is jumping up and down, 'why is Ellen in that thing?'

He holds his Daddy's hand as tight as he can. 'Where is the push, the pushy? You haven't lost it, have you, Daddy?'

'No, I haven't lost it. I've left the pushy and bought a buggy. So that we can move faster. Can you run?'

'We're not going to run all the way there, are we, Daddy? It's too far.'

'Just as far as the bus stop.'

'But I'm tired today. I've run and run in the playground. I want to go home and have tea, and watch telly.'

'Wouldn't you like just to go as far as the playground, Moth? And go down the slide?'

'No.'

'Don't be silly, Moth, you want to see Alex don't you?'

'No. Yes, but not all that way.'

'You're just being perverse. You'll love it when we get there. I know you will. Here, grab my hand.'

Cold days, brisk days. Ellen wears dungarees and a padded jacket, Moth wears tracksuit bottoms, two sweaters and an anorak. Both children have bright-red scarves and woolly hats knitted by their great-aunt. It is a blessed autumn, luck is with Tony and Alex, so many good days, so many days when it seems sensible to catch the last of the daylight and often even the sunlight, on the Heath.

Today Moth has asked if he can bring Seth with him. Seth has no scarf. His jacket has a hood and he pulls that up and zips the anorak up to the very top. But still he complains, it might well be sunny but what a wind, he's cold, cold. He looks very sorry for himself. Alex takes off her own fine wool scarf and ties it around his neck. 'Is that better, Seth?' He nods, pleased, and runs off after Moth. Ellen, flapping her arms at the birds overhead, toddles after them.

Alex and Tony, watching them, stand close together. The closer, the less wind to buffet them.

*

November 5th. The Heath is full of people. Little groups cluster, the sky is lit up with rockets and shooting stars. Alex has never been on the Heath by herself in the dark. She has even considered bringing a girlfriend. But will not have anyone break into the private world of her 'Heath family'. They are other than the rest of her life. She likes it like this. She has become mysterious, will not tell others why on Tuesday and Friday afternoons, come hell or high water, she cannot consider any arrangement which will take up the latter part of the afternoon.

She skirts the lower reaches of the Heath, relieved at how many people seem to be around, how the lit sky gives light to all of the ground around. She finds Moth and Tony by the water fountain close to the bandstand. There are a number of children around Moth's age. All excited, being handed lit sparklers by two of the daddies. Another father is busy fixing stakes into the ground, and attaching Catherine wheels to a nearby tree, getting ready for the show. Moth runs over to Alex and holds her hand. But then has second thoughts and rushes off to where his friend Seth and others are standing.

Alex begins to feel like an unnecessary appendage as she watches the tame display of fireworks. Moth stands during the whole show with his friends, and Ellen is not there to be comforted and held. She is not a mother, after all. Why is she here? What is she doing? Tony speaks to her, his eyes find hers in the half darkness lit up from time to time by bursts of lights. She half wishes she hadn't come.

At the end there is confusion, so many people, so many excited voices. Moth is trying to tell his Daddy that he has been invited back to Seth's for beans on toast and please Daddy say yes he can go . . . please. Alex listens to this, feeling strange. If Tony agrees then it will be the first time that they have been alone together. Maybe he'll walk her back across the Heath. Let him say, of course not, it's far too late, tomorrow is a school day, not this time, Moth. But Tony has acquiesced.

The others are departing, she hangs on at his side, uncertain. He is aware of her waiting undirected presence. Well, why rush off after all, when Carole is home looking after Ellen and for once he has a choice?

'What about a drink in the pub?' he asks.

'S'pose so. What time is it?'

He looks at the luminous face of his watch. 'Just after seven. Why?'

'Chris and Dave and a whole group of us are going to Alexandra Palace, but we're not leaving for a couple of hours yet.'

The pub across the road is full, it is hard to find a seat. Guy Fawkes night, so many people have the same idea. Alex and Tony feel anonymous in the well-lit room. They lean against a wall, Tony with a pint of beer and Alex with a half. Alex, near to a radiator, warms her bum. Tony has to move close to her to be heard over the noise.

Alex sips her beer, uncomfortable, pressing the glass against her thin fingers and enjoying the sensation. She does not know what will constitute pub talk with Tony. She is conscious as always of other people's looks, especially the guys'. She thinks about the kind of couple they must look like. She is aware of Tony's unkempt hair, neither long nor short nor anything in particular; one day she will bring scissors onto the Heath. Maybe have a go at his moustache too. She is aware of his jacket, its ancient shape. She is also aware as always that there is some kind of internal excitement going on for her, as they find their way back from the externals into something that constitutes intimacy; none of the rest counts. Now he is standing beside her, near her, drinking, waiting his time. She wonders what he is thinking. She wonders is he still 'desperate'; she would like to ask him that, but not yet.

'My mum's got another one, another bee in her bonnet, you wouldn't believe what it is,' she giggles. 'It's about finding the power spots. She takes it so seriously, you should see her wandering round the house, finding, or not finding the power spots. You know, when I said last week that I was having difficulty with my History essay she actually said it was probably because I hadn't yet found the power spot in the basement. "Just find that and all else will flow." Can you believe it? Oh, there's nothing wrong with finding power spots but she gets so – exaggerated about it. Like she's the only person in England who's had this revelation. And she's got to share it with all and sundry.'

'That's why she's a writer, I imagine.'

'I suppose.' Then shifting, 'How did you get into the record business and what happened? I'd really like to know, Tony, really. If you felt like it.'

He contemplates the girl beside him. Not full-face, not the eyes and the expression, but the side of her, her profile, her shoulder in its vibrant blue jacket, the long jean-covered legs. Hell, what to say? It was a long time since.

'Oh I don't know, Alex. Music was just a hobby for ages, well, ever since I can remember. I used to play drums at school. There was a group of us; we played gigs at youth clubs and things. Drove my parents to distraction, especially my mother, because that way I got to be tired in the mornings and miss even more school and she wanted me to have an education. Hadn't had one herself, had married "above herself" because of her looks, she was a very pretty lady, pretty and gentle, but my adopted father always treated her rotten, and her other sons acted like she was just the skivvy. Being the youngest, I got to spend the most time with her. From the age of five when I joined the family we were real close. Then at fourteen, I suppose it was something to do with my father's drinking and rages – this is after he'd been sacked from his job – I spent more and more time hanging out with the crowd from school, earning the money to get my hands on every ticket for every pop concert going. Pop first, then gradually jazz took over. It was only in my twenties that I started to listen to classical music too. At the time, at school, I wanted something young, vigorous, something that blew the top off the surface of middle-class, supposedly cultural life, which seemed a sham in our household from the start. Yeah, here am I talking about way, way back. Boring you rotten, no doubt.'

'You're not boring me. You know, I was thinking about one of Mum's horribly snappy wisdoms.'

'Yes?'

'Life always repeats itself.'

'You've lost me there.'

'Your father being sacked, you becoming redundant.'

Tony falls silent. Until that moment he has never made the connection. He is silent for such a long time.

'You didn't mind me saying that, did you?'

'Mind? Not a bit. It's certainly food for thought. How old did you say you were?'

'Eighteen and know nothing.'

'Don't you believe it, Alex, not for a moment.'

They both fall silent. Tony rattles his glass, realising that it is empty. He rattles it because he needs to do something with his hand. He has an urgent desire to reach out, to touch her. But doesn't. Ever since he started living with Carole he hasn't. He won't now. It would complicate things and be good for neither of them. He must hold on to that. It won't be too difficult. Apart from anything else, the gap. No one could be more aware of it than himself.

'Hey look, there's a couple of seats by the window there, why don't we grab them?'

'Okay then.'

'What about jazz?' she asks, when they've sat down. 'Do you have a special period, or some players that are your favourites? I like jazz too but I only know the big names I guess.'

'I got hooked into the jazz that took place immediately after the Second

World War, and right into the fifties. A lot of it's coming back into fashion now, that's the irony. Early Mod, jazz bordering on rhythm and blues . . . think of the music in recent films. *Absolute Beginners, Round Midnight*. Oh, there are countless other examples. Charlie Parker, Thelonius Monk. Ben Webster, they're all having a new wave of popularity.'

'I suppose so. But where's the irony?'

He sighs and looks again into the distance. 'Well, the truth is, Alex, I overjudged it I suppose. Backed my own hunches. Just bought too much of that stuff in, out of proportion to the rest. Wanted everyone to enjoy what I enjoyed. You know? Then the stock turn was too low and those buggers moved in. They had it in for me anyhow, I reckon. They simply wanted me out. Wanted their own guys in.'

He is silent again. And then almost as if not to her but to himself: 'There were other things. Too complicated to go into now. Will you drink another half?'

Alex is conscious of the time. She will have to walk along the road home and that will take much longer. Chris has said nine-thirty. He is not one to be punctual. Still if she wasn't there, knowing her gang they wouldn't hang around. They'd just reckon she'd changed her mind or something. And she doesn't want to miss Alexandra Palace this year. Still she doesn't feel ready to go either. They might never be alone together like this again.

'Another quick one, I reckon I've just got time.'

Neither of them see the man who has stepped in through the door and is staring in their direction. He is there for a matter of seconds. Twenty, thirty. Then he turns on his heel and leaves.

The following morning, Angelica, Jerry and Alex are having breakfast in Angelica's airy farmhouse kitchen. It is airy partly because the cat flap no longer closes, and Angelica and Jerry are both the kind who believe in the cold. 'Just put on more sweaters,' they say to visitors. Alex, of course, isn't quite a visitor, though since her move downstairs it is unusual for her to breakfast with them any longer.

When there had just been Alex and Angelica in the house, Alex had persuaded her mother on numerous occasions to indulge her and turn on, or up, the heating. But after Jerry's arrival, that, like much else, went by the board.

She wishes that the basement had its own heating system and has just said so. What is just about acceptably cold here is freezing down there, she tells her mother; 'You ought to try sometime – no wonder our lodgers used to leave.'

'They always stayed for ages, darling, I am only grateful none of them took root.'

'No doubt they would of . . .'

'Would have.'

'For Christ's sake! Would *have*, if they'd been warmer – or found the power spot.'

'Girls, why are you quarrelling?' asks Jerry. 'Not at this hour of the morning, please.'

Alex hates it when he calls them 'girls'. She also hates the inference with 'this hour' that it is no longer her home, she can no longer come up to breakfast if she wants. She has wanted. Or rather she's wanted to borrow milk. But once upstairs the smell of eggs and bacon and mushrooms that Angelica is frying has attracted.

'There's plenty. Do stay.'

'I could. If you're sure.'

Actually it isn't just the food. But also the company. Her mother's. Forget that guy, if you can forget him – which is difficult.

Her nerves jangle this morning. That time in the pub. Where are they going, what is happening? Then afterwards, with Chris and the gang, and of course she'd been late back. And Chris had honked outside, then gone away and come back three bloody times, he'd said. Where the hell had she been? She'd told him. Then the Spanish Inquisition, why? what? All hell let loose. And died down. But after the fireworks, again it came up. What he wanted. And when she'd tried to tell him how she felt he'd said, 'Oh fuck all that, you're sounding like a granny you're so responsible.'

'Fuck off yourself.'

And then they'd fought.

While they eat Jerry watches Alex, aware of the translucent skin, the dark rims under her eyes. He feels that he knows something about her that he shouldn't. He almost wishes he didn't, for now something ought to be done about it. Tell Angelica? If only she wasn't enmeshed in her work and so volatile. Speak to Alex himself? This has never worked so far. Over breakfast maybe he can gently guide the conversation round to what he's seen. In this sense it is a godsend she's come up. But he knows before he starts that all the leads he will offer her she will not take. Damn! damn! damn! Hasn't he enough to worry about, with his mother?

Yesterday he'd found her lying on the floor in her flat. Goodness knows how many hours she'd been there. It had been impossible to get a coherent explanation out of her. He'd tried to lift her but she was in too much pain. He'd called for an ambulance, gone with her to the hospital, seen her settled for the night. Then he'd taken a taxi to where his car was parked outside the flats. But when he put the key in the ignition he found that he was trembling. So, noticing the pub on the corner of the junction with

Highgate Road, he'd decided to drop in there for a brandy before making for home. Instead of which.

What is she doing with a man like that? Old enough to be her. Not much younger than him. So unsavoury, no doubt on drugs. That hair curling down his neck. He looks again at Alex and shudders. Where could she have? Why would she have? Her school crowd are bad enough. At least they are her age. But this! For God's sake, what is she getting into now? The way they'd been, the something deeply intimate between them that he'd observed as he stood at the door, not wanting to see. Yes, he will tell Angelica. But last night she worked till after he'd fallen asleep. And this morning she needs a clear mind in order to finish her piece.

Why feel angry with Alex, try to feel tender with her like you used to. Look at her expression, she's such a child, such a lost soul. Try to help her. Can it be my fault really? Angelica says she wasn't like this before. I can't take that on. It doesn't make sense. It must have been coming anyway. I'd like to feel that she'll pull through. That it's just, what, a rather late adolescent rebellion. But she's so very off course. Then feel sorry for her, yes, be gentle.

'Alex, love, you look awfully tired, how are you feeling?'

'Tired, yeah, it was one hell of an evening. A night I mean.' She laughs.

Instantly he is bristling. 'Then why the hell have a night like that when you know you've got studying to do today?'

'Here wait a moment, Jerry, what bloody business is it of yours? Anyway, I'm off.'

She takes her plate, cup and cutlery to the dishwasher and stacks them, then without another word makes her way down to the basement.

'No, wait a moment,' Jerry says after her, 'I didn't mean . . .'

'See ya.'

Jerry sits with his fists on his forehead.

'Short fuse?' says Angelica. 'It makes a change anyway, darling. It's usually me.' She leans over and kisses him on the mouth. 'What time did you say you'll be visiting your mother tonight?'

'Around seven.'

'I'll come with you.'

★

Sarah is aware that Carole is losing weight. Perhaps she is the only person who notices. She watches over Carole with motherly solicitude. It seems sometimes to the younger woman that she is obsessed with the older. The feeling takes her by surprise; she doesn't know what to do with it. Nick says that she is going through a mother transference and to let it happen and not judge herself. Thank God for Nick! Work is both exciting and uncomfortable because she is so aware of Carole; it seems to her that she must continually be holding herself back, terrified to let her feelings show. At the same time her ambitions are accelerated by Carole's. The two work together at fever pitch. In the weeks leading up to Frankfurt, and since, they've been getting to work at eight a.m., yet the days never seem long enough.

Sarah has got over the disappointment of Carole not becoming editorial director. She wonders if Carole feels it was a slight. But Carole will not say so. She simply says that it is for the best, it wasn't for her anyway. Rights is what she likes and what she is good at.

Still Sarah, getting to know her better, is aware now that in the last month she has made two bad misjudgements. These have been hushed up. She does not know if these happen in all publishing houses and whether they are as horrendous as they seem to her.

They haven't had an editorial director as such for the last three months. The senior staff have all been temporarily sharing the load. It has been a fun time for Sarah as Carole has had new informal responsibilities. Now Lee Getting has arrived to take up the position.

Carole told Sarah that if she wished to become an editorial assistant she could make the move at this point and work for one of the other editors. Sarah weighed it up. To work for the editorial director was one thing. To work for an editor with little power, another. Besides, and here ambition blurred with personal feelings, she was not ready to leave Carole. She tried to convey her dilemma in a way which would cloud both her worst and best instincts. But Carole read her like a book. She valued Sarah, she valued stability, still she didn't want her stuck in a secretarial role. So she came up with the compromise that a third of her time would be taken up with editorial work; meanwhile, Carole would get extra secretarial help from a new part-time typist.

Sarah was happy. It seemed just right. Her gratitude to Carole knew few bounds. If only she could do something for her. That was the thought that was occupying her mind the morning after Guy Fawkes night in which at the last moment Nick and herself had drifted up to Alexandra Palace and found the fireworks good enough but the crowd insufferably noisy. 'To think that we were like that only a few years ago,' she'd said to Nick.

Now it is twelve-thirty and Carole has Sarah in her room going over a number of matters that might come up whilst she is out having lunch with new boy, Lee.

Sarah looks at Carole's figure, guesses that she's lost a half stone quite rapidly and wonders, does she eat lunch these days, or does she just pretend, or not notice? And then a pang. She's ill. Does she know it? Cancer? Don't be ridiculous.

At Angelo's Carole orders a *salade niçoise*. Lee orders veal and noodles, a half-bottle of rosé and a bottle of Perrier.

It is true that Carole has made a couple of big mistakes this last month. Miscalculations. It is all to do with the prices books are going for. Every new record seems impossible till after the fact. Carole is uncomfortable with the new high figures. Now the old chairman has retired there has been a shift around in the group, and the new chairman who has bought back his original company is making things tough for everyone. No wonder the MD himself feels threatened, and similarly all the staff.

The new chairman takes a greater interest, or rather a closer one than the outgoing one. He wants to go over the accounts with a toothpick. The MD has done some doctoring which she hopes will be overlooked. So far the doctoring is concerned with other people's mistakes, not hers. And things, too, which they all reckon are outside everyone's control. Some things you can't gauge for. But if she goes on making errors of judgement she too will be losing the firm's money at a time when they can hardly afford it. The latest Drucilla Stronghold, for example, which she was sure would fetch six figures and in the end hardly brought in a figure worth paying for the auction. And then there was Monty Pearson's *Hang Them, Thrash Them, or Send Them Here*, which she knew she should push for but at the last minute lost her guts and let it go to Kimberley-Clark. And then only last week, to compensate, or in reaction, she'd been tempted . . . forget it, she hadn't, she'd stuck with herself and not been influenced.

Now she toys with her salad and considers the new editorial director.

She had been happy with the decision in the end to take on someone from outside. She knew herself well and had considered it too great a challenge. She wasn't convinced that she'd be comfortable in editorial; it would have meant a whole new bag of skills, not least a way with the authors which was not something that would have come easily. She loved the 'game', she got on well with people in publishing, but writers seemed a different species of animal. She got none of the kicks that many do from mixing with them. Give her a room full of good solid people in the trade any day.

However, it had been a difficult decision to make. The days had long gone when she might have discussed this with Tony. As he had got deeper into his depression, so it became harder and harder for her to talk over work matters. And as she'd risen at A&P her own experience had so outstripped his that very often what he did say she found of little constructive value. Or led to bitterness and innuendo which she had little time for.

So at some point along the way she'd stopped talking to him about much of what went on. It was easier. She made a neat division, work and home, and kept it that way.

Still, over the last six months, the time of the worst atmosphere at home, she had often wished for someone outside work with whom she could chat things over. But it wasn't to be. She had her colleagues at work, the friendship with Charles and, to a lesser extent, Ian, plus a couple of women friends whom she was frequently too busy to see. She had yoga which, if nothing else, helped her to get out of her head and into some other space. And, indeed, it was at the end of a yoga class a month or so back, when she was lying on the floor in the corpse pose, that it had come to her as clear as daylight that to take up the post of editorial director might please her vainglory and make her more money but was something she wasn't up to. Nor was she convinced that it was best for the firm. She suspected this was another instance of Charles playing safe. She suspected that he should take the leap and bring in some new blood, and urged him to do so.

What had gone wrong then? She had failed to take into account that the choice would be none of her making. She imagined that she would have a say, even if an informal one. In the event, it all happened fast. Charles and Lee had had opposite rooms in Frankfurt. Charles's luggage had been mislaid on the plane. Lee had offered to loan him a rather nice dinner jacket. Lee with excellent credentials, bright young go-ahead, only one year to prove himself at M—— but already he'd brought in some winners. And what a publishing pedigree!

Carole looks at Lee now as he makes light and easy conversation. So charming, so sure of himself. He thinks he can win her round, does he, by flattering her? She has seen people be used. She has, no doubt, used others, though she's tried not to; more and more that part of it doesn't attract. Now her guard is up. She senses that she will have to play Lee's game or lose, not a choice she relishes.

Twenty-eight. Is he really? He looks such a boy. She is only five years older but feels so very much older, sometimes feels that she is running out of steam. Needs a holiday. Away from the family too. Just somewhere she can put her legs up. Is he really twenty-eight or has he lied? His cheeks have that scrubbed-by-mum look. His hair, dark, like Tony's, tumbles over his forehead. His lips are fleshy and extremely red. His eyes are blue, again a similar shade. He is indeed like Tony in some ways. Like a younger Tony when they'd first. But what a different personality. Tough and going places where Tony has just.

'Give me a chance, Carole,' he is saying. 'I know how difficult it is to let an outsider in. And Charles told me about how you had a particular bond and worked so well with the outgoing – the unmentionable – outgoing editor.'

'She's not unmentionable to me. Nor to anyone else, as far as I know. We all think she had a right to . . .'

'I was just making a joke, nothing personal. All I want to say is that I'm going to follow right along with what she's been doing and at the same time obviously bring in some of my own authors. But there won't be any major changes I hope,' (That's what they all say, thinks Carole wearily) 'and I'm going to rely on your expertise. I am sincerely hoping you and I can become good friends in time. And if there is anything –'

'Okay, okay.'

She is easier when they are drinking coffee, and somehow they end up (his suggestion) sharing a zabaglione. They have stopped talking publishing and he is telling her about the holidays he spends on the Isle of Skye. She and Tony had been there once. 'You must come up again,' he is saying, 'my people have a place . . .'

'It's pretty well impossible now with two young kids.'

'Who says there's anything impossible about that? We' (Who are *we*? He doesn't specify.) 'love kids, no, you must come, I insist. After Christmas. How about it? Come for New Year.'

'We'll have to see.'

'Bet you could do with a few sea breezes. Well, couldn't you? Go on, admit it. I've only got to be in London for a couple of months and I'm planning my next visit. Not quite the right fodder for publishing, eh?' He is laughing, he is full of good nature and pleasure with the world. It is impossible for her not to relax into it. And as they walk back together towards the office he says again, 'You will think it over, then? Please do.'

How would that be, Carole wonders on the bus going home from work, how would it work out? Would Tony agree to come? It seems such ages since. And then the kids, could you take them anywhere? Yet the more she thinks about it the more she thinks that a) it is good of Lee so generously to offer, whatever his motives, and b) she could do with a break. *They* could do with a break. Of course there is nothing to worry about. Not with Tony. She can trust him. They've always said that they could trust one another. And stuck to it. It's just that. She tries to look back along the path of her relationship with Tony and remember when this was said. It was certainly at a very different time. For the first time it occurs to her to wonder whether the inevitable shifts that have been necessary in the relationship between them would, in Tony's view, change any of what they had promised one another. No, of course not.

She'd been surprised the night before when Moth had been delivered home after his beans on toast with Seth's family. He'd rushed up to the flat by himself, all joyous and eager.

'Where's Daddy, Moth?'

Moth couldn't remember. All he knew was that Daddy said he could have supper with Seth and they'd had a lovely time and the fireworks were super and, 'Guess what, Mummy . . .' and the long and the short of it was that he didn't remember anything about what Daddy said he'd do. 'Isn't he here?'

'No, of course not, silly. But don't look so grim, it's not the end of the world.' She had to laugh and ruffle his hair to take the seriousness out of it. 'He'll show up.'

Moth had been asleep when Tony showed up. And Ellen for far longer.

'Had a nice time?' called Carole from the kitchen as she heard him enter. It was on the tip of her tongue to say, 'Where have you been?' but she managed not to. Let him tell her if he wanted to. Each person must have personal freedom. These things can't be bulldozed.

He came into the kitchen, beer on his breath, and put his arms around her. 'I did, old girl, as a matter of fact I stopped off for a couple of pints with Alex, you don't mind, do you?'

'No,' (She'd lied. She noticed that she did mind) 'but I mind being called old girl. You know I noticed my first grey hair this week.'

'There's my Carole. It will take a lifetime to make you old. Believe me. That looks good, are we partying or something?'

'Yes, partying. It is Guy Fawkes, though I haven't given it a thought all day.'

'Dance with me.' He shuffles her round the kitchen floor. 'She's such a child, but sometimes very perceptive.'

'Who?'

'Alex. You know what she actually said to me this evening?' He is still dancing. 'That there was a connection between my father having been sacked and me being out of work now. What do you think of that?'

'Probably balls,' said Carole.

Yes a holiday away, new scenery, something to share. If it could be arranged, after her brother came, it would probably be no bad thing.

*

Jerry's mother has bruised herself badly and has been semi-concussed. However there are no breaks and after a ten-day stay in hospital the authorities are anxious to return her home. Jerry steps up the care.

One afternoon he decides there is still sufficient light to walk back across the Heath. It's just what he needs after the gloom of his mother's isolation, the sadness of old age, the talk with the health visitor which has not been especially reassuring.

The leaves have now fallen from the trees. Only a handful cling on bravely here and there. It is a dull day, cold and bitter; he is pleased to have his gloves and regrets that he doesn't have his deerskin hat with its warm earflaps. Through his gloves he rubs his hands together and walks with determination. What is the point of letting these things get one down? No point at all. No doubt it will all unfold as it must.

At that moment – yes, it is. Alex with that man. And . . . he takes a few more steps up the hill . . . a couple of kids, by the looks of things. The bloke is flying a kite. A few yards away is Alex with a kid in each hand. All three are looking at the sky to where the kite flies overhead. The kids are jumping up and down in excitement. The whole scene looks extraordinarily domestic. He stands watching them, at a distance. Then, skirting the hill, makes his way home.

*

This is the period of late November and early December. Trees bare. The last of wood fires. Mild days alternating with colder ones. But also days of an exceptional winter stillness, when a pale-blue sky hovers over the Heath, so close there seems to be no space between the grass and it.

The weeks of later November and early December are also a time of extraordinary sunsets.

Alex carries a powerful Leica camera onto the Heath and takes photos of 'her family's' silhouettes from all angles, attempting to make the most of the streaky, unearthly pink light.

The weather is kind to them. Though there is some rain, it takes place mostly in the mornings and the early afternoons, giving way later to still, fresh afternoons. On the brown, empty winter branches Alex likes to watch the early afternoon's raindrops gather, and remain, plump, too lazy to fall off. These kind of days are ones when they can't sit down. Instead, when they are tired, they rest their backsides (clothed in shiny waterproofs) against supporting tree trunks, and talk.

'It's ridiculous,' Tony is saying to Alex, 'I still don't know your address, nor you mine. I wouldn't even be able to give you a ring if I couldn't make it.'

'I'm not on the phone anyway.' This is one of Alex's withdrawn, uncertain days. And she has lots. She often wonders, what does he want, rather than what does she want. One thing is clear, he does not – unlike Chris, or most of the guys she hangs around with – want sex. He hasn't picked up any of the normal leads, or made any approaches. About which she has a mixture of feelings. One is relief. Her head tells her that she doesn't want to start an affair with a married guy, old enough to be her father. And a guy who looks . . . like he does. She's not even attracted to him, really. On the other hand he looks a lot better without his moustache and with his new haircut. She'd been delighted when she saw him like that.

'And I didn't need to tell you, after all.'

'Tell me what?'

'That I thought all along you should get rid of your moustache. You look great.'

'Thank you. I treasure the words from someone as modern and . . . critical as yourself.'

She blushes. 'Don't tease me.' And thinks, half amused, half disconcerted, does he really know how critical I've been? She looks at him. What he needs now is new clothes, if only.

No, she's not attracted to him in the regular kind of way. All in all, it's a relief that he isn't making a pass at her, which she'd have to fend off. It's just that at the same time she is used to being found attractive. Even with Jerry, she can make him react, and then finds it a pain. But with Tony you kind of. There's something elusive, you can't draw him in. So that she is continually doubting her own worth. It's scary. She's never had this feeling with a male; like how far can she trust him? And then when her father died. Her mind shuts off. It's as if she's pressed a button and the camera door has closed over the lens. Anyway, it's kind of neat that we just see each other on the Heath. I like it that way. Like there are natural boundaries.

Tony at this moment is more concerned with practicalities. 'If you gave me your address I could in an emergency at least drop you a note.'

'We manage okay.'

'Oh, and by the way, while we're talking about it, Tuesday's not on, Moth's being kept late at school.'

'Moth, you haven't done anything naughty, have you?'

'No, no.' Moth is eager to tell her the true cause. He is to read the Christmas Ode in front of the school and has to have a practice run.

'That's great. Anyway, it's fine with me. Actually Mum's been pressing me to go shopping with her that afternoon.'

They have walked to the tennis courts. Tony looks at Alex's tense face, which she has relaxed today only when playing with the kids. Now as they are to part, or even before, she assumes her mask. The thought comes to him that her pain is like his own. Though it is not something that weighs him down. On the contrary he is beginning to feel more and more purposeful. He would like to give her a gift, he reflects, as he steers his children across the busy road: but what?

*

It seems to Tony as he thinks about it on the way to pick up Moth from his Christmas play rehearsal, a stroke of supreme good fortune that when he hit rock bottom Alex appeared. And if she was nothing more than a nursemaid to the children he would be perfectly satisfied. It helps, of course, that she is pretty. He'd be a fool to deny that. He isn't going to try. He likes looking at her, frankly it raises his spirits no end. And gradually he has noticed in himself the desire to look less unkempt. Recently he bought a new jacket. Carole always hands over the Barclaycard but he hates it that it is her money and rarely spends anything on himself.

'What's this?' she'd teased when he asked. 'Splashing out, are we?' When she noticed the look in his eyes, she put her arm round his shoulder. 'Sorry, love, I didn't mean it, really.' He shrugged her off. Sometimes he tells himself that he is immune to these barbs, that they are just Carole's way, something that has evolved over the years with a lot of other shit. Sometimes he responds, realising, still, how much power she has to put the spikes in if she wants to. Recently it hasn't been so bad. Recently he's begun to think a lot more about things outside himself. And this seems not unconnected with the developing friendship – if you can use that word for such a strange connection – with Alex.

What a mixture she is. Here is this female, part-girl, part-woman, her lively nubile body cradling a child; holding Moth's hand and running for all her worth; clasping both children to her slim frame; putting Ellen on her knee whilst the two of them throw bread to the ducks or the pigeons; manoeuvring her 'family' across the Heath, out of the wind, away from potential scrapes or areas of possible harm to the children and into those of safety. Pacing the occasions so that they are happy, trouble-free. So that the children get neither bored nor over-tired, nor too cold, too hungry. How he admires this ability.

Yet another part of her is in such confusion. And what she says, when the defences are down, he finds disturbing. His own recent anger, blackness, periods of frustration and hopelessness seem to be of an entirely different character to hers. It is as if the foundation of herself is quagmires and quicksilver, and everywhere he treads the support of elegant branches gives way to bottomless muddy pools. When they talk it makes him see so clearly the solidness of the time he grew up, compared to her times.

Out of work since his early thirties, he has become insulated from changes going on around, stuck with his own brand of anger. Now what comes with considering Alex is considering her world too. And his thoughts have begun to move, when he is alone, away from Alex and towards the world that Moth and Ellen will inhabit. And back again to Alex, who, he feels strongly the more he knows her, shouldn't be frittering away her life. She seems in some uncanny way to be a reflection of himself, at another time, in another shape. And gradually he feels dawning a desire to see her steady herself and find a way forwards, not to end up a useless block like himself.

Yet is he quite that useless? He carved her this week a whistle in the shape of a pigeon and she said it was one of the most beautiful pieces of carving she had ever seen. Allowing for exaggeration, still it was pleasing. He has always been good with his hands. In the first years of being at home he'd made many wooden toys for Moth. But when Carole urged him to put shelves in the kitchen he just couldn't get round to it. 'Not with the little bugger under my feet,' he said. 'You have to have time to concentrate for that kind of thing.' Whereas the toys were small and usually done in the evenings. Animals, blocks, a post-box, a range of cars, a whole family of wooden people, known as the Fisherwoman's family.

Now when Carole sees him carving the whistle she asks about it. He tells her that it's for Alex, to enable her to call the children without having to shout. Carole watches him, intent on his carving. She wonders, as she has begun to do more frequently, what the relationship is, but still thinks it wise not to say anything. Moth now wants a whistle, so Tony sets about making a second, smaller one, and for Ellen a couple of ducks on a stick arrangement that move and flap their wings in the wind. This is one of the most complicated toys he has made. He works on it for many nights in deep concentration.

Carole hasn't mentioned the shelves for some years. Jars of dried food are arranged along the floor, others stand on crates, a hopelessly makeshift arrangement. Seeing Tony busy with his hands, she wonders if she should try again. She suspects that whatever is happening on the Heath is making him happier and reckons that it might be worth at least capitalising on it for the present by harnessing his new energy.

'Tony, the ducks are such a hit with Ellen. You seem so much happier when you're doing something with your hands. I was going to ask you . . .' Their eyes meet. She trails off, laughing. 'All right, you know damn well. With my brother and Kerry threatening to descend we've got to do something about the place. Fixing the shelves in the kitchen would be a start. Come on, I haven't nagged you on this score for ages, you've got to admit.'

Tony considers. 'If you take the children out for a couple of days, one weekend between now and Christmas, then I'll do it.'

'You know that's impossible. There are only three weekends left.'

'Take it or leave it.' He gets a beer from the fridge, wanders through into the sitting room and turns on the telly.

A few minutes later Carole comes after him. 'Well, perhaps . . . next weekend.'

'Up to you.'

'Both days?'

'That's what I said.'

Pause.

'I could take them over to visit Barbara.'

She looks at him. Knowing that he has won and she will visit Barbara. And trail around the shops with them on Saturday, which she hates.

'Couldn't I leave Ellen at home? She's no trouble,' she tries as a last attempt. But Tony isn't listening.

Nothing more is said on the subject. He makes love to her vigorously that night. Both are aware that it has been some time since he has so much stuck up for himself.

Tony doesn't mind making the shelves, as long as he is left to it. It is true that there is a slight but noticeable increase in his energy level. True too that it has been a couple of months since he's felt the kind of despair that's totally immobilising.

As he prepares the wood, saws, drills and attaches the shelves to the uneven surfaces – why do they always turn out to be uneven? – many new thoughts pass through his head: about what he has to be grateful for; in the validity of certain things that he has until now not given much time to. Thinking about Alex he begins, for example, to see in what he is rooted.

Life, it seems to him, had been altogether a more simple affair when he was growing up. In his earliest years a matter of survival. Then, with his adopted family, it was a fight against the odds for the continuation of a way of life of middle-class privilege, for those fortunate enough to enjoy it; a sense of the unswervable rightness of certain things, that for example, the British were not only the best but almost the only race. Though he wasn't aware of taking on board much of this value system, it was there, nevertheless, to be rebelled against.

What had been in his mind when he was growing up was the intention to operate the system better than his father had done. With more energy and acumen and less prejudice. He would work hard. He would give more time to personal relationships; family life he thought important. Inevitably, he would enjoy things more than the lot before him had done. It was as simple as that. It would be better being a grown-up and calling the shots. The world would be stable, he would be changed, older and wiser and more able to move around in it. That was the assumption. And that seems to him, wondering about these things in the delightful quiet of the flat, to have offered a kind of sanity, the value of which only now can he appreciate. Particularly when he sees so clearly in Alex the effect of its absence.

Her world seems to be a shifting world, a world in which every move ends in pointlessness. Her mother is so liberal, so understanding, so attuned to what is going on; there is nothing she will not discuss, will not consider.

Alex has been given a bit of this religion, a bit of that. She'd been taken to an ashram in India when she was fourteen. She'd been introduced to religious groups, political groups, militant feminists, battered wives, gays of both sexes, Rastafarians, anti-vivisection campaigners, members of Green Peace, Friends of the Earth, Animal Rights campaigners, Human Rights campaigners, all kinds.

Her mother had urged her to join Youth CND and was proud to get up early to make sandwiches and pack her off on coaches to wherever a demonstration was gathering. She would tell all her friends: 'My daughter . . .' It was so satisfactory.

Naturally they'd become vegetarians. They'd talked about the cruelty of battery farming, together they'd sat through every programme, Alex sicker than her mother, the first to say, we must, we must. And Angelica enthusiastically wrote about it. Living with a vegetarian, being a vegetarian, entertaining meat-eaters, and so on. At first they both seemed to thrive. Angelica told their friends how well they were doing, that they had never felt better. Then about two years later Alex became ill, at first it was only the flu, then a series of colds and general malaise. Iron tablets, vitamins – nothing made a difference. She found school increasingly difficult and became so wan that Angelica, in rude health herself of course, became worried for her daughter. Looking at her one day, lying on the sofa after school, she sighed. 'You seem to have no resistance. I'm going to make you a hamburger, you're going to eat meat, just till you're better.'

The sight and smell of the meat troubled Alex at first. But gradually she eased herself in, telling herself it would only be for a short period. However, there was no doubt she was better on a partial meat diet. 'Some people vegetarianism suits; not you, darling,' Angelica said merrily, writing about it in her column. Poor Alex was forced to agree. And yet where did that leave her? Back on a diet in which meat played its part, but unable to eat it with her previous innocence. All those pictures on the TV screen, she could almost hear the agony of the animal, shut up all its life in a cage so small it couldn't turn around. She could almost taste the large doses of antibiotics and hormones it was injected with which were poisoning her in a different way.

The world was being polluted, desecrated. It was almost too grim to keep thinking about. Yet why didn't it affect Angelica in this way, she who talked about these issues constantly yet went round with a smile on her face? 'Because I've got my job, sweetie,' she'd insist, 'because in my small way I'm doing what I can to make the public more sensitive, more aware . . .' When you have a job, when you too are doing your bit.

But it wasn't that simple. Alex, watching out of slanted eyes, saw how Angelica compromised, swearing sisterhood but then look at the way she was with Jerry, she was even happy to cook him meat, swearing this and doing that, part of the establishment for all her ideas, wasn't she just blowing with the wind? And Alex, her age, her nature, her own sadness, the daughter of her father whose death she felt so painfully, looked out at the world with all the more serious, and, for a time, devastated eyes. The water was being polluted, the air, she went to bed with terrible visions. Keeping quiet, asking intelligent questions, she would never let them know how horrified she was inside.

So she grew a skin, a thin skin but a skin all the same. A way of telling herself: it is all too painful, if we'll all be dead, we'll be dead, what the hell about anything, I'm simply not going to care. And it was this that drove Angelica to distraction. How could she have produced another member of the unthinking young generation with no social conscience, she wanted to know? How could she have produced a daughter who, having been taken to so many exhibitions about ecology, about the beauties of the earth, the preservation of our heritage, nevertheless threw her sweet papers straight onto the pavements and said she didn't care.

So she questioned Alex until she saw that the questions would get her nowhere. Then she resorted to writing notes.

Alex, of course, threw away the notes, or refused to discuss them. She would tell Tony that she had stopped being influenced way, way back. 'I'm my own person,' she would say to him. And Tony would think to himself, brave words, knowing them to be poignantly untrue. She is nobody's person yet.

All through the autumn as he's been getting to know her he has felt more and more how carefully he has to tread with her. He's experienced a new flooding strength in the face of her vulnerability, a feeling of protectiveness. And with this has come the desire to help her sort herself out so that she doesn't squander her own life. It even seems to him, when he takes stock and considers it, as he works away happily at the third shelf, that in a curious way this isn't only for the girl, but also for himself. It has become a personal challenge. A sort of second chance, as if she is in him, a younger him.

And so he works on through the whole quiet weekend, with Alex much in his mind. At the same time he is acutely aware of his childhood, of Caroline, his adopted mother, now dead, of his adopted father. Scenes come back to him that he hasn't thought about for years; his mind darts in all directions, so that the carpentry does not go as quickly as he has anticipated. Sometimes he sits down to catch breath, as certain thoughts take root in his brain and tight knots of anger bubble up to the surface, hitting him hard. Sometimes the pain is voluble. Then at other times there is a sense of release, certain things become clearer.

On Sunday when towards the end of the day Carole returns, the shelves are up; the kitchen even looks quite neat, give or take a few dustpan-loads of wood shavings.

'Sometime I'd like to get the old man over to stay,' is how Tony greets her.

'After all this time, I thought, I thought . . .' But her mind is working away, why not? It would seem to suggest, if anything was amiss surely he wouldn't be thinking . . .

'Want to make a party of it, eh?'

He puts his arms around her before taking up the kids, who are clamouring to tell him things. 'Idiot! No, after your lot have come and gone. And we've had a rest. But sometime, sometime in the spring.'

'Why ever now, Tony?' She is interested, not accusing or negative. But he shrugs his shoulders, doubting if he can express it.

'Just a hunch. I'd like him to meet you, and see the children.'

'Before you said . . .'

'I know. I couldn't be bothered before. There it is, it's one of those things, well shit, woman, enough of this. What do you think of the kitchen, mmm . . . mmm . . . a nice bit of handiwork . . . What do you think?'

Carole looks at her mate, trying to ascertain something, not quite able to, but pleased all the same. The kitchen shelves *are* a nice piece of handiwork. It's a long time since she's felt so positive about anything he's done.

*

The Heath is more empty than usual today. The winter light seems to Alex an unfriendly thing. Looking out of the window of her basement bed-sitter she had known that it would be stingingly cold. She wears a grey tracksuit, her glossy hair today tucked into the hood. Even with her blue padded jacket over the tracksuit the cold is not kept out. The trees are completely bare of leaves. She wonders about snow, she would love snow for Christmas, but it seems far too cold. The trees with their thin, spiky branches, dark, gloomy fingers of brown in the dull, low, hovering light, seem to her, as she passes by the nearest, ominous and hostile.

She crosses the first pond and yes there is the notice for the first time this year, BEWARE OF ICE. She looks at it with uncanny satisfaction as if it is proof of how grim things are. She starts to walk away from the pond up the hill. Her knee is hurting, causing her to walk more slowly than usual. Through the trousers of her tracksuit she is acutely aware of its throbbing presence.

She and Chris tusselled again last night about having sex, half in fun, half in a kind of cat-like anger. It was meant to be cool. Not to mean anything, just something you did if you felt like it. The way Angelica talks about it, making love and all that. You'll get involved emotionally, and then you'll get hurt; better to wait until it's someone special; all that nonsense. It is just a different kind of thing these days, a different kind of attitude, that's all. But now there is Aids and you can hardly turn on the telly without hearing another programme about it, to say nothing of Angelica's bloody notes.

Now if they are to have sex, Chris will have to agree to be monogamous, and that puts other pressures on them and determines the kind of relationship it is to be. For one thing, he isn't old enough or responsible enough for any of that bit. She likes Chris a lot. He looks really cool, really, handsome, and when he is sweet he is very very sweet. But he is also both a bastard and, well, terribly young. And as a real boyfriend he would be hopelessly unreliable and unsatisfactory.

Last night, scrapping, he'd fallen on top of her, pinning down her knee which had collided with something hard – it might have been a marble ashtray from upstairs, or the edge of the transistor radio – and the result was that when she woke up in the morning she nursed a huge bruise which covered the entire knee area and spread downwards towards her shin. She swore at Chris who said, don't be silly, don't make such a fuss. Then she cried and he felt sheepish. And he got it together just enough to make her a cup of coffee and give her a kind of sheepish hug, then left, saying he'd ring her. Which she'll believe when it happens. Sometimes he does, more often he doesn't. And, well, that is the way Chris is and what does she care?

So in the afternoon she limps onto the Heath. By the time she has reached the pond she finds she can walk without limping, as long as she moves slowly, which is a nuisance because it is bloody cold.

The squirrels give her some amusement. They seem to love the leafless trees and are everywhere to be seen chasing one another and leaping from branch to branch, forcing Alex to laugh despite herself. She always feels better nowadays just to be out here.

There he is ahead. There they are ahead.

There *she* is ahead, thinks Moth, jumping up and down running ahead a few steps as if he will go to her but no not quite, not quite sure. He runs forward again. And again he stops. Then he runs forward all the way to greet her, takes her hand and opens his mouth to ask her. But instead he says crossly, 'Oh Alex, why are you walking so *slowly* today?'

She puts her hand through the thatch of his hair, which looks, she thinks, as if it needs a decent comb, and smiles at him. 'I've hurt my knee, Moth, I've got an enormous bruise.'

'How did you do it? Can I see it?'

'I did it in a fight.'

'A fight?' He jumps up and down, his eyes wide with the thought of it.

He can't imagine his mother fighting like that. It opens up a whole new range of possibilities. 'I fight at school, sometimes we get bruises. And sometimes there's blood. Who did you fight with?'

Again she tousles his hair and smiles at him. Already happier inside herself. How quickly a mood can melt into another. So that she is smiling at Tony and at Ellen, who is prepared to give her a kiss and can say a word now which is almost like 'Alex'. She lifts Ellen out of her buggy, Tony helps her put the little girl on her shoulders. Routines of this kind are done without words now. But Moth loves words, he is the noisiest voice amongst them.

'Alex has got a bruise,' he tells the others importantly. 'She has to walk very very slowly.'

Tony looks at Alex. She shrugs, 'It's nothing.' As she shrugs she blushes slightly.

'Where shall we go, where shall we go today?'

'Where would you like to go, Moth?' Alex asks.

'I'd like to go to our climbing tree.'

'Maybe it's too far for Alex if her leg hurts.'

'No, it's fine,' Alex assures Tony.

So they walk north in the direction of the tree. Alex's pace is slower than usual. Moth runs ahead.

'Here, give me the bundle,' Tony says to Alex.

'Don't talk about her like that.'

There is a teasing gentle mood between them. Ellen back in her buggy bag beats her fists against Tony's neck, understanding – what? Anything?

'I've got the dates for my mocks.'

'Your what?'

'Mock A-levels.'

'I thought you were only doing one.'

'I could retake both.'

One of the things about Tony that Alex likes is that he doesn't rush in, like Angelica and Jerry and her teachers do. He just walks along beside her, companionably. After a time she says, 'It would mean a heck of a lot of work, I've hardly done anything this term, especially for History.'

'Can I help?'

Surprised, 'I dunno.'

''Course, it's years since I opened the old schoolbooks, but there's a brain in here somewhere, ticking over no doubt. I used to rather enjoy History.'

'It's my Politics project that's bugging me most at the moment. That's meant to be in by the end of term and I haven't even begun . . .'

For the rest of the walk to the tree, and whilst Moth climbs and Alex with Ellen between her legs plays with a couple of miniature knitted dolls that came out of Alex's blue jacket pockets, she also manages to convey to Tony the gist of her Politics. Tony finds the attitudes of sixteen to nineteen-year-olds towards the present government not something to which he has given any thought, but not without interest either. It is later when they come to part that Alex suddenly remembers that she has something else in her jacket pocket.

'I got one of my friends to print those photos of the sunsets. I thought you might like to see.'

Back on the bus, wedged between his father and little sister, Moth fingers a photo. He has asked and she has given it to him. To him, not to his father. He holds on to it tightly. She had set the camera on what she calls 'automatic switch', propped on a bench. They'd been in the long grasses, shaking a tree which had a kite stuck in it. They were laughing and looking up, and behind them, peeping through the branches of the tree, were the red fingers of the sunset.

The picture is coloured. It is strange altogether, full of darker and lighter patches, making everything look eerie. When she'd shown it to them, he'd said, 'I like that one best.'

'Do you want it?'

He could hardly believe his ears, he'd looked at Daddy to see what he would say, 'Can I, can I really have it?' He would keep it for ever, he'd told her, and she'd kissed him and said, 'Don't be such a billy, it's only a photo, Moth.'

And now they are on the bus and he is swinging his legs and looking again at the photo and he still likes it. Likes it a lot. Only.

'What made you do that?' His father's voice is harsh.

'I dunno. I just.' In the swerving motion as the driver negotiates the congested road, the scattered pieces of the torn photo make their discarded journey down the gangway.

*

The weather is uncertain this beginning of December. Will it snow or is it too cold? Will it remain below zero long enough for the ponds to freeze over? 'We could skate if it does,' Alex tells Moth.

'But I haven't any skates.'

'Don't worry, I think there's an old pair at home that would fit you.'

'What about Daddy?'

'Now that's something else.'

Today the sun is shining brightly on the playing fields. Each grass-blade is caught in a frozen shiver. So that they make a delicious crunchy noise when you run and jump, which Moth and Ellen are discovering. It is earlier than usual, the lower half of the school has been let out so that the higher classes can have a parents' meeting. Despite the sun and warm clothes both children are cold. Alex and Tony do warm-up exercises with them on the bouncy grass. Ahead, nestling close together, is a flock of gulls. Alex takes out her camera and creeps closer. Moth starts to run but Alex signals him back. It is the whiteness that intrigues her, against the pearly-green grass. She curses that she has a black-and-white film today. In the sunlight the wings of each bird seem to be a pure blue. Persil blue. Nearer and nearer, with Moth following her and Tony restraining Ellen, who starts to complain but is more quickly comforted these days.

Tony is at last communicating with his daughter. When it seemed that she needed more of him than he could give, it set up an intolerable situation between the two where Ellen could only cry more and Tony could only abandon her more. The advent of Alex has changed much of this. Alex seems to love the little girl, who's blossomed in her presence. Somehow, Tony doesn't quite know how it's happened, there she is tottering after her brother, a doughty little girl with a sense of humour all of her own. She is beginning to giggle and giggle. She is our little clown, Alex says, the clown of the family.

Sometimes when he is alone with Ellen, showing her picture-books or watching her progress from object to object in the tip that is still their front room, he says to her softly, 'Are you my little clown?' She grins, a funny, lopsided grin and he feels an overpowering sense of sadness for the barren times in which her cries have been overlooked.

Yet she has come through, walking now, beginning to talk, adoring her brother, not a good-looker, her funny little podgy face with its small, bright, brown eyes, and well-etched mouth, her wavy hair that is everywhere and won't lie down when you brush it.

Now, lifting her high, he puts his face against her warm tummy and pretends to butt her, knowing how she likes this, and gradually she lets go of the thought of what she really wants to do and begins to laugh and say, 'Bad, bad da,' then as he lifts her high she catches his hair and gives it a tug and that makes him laugh, 'Well, you're quite a bad little Ellen yourself.'

Meanwhile Moth, crouching some way behind Alex, turns round and says, 'Shhhhh.' He kneels as Alex does, aping her movements. She has got too near. The gulls soar into the air. As their wings open, each is flashed by a shaft of pure blue. Alex snaps and snaps.

She is in a happy mood today. Putting away her camera she is ready to play any amount of games with the children, and eventually to race them across to the playground. Pushing the children on the roundabout, she tells Tony, 'Well I've got the project together, in and passed by Mrs M.; it's being printed out at the moment. I might even get the questionnaires answered before the end of term.'

'I suppose you'll then have to settle down and analyse the data.'

'God knows when I'll have the time, over Christmas. And I haven't even started my revision yet.'

'You'll get it done. And remember, if you want any help . . .'

'You're not pushing *hard* enough,' says angry Moth.

'Yeah, with these two around can you just see me describing the working of the Attlee Government while you checked it against the books? We wouldn't last out against them for a moment.'

'It could be done. I could find a way.'

'Nope. I'll manage. Thanks.'

What is this? Why is he offering? It's good of him. I wouldn't mind. With him I wouldn't mind, it would take some of the drag out of it. It would mean. Well, forget it anyway, it isn't possible. And we'll be away straight after Christmas, wonder how that will turn out. It's such a draggy time, everyone says the same. I remember Christmases when. Listen to me, reminiscing. Still, when I was a kid and. Stop it. On with the future, here's to it. And the present. He did offer though. He must. There must be some reason why. Wonder what will happen in the Christmas holidays. Nothing. We probably won't see each other for ages. Maybe if I'd said I could do with some help, shit Alex, forget it. There's no space with those two around, you know that. It's okay, it's fine. I don't need any help. But it's cool that he asked, as Chris would say. Stupid word that, cool.

Then she remembers again how yesterday she'd given Chris money to buy films for her and he'd bought black-and-white, so that's what she has in the camera today. The blue of the gulls' wings in flight will be lost. Damn. Suddenly, damn. Suddenly it matters more than anything.

The cold weather thaws before the ice becomes firm enough to skate on. It is so disappointing. It rains and rains, day after day. They meet in Mel's cafe and sit over cups of tea, hot chocolate and sticky buns.

★

December is a crazy month in the publishing world. Everyone is having parties, and going to them. Christmas is a kind of deadline, too. Between the endless lunches and dinners, the fun, the booze, the scandal, deadlines must be met, deadlines that are often more and more hectic. Carole usually enjoys this period. She has a reputation for being an ace party-goer. There are frequently pictures of her in the trade press, dancing with this one, helping that one open his bottle of champagne. This year she cannot work up the same enthusiasm. There appears to be more of an edge to each occasion; on top of which, the firm's bad profit-record for the last quarter has led to discussions about whether the staff should forgo their Christmas bonuses and be asked to provide their own drink at the Christmas beano – decisions that lead to a surly rather than joyous atmosphere. Still, she's promised herself a complete break from work over the Christmas holidays. She is pleased that her brother and his wife are coming to stay. She and Johnny used to be very close. She hasn't seen him for five years, since he was last in England. She herself has only gone back once since leaving Australia over a decade before.

Having them to stay will mean more work. But with Tony in a more amenable mood there is hope that he will share some of the load. It will be good too for the kids, a real Christmas. Last year they were too young but this year Moth will appreciate it. Even Ellen, in her funny little way.

'Sarah,' Carole calls out, 'have you ever had one of M&S's Christmas puddings?'

'You don't want to have one of those made-up jobs surely?'

'I do, yes. As long as it tastes good.'

'I always love the stirring and mixing.'

'If you've got the time, that's another matter. But I'm not one to spend four days standing at the kitchen stove, if M&S will do it for me.'

A few days after this, Carole comes to work to find a Christmas pudding on her desk.

'Hey, what's this? Sarah, you bad girl, come in here this minute.'

'Carole, I was making my own. It's the first time Nick and I are having Christmas by ourselves – we've just said no to both families, though we'll go up afterwards to mine for Boxing Day and Nick's for New Year. Anyway I wanted to do it all properly. It gives me a real buzz. And when I was buying the ingredients for the pudding I thought I might just as well . . .'

'What a treat. You're a honey, you really are. But you shouldn't have. Hey, you don't actually make the chestnut stuffing, do you?'

'I intend to. Why, would you like some of that?'

'No, I was thinking maybe I could come over to your place and you could show me how. You're making me enthusiastic suddenly; why shouldn't my Aussie lot see how it's really done?'

'I'd love you to come. But you won't.'

'Don't you believe it, we'll fix a date next week.'

Will she really? She won't come, she's just saying that.

Meanwhile, Carole hums to herself as she works. Sometimes the path seems clearer. One thing leads to another and in each new situation you can see what to do. Everything goes fast. Today is like that. She makes phone calls, dictates letters, makes decisions, with a wonderful clarity. All opposition simply melts away. The last of the sales she negotiated at Frankfurt this year has just been nicely tied up. There are days when you can see the distant shore; others when you can't.

And thinking of distant shores, she has mentioned the Isle of Skye to Tony. And he seemed, if not enthusiastic, then also far from reluctant. Skye was a good time for them. Carole wonders if it would be healing to return there. Tony has pronounced a longing to be in the country, and in response to Carole's anxiety about how the 'little horrors' would behave, he's reassured her: 'They're getting more civilised all the time. I'm sure we could cope. What's the set-up there, with this Lee . . . what's his name?'

'Lee Getting. I haven't been able to make out. I think it's his parents' place on Skye, but whether they'll be there and whether Lee will be by himself or with a girlfriend, or boyfriend for that matter, I haven't any idea. Someone said he's living with a much older woman. No doubt it will all become clear.'

'You just want to nose around and get all the gossip firsthand,' he accused her, amused.

'And why not? Go on, I know it's a bit low of me, but we're all human.'

He liked her in this mood. He put his arms around her. 'But she only admits it every fourth Sunday,' he whispered into her ear.

She laughed. 'So you'll come?'

'Of course I'll come, woman. Why, have I suddenly got the reputation for being a total killjoy, or what?'

Lee comes into her office. Sarah makes them coffee. He often arrives mid-morning, around the time he can smell the coffee brewing.

'You've made this such a comfortable place, Carole, no wonder we all come to you rather than the other way round. What is it about a woman's touch?'

Carole laughs deprecatingly. But as she looks around the office, at the brightly coloured rug on the wall, the large weeping fig, and ferns, the two avocado plants, the splash of colour from the red berries and the poinsettia, the wicker sofa and matching armchair with its red-and-orange checked seats, the displays of books and covers, the huge display of postcards, some picture-side up, some just showing the message, that have been sent from all over the world, she does feel pleased. This is her space. It represents what she is. Yet her home – God, he'd have a shock. She never invites anyone back. She makes the excuse to herself that it is because of Tony, or more generally that it is because of their 'lifestyle', but she knows that it is as much something to do with the two halves of her.

Now, as she drinks her coffee and exchanges pleasantries for a few minutes, she knows what Lee wants. To see what she thinks of a book written by a friend of his. She has to be careful, skilful.

Her first reaction had been to be repulsed by the book. Its message was so bleak, its style so dense, such damn hard work, that she'd wondered again and again, need it be like this? And something about the essential male in Lee as he'd handed her the book, his youthful swagger, his 'How can we sell this? I admit it will be a challenge', not, 'Should we?' made her feel combative. God, were all the new writers he was going to foster going to be like this? We can't sell it, no one will: I'll go right back into the office and tell him, is what she thought at three a.m., when she lay awake in her bed next to Tony, restless and angry. But at five she was up and in the sitting-room reading it again and reconsidering.

It is good, you know it is. There will be times enough to fight. You've got to accommodate. And you can sell this. Think, think.

'It needs a very particular kind of marketing,' she now says to Lee. 'I think we should get Ian in and have a three-cornered discussion. I've some ideas of my own but . . .'

'Shoot. Get him in then,' says Lee. How she resents his way of never letting one finish a sentence. She rings Ian, who says he'll be down in a couple of minutes.

From where Sarah sits at her desk with the door open between the two offices, she can hear Carole's voice, it is a particularly attractive voice, low and sonorous, saying, 'The size, whether we divide it into two books, or manage to . . .'

'The size is no problem,' comes in Lee quickly.

'The size, the cost, the covers, they all need to be thought about radically in this case.'

'What do you mean, radically?'

'What I mean is . . .'

Sarah hears the words but no longer lets them penetrate. This morning she's got the mail out of the way quickly. She's put through a couple of calls but neither of the people she has to speak to are in, predictably. Now she can settle down to a stretch of proof reading. Though in this job you just never know when you're going to be interrupted next. She picks up Brian and Annette Tobin's *Personal and Planetary Peace*, and hopes the phone won't ring at least for the next half-hour.

'Lee, you know your kind invitation for the New Year? Well, I spoke to

Tony and yes, thank you, we'd both love the chance to get to the country. It's only when something like that comes up that you realise how much . . .'

'Hey, did I? Oh, hell, yes. How terribly awkward!'

Sarah's ears prick up. So they're getting that friendly, how interesting. She feels a pang of envy. Her fantasy is that she and Nick could. But of course there would be nothing in it for Carole.

Now she hears Lee's laughter, laughter that is meant to sound embarrassed, but to her it doesn't.

'It must've gone right out of my mind. Silly of me. Carole, I'd love you to come. New Year's rather complicated – you know how it can be – but some other time. The spring's great. It's always pissing with rain at this time of year, anyway. I promise you, you're missing nothing.'

Sarah looks at her watch. Twelve-thirty. There are just the two of them in the inner office now. She hasn't even noticed Ian leave, she's been so engrossed. She sees Lee go round to Carole's chair and put his hand on her arm.

'I haven't let you down, have I?'

'No, of course not.'

'It was just in the conceptual stages, wasn't it? Like so much else around here.' He laughs happily.

The bastard, Sarah thinks, don't trust him an inch, Carole.

Now you know where you stand, thinks Carole. But she flashes him her most brilliant smile. And when he suggests lunch because there is something he wants to pick her brains about, considering how spot-on she's been this morning about marketing that book, she manages to convey that there is nothing she would have liked more if only she hadn't already been tied up. And he, ego unimpaired, decides she's bright, Charles B. is right; maybe in the spring, if I'm still around, I will invite her over to Skye, with a few others.

He stays on for a few more minutes bantering with her. Meanwhile she is thinking, I know your kind; you're the sort who picks people up and drops them as it suits. What will you do with us here? Create havoc? Twist us round your little finger? Then her mind flips to Tony. In many ways they're such opposites. And yet.

Damn it, damn it, Skye would have been so good for us.

*

The photos, though black-and-white and missing the blue of the gulls' wings, still seem to Alex to be the best she's taken. She can't wait to show Tony.

It is mid-December and has been raining for days and days.

This is the third time in a row they have met in Mel's cafe. Outside it is pelting down. From inside the steamy little room they can hear the noise of the rain beating on the roof and against the panes. The cafe area is empty except for themselves, though occasionally someone comes in to buy bread or cakes, spraying great puddles of raindrops everywhere as they do so.

Alex had brought a comic for Moth. Tony, too, has thought to bring colouring books and crayons. To no avail. Soon Ellen is wriggling down from the table, Moth starting to ask endless questions. Alex tries to encourage him to do the puzzles on the back page of the comic, but every time he picks up his pencil his attention becomes diverted. He has had to sit at a desk for much of the day and now wants to be out and running around, free. Or to be watching telly like all his friends. There is something good on telly this afternoon. Everybody is watching it. This is one of the days when he has said to Daddy that he doesn't see why they have to drag along to Mel's in the horrible rain and why can't he just go home? 'Because you watch telly every other afternoon and it's nice to have a change.' Moth was insistent. There came a moment when Tony almost gave in. It was a foul day to be sure, but they'd made an arrangement, they couldn't let Alex down.

Now, facing her across the table with Moth in between them, he wonders whether it is just for himself, not for the children after all. The thought makes him uncomfortable. At the same time, when Moth on the third or fourth time – Alex has lost count – seems to be settling to his puzzles then after only the briefest of seconds looks up and says directly to Tony, 'Why *can't* we go home and watch television, please?' while at the same moment Ellen manages to pull a cream cake off the counter, upsetting a number of others, and now, sitting on the floor, begins to eat it to the consternation of the owner, so that Alex has to rush over, apologise, pick her up, clean her off, and there are tears and complications – for the first time since she has begun to be involved with the children, she feels a rush of resentment, even of disliking them, thinking them horribly demanding, wishing they were hundreds of miles away because what she realises is that she wants time alone with Tony. She has brought the pictures with her, they are the best she has ever taken. She wants to show them to him. In *peace*.

It is all a rush and a scramble. They decide to go. Tony calls for the bill. Getting up and putting wet and still dripping coats on the children and themselves, Alex says to Tony, 'Moth must be breaking up from school soon. I know our term finishes on Tuesday.'

'They go in for a couple of hours Wednesday, just for their Christmas party.'

'Days will be pretty busy after that.'

'Yes. We've got some people coming to stay over Christmas, relatives of Carole's.'

'Oh.'

'How's the work going? I haven't had a chance to ask.'

'Okay, I've got all the . . .'

'Daddeee, Daddeee, Come *on*.'

'Look, if the weather's fine, let's at least try and get in one more walk on Tuesday before . . .'

His words get caught and are not discernible because he has ushered one of the children outside and Alex is still inside with the other. She joins him in the rain. Ellen won't be carried today, insisting on walking, which is a slow business. Alex walks with them as far as the bus stop. She can't remember if there is a shelter or not. If there is a shelter and if we have a moment or two I'll show him the photos there.

But there isn't a shelter and the rain is relentless. Oh fuck, what does it matter, why should I be so keen to show them to him anyway?

The bus comes. She sees them onto it and waves them goodbye and walks back across the Heath, the photos unseen in the pocket of her jacket.

All of them feel irritable that evening, and take it out in different ways on different people. Maybe it is just the rain.

Then all of a sudden it snows. Not just a sprinkling but a couple of feet. Angelica and Jerry are spending a few days in Rye. Alex has the house to herself. What luxury! No family noises. No notes in the letterbox. Only the cats to feed and the lights to put on in the upstairs bedroom in the evening. Of course the basement is freezing cold but she can turn on the upstairs central heating full blast and luxuriate in the sitting-room.

It strikes her that it is no longer her room, but now only Jerry's and Angelica's. She curls up on an armchair and tries to accommodate herself. The room is bright, and still. Outside, both the street and the long garden are covered with snow. There is scarcely any movement of cars in the road. She tries Vivaldi's 'Four Seasons' on the stereo. The cats, delighted with her company, vye for her attention, pushing each other off her narrow knees. It is hard to get down to revision.

She hates to try and force her thoughts along one track where they don't want to go. It makes her feel inadequate and angry. She contemplates the room again, the pinks and blues and oranges of the furnishings, the daffodils in a vase on the round table. Some have come out. Three daffodils amongst the green of leaves and green of plants frozen at the windowsill. Three forced yellow daffodils bright against the background of snow in the back garden. The yellow of spring. And it is only December. Everything is topsy-turvy, she thinks crossly, telling herself that she will watch East-Enders at lunchtime, if only she can get down to the revision now.

Then, head down, she is finally working. The hours seem to hop along. It becomes easier and easier to concentrate.

She is pleased with herself as she puts on extra sweaters and thermal tights in preparation for going out. Leaving the house she throws a snowball at one of the cats. She is carrying bread for the ducks, having already left some for the birds in the garden. At the gate she has a thought which causes her to return once more to the basement.

Of course they are there, the children dressed in thick, brightly coloured clothes. They are not at the top of the hill but at the bottom, sheltered from the wind which is icy though the sun shines on them. They don't have a toboggan but they watch those who do. They feed the eager ducks, they build a giant snowman, they throw snowballs at one another. In the icy air they run and shout. The mood on the Heath is infectious. Everyone is glorying in the fun of it all, its unexpectedness. Everyone has huge smiles on their faces. And the smiles, it seems to Alex, add up to something larger than each individual smile. It is that kind of day. In this sense not unlike the one on which she first met Tony.

The cold squeezing the breath out of the bodies, the dazzling whiteness against the darkness of bare trees, the substance of the snow itself, compressed into small hard balls and then as it reaches its target shattering into multitudes of pieces – all this seems to contribute to the mood, the lightness of being of Tony, Moth and Alex. How far away the mood of the trapped cafe.

Moth has been looking forward to the adventure since morning. His feelings are totally of love for Alex today. Everything today is uncomplicated. At the school door he runs forward eagerly to greet his Daddy and Ellen. Everyone is saying, 'Happy Christmas, get your Mummy to call us tomorrow, don't forget this and that.' Everyone is full of jelly and crisps and chocolate biscuits. Everyone has something that they are looking forward to doing this first day of the holidays.

Here is Alex playing such a game of run, chase and hide, and yet another snowball to be thrown, Daddy and Ellen are left far behind, look they are way way down the slope, it is just he and she. He is shouting with laughter, his ears, peeping out from his woollen cap, are red with the cold, but twitching with the laughter he feels. He runs up to Alex in a moment when she is distracted and quickly throws three snowballs against her. Oh she is angry! Or pretends to be. She runs to catch him but he is too fast for her, poor old Alex she just can't run as fast as him. Perhaps he ought to slow down, give her a chance? He looks at her sneakily, then decides to slow. Of course she catches up with him, turning him upside down and shaking him so that it seems that all his insides will fall out; they are both laughing, above the snow.

Then all of a sudden, where is the sun? They have rejoined the others and all of them are looking at the sky. 'More snow. Any minute now. I'll see you to the bus,' offers Alex. They start off along the path, Moth running ahead, Ellen trotting along with her sturdy defiant steps.

'I've actually been working,' Alex says to Tony. 'I've been trying to catch up on some of the History I've missed, what do you think of that?'

'Good for you. I thought you looked pleased with yourself.'

'Now hang on, that would be going too far.'

They are quiet with one another. She is conscious of a whole range of things she'd like to say. And that in a minute Moth will be darting back up the path. She won't be seeing Tony again till after the Christmas holidays. He hasn't said but she. In a few minutes their routine will be broken. Suddenly it seems important to her. Too important. The Christmas ahead with Angelica and Jerry and the projected week in Norwich, with some of their family over New Year, unnervingly long.

'There is something, though, that I am quite pleased about.' She tries to make it sound casual.

'Oh, what's that?'

She stops where she is on the path and pulls a thick envelope out of her jacket breast pocket. 'Here.' She passes them over to him. Tony takes the photos of the gulls and looks at them carefully, one by one. Then he hugs her. Moth further down the path comes scampering back saying, 'Hey, hey, hey.'

'They are good, then?' Alex quickly asks. 'You think so too?'

'They are – really something. You ought to enlarge them, you know, you ought to learn to do the printing yourself, it would be worth it, you . . .'

'Haven't got time.' She is afraid that she has already made too much of a fuss.

'Of course not, not at the moment. Anyway, I like them a lot.' He gives them back to her. They wait for the bus, as so often letting the children do the talking for them. Alex at one point looks up at Tony and sees that he is looking at her in a particularly gentle way. She looks away. Let the effing bus come, she thinks, angrily. Then when she sees it making its way down the hill she doesn't want it to come at all. She hugs her arms across her chest because of the cold and does her little half laugh.

'Alex, leave the negatives with me. I might make some more prints if I have time . . .'

'Daddy, here's our bus, look! look!'

'Do you know how to?'

'God, years ago when I was a kid I used to . . .'

'We'll miss the bus, Alex,' says Moth.

'Then give me a kiss, a big one, mind, to last for all of Christmas.'

'I love you.'

'I love you too, Moth. And you Ellen, my little clown. Happy Christmas, all of you.'

She starts to sort the negatives from the photos but the bus is beginning to move off. She thrusts the whole packet into Tony's hands. 'Take care of them.' Another half laugh.

'See you,' he says, 'the first Tuesday in January.'

'Yes,' she says, 'yes.'

Then comes the next fall of snowflakes. The bus passing out of sight is lost in a swirl of white. Alex stares at it till she can see it no more. She starts moving swiftly across the Heath, homewards to Christmas with Angelica and Jerry.

Christmas Holidays

OH, THE complications of Christmas up and down the country! The pressure to be happy, to be with family, to be, to be. And where is Christ in all of this? Where are the loved ones? Dead and gone, or perhaps just not around. Then family groups splintered through divorce and remarriage make for endless compromises over this time when everyone wants to be with everyone. And everyone ends up saying, why oh why? Never again. So many days, so much eating. How pleased I am to be going back to work, they say, now that's over. Ban Christmas, it would be doing a favour to most.

But, no, say the children, Christmas is for us, it's a magic time. And the grown-ups reconsider, remembering what makes it all worthwhile, and sigh. Yes, they're right, Christmas is for the children. And those who control the consumer market say, Ban Christmas? Whoever heard of such an idea, of course it's a mad rush, we all go quite crazy with it, but look at the cash tills. Of course we have to have Christmas, indeed, we're thinking of making a second one in the summer. Just to make the year more even.

Moth has a dream. He is skating on the Heath on the large pond. There is no end to it nor any beginning. He has on Alex's skates. They are shining white, more white than the frozen pond itself, and so fast. They are magic skates, must be, because he can skate faster than anyone else on the pond. He wants to show someone how well he is doing. Where is Mummy? No, they are Alex's skates, maybe Alex is there with him. Or is he alone? So many people on the pond, which of them belong to him? He skates faster and faster in a state of panic.

Just when he's about to cry out because he is alone and doesn't know how to get off the pond, he sees two figures coming towards him, Mummy and Alex gliding, dancing over the ice towards him with their arms outstretched, both calling, 'Moth, come here.' He skates up to Mummy.

'Mummy, come and dance with me.' They dance, twisting and turning like other people on the huge lake.

All the time Alex is watching. Whilst he dances he can't help looking towards her. She is mouthing something. He wants to make out what it is.

But Mummy is taking them further and further away. Then they have turned round and come back close to Alex. She is mouthing, 'They are my skates.' She looks so sad. Mummy says, 'Aren't you pleased that we've left Tony and Ellen behind and it's just you and I, my little man?' He wants to reply that he is pleased but instead he lets go of her arms and skates up to Alex. Alex puts her arms around him and starts to dance, a fast crazy dance so that he has difficulty keeping up, but all the time he is laughing. Everyone is watching and laughing and clapping.

Now Mummy skates across the frozen pond in large angry strides, her light short hair flicked out behind like a duck's tail. Her blue eyes are fierce. Is she going to hit him? She grabs him. But Alex still holds on. 'Let go Alex,' Mummy says. 'Yes, let go Alex,' he echoes. One has one arm and one has the other. They are beginning to pull him in different directions and it is beginning to hurt. Neither will let go. He starts to shout, then to scream, 'Oh let me go, let me go!' But neither will listen. 'Help!' he screams to the crowd. Why don't they listen, why do they just go on skating? One of his arms is being torn out of its socket. 'Alex, please please,' but now she turns to look at him and it isn't the Alex he knows just a row of terrible teeth . . .

Carole is at a launch party. It is being held on a floating barge down in Docklands and despite weather conditions making access difficult, it is a huge success. In the snow, Docklands, instead of looking like a large area of wasteland, has taken on an altogether different character, so that the modern buildings, the lights on the river, the strange shapes make the whole seem like a playground of the twenty-first century. Even the barge is not just any old barge but a huge modern construction of fibreglass and tubes. The author, well pleased with the reception, has drunk a great deal and rolls round the boat saying in a large booming voice to anyone who wants to know, and many who don't, that A&P have done him proud and there aren't better publishers in the whole of London. (Only six months later when a good offer makes him shift his loyalties he is grateful – or might have been if he hadn't already forgotten the occasion on the barge – that, unlike politicians' comments, those of authors aren't taken down in evidence.)

But as he hugs Carole and all the other 'loyal staff' who have, he claims, treated him so generously and courteously, his mind is on the present not the future. He likes hugging Carole. She is an attractive girl and looking splendid, if he might say so, in her black dress. 'You've got just the . . . just the figure for such *décolletage*.'

Carole murmurs her thanks, letting his hand remain where he has laid it long enough to please him but not long enough to compromise her. Lee joins the group. Soon after, Carole leaves the two men talking, to the author's disappointment, and goes off to find another drink and other people to talk to. Today is not the day when she feels comfortable in Lee's presence for long.

It has been a day of ups and downs and somehow at the moment Lee always seems to be in the middle of things connected with her. Charles, Ian and she have formed the habit of meeting for an informal lunch each Tuesday. This has been going on for years. The meetings were not ones which the outgoing editorial director ever joined, partly because she never hit it off with Ian and partly because she disliked meetings and found the number she already attended sufficient for her purpose. So it has always been just Carole and the two men.

Carole enjoys this trio and has grown over the years to find these some of the most pleasant times in the week. Their sandwich lunches in the boardroom are essentially informal and social. But, inevitably, some of the power structure of the firm works through this medium, something Lee perceived immediately upon arriving at A&P and was determined to get in on. He simply invited himself, and Charles said, why of course he should have been invited, it was only an oversight. So the trio became a quartet, and today Carole felt uneasy as the group realigned and Lee skilfully, oh how skilfully but he knew just what he was doing, called to mind some kind of sexist division, 'Of course, we men . . .' reminding the others of the most primitive bonding, cutting off her strength, and yet as always so charming.

She would not let him win at his game. She would fight this one. At the same time, how she dislikes him. And has even – she, usually so cautious – shared this with Sarah.

Back in her office, Charles had come to see her. There was something he wanted to discuss. Did she feel like a run? It was best discussed out of the office. A run, fine; it was a couple of months at least since they had run together.

'Tomorrow lunchtime?'

'No, this afternoon.'

'In the middle of the afternoon?'

'Why ever not?'

She had a number of things she was keen to tackle before the day was over. Still, if that was what the boss wanted. 'And in the snow?'

'The snow ought to make it fun, we're talking about inches not feet. Come on, where's your spirit?'

So Carole got into her running clothes, which she kept in the office, and the two set out towards Regent's Park.

'This is in confidence, mind,' said Charles to Carole as they ran.

'Of course.'

'I've had an unsettling phone call from B.B. I hate to repeat myself but this is highly confidential, I can absolutely rely on you, can't I, to see it doesn't go further?'

'You know you can.'

'It's rather unfortunate but she insists she can't get along with Lee. Called him an arrogant pup, actually.' Charles laughs. 'Can you believe that?'

Yes. 'Dear oh dear. But surely it isn't anything irreparable. Does Lee know how she feels?'

'No, that's the trouble. Of course I'll have to mention something about it to him. Urge him to go more softly. But B.B. doesn't even want to give him another chance, she wants to . . .'

'No, don't tell me.'

'You have it, Carole. Listen. You and B.B. have always hit it off. Couldn't you?'

'What? Flatter her ego?'

'Don't be so cynical. Find some way of ameliorating . . .'

I'm damned if I'm going to do Lee Getting's patch-up work. But apparently you are, Carole. 'And how were you thinking I might . . .'

'That's what I like about you, Carole, so game for anything. No hang-ups, unlike most people around here.'

Yes, and then if Lee gets to know. At the moment he's just out for me because he's out to get everyone, pushing them down on his way up. But if I give him any reason. Christ, not an easy one.

Back in her office, Carole had been lost in thought for at least half an hour. Sarah, aware of this, wondered what was occupying her boss's mind so intently and had two guesses, both vaguely connected with herself.

Then it had been a race to finish off today's most pressing matters and to shower and change before the launch. Sarah thought Carole looked superb. She would have liked to be going to the launch herself, instead of home to a TV supper with Nick. In just one more year, she promised herself, I too.

Carole knows the black dress suits. She intends to enjoy herself. She is not hungry and refuses the canapés but has three glasses of white wine in quick succession. She flits from one group to another. Sparkling. She is in a large group of television producers and reporters. Why has the conversation changed from the problems of filming in China to Aids? She must have lost concentration for a second. Someone's husband, married twenty-five years. A business trip to Bonn. It only takes one. Such a knock the first time you actually know someone who. She thinks of Tony. All of a sudden the white wine drunk too fast rises up in her chest. It is as if that safe world at home, one she has relied on for a backdrop, one without which, if she did have to worry, none of this would be possible, rises up and threatens her.

She moves away. She picks at three peanuts. That is when the author whose launch it is finds her. She tries to put the other out of her mind. But Lee joining them is too much, she doesn't want to be around him tonight. She moves on again, determined to enjoy herself, to get back into the mood.

Afterwards she shares a taxi with Linda, A&P's publicity manager. It has been a good party, the two women agree. Linda gets dropped off first. Alone for the last lap, Carole thinks again, I must spend more time with Tony. I hardly know what's in his mind these days. Will it be worse or better having Johnny and Kerry to stay? Who knows?

She is hungry now and weary, and looking forward to getting home. Out of these clothes into a dressing-gown.

In her low black dress, tonight oddly incongruous in their flat, Carole enters Moth's bedroom, with Tony close behind her. Her huge, moon-shaped, silver earrings glow in the pink of Moth's night-light.

'Wake up, Moth, wake up, do you hear me? You're just having a bad dream, it's not real. Moth, can you hear me?' Gradually Moth's screaming and thrashing subside into pathetic blubbery tears. His whole body is soaked with perspiration, his eyes dilated.

'He must be about to go down with some bug or other. What a shame, just before Christmas. You didn't stay out in the snow till he got cold, did you, Tony?'

'I wouldn't have thought he'd have caught cold. We kept on the move.' Tony puts his hand on his son's brow. 'Poor Moth, that was a nasty dream, wasn't it? Was it that tiger again trying to get at you?'

'It wasn't a tiger.'

'Do you want a hot drink, a nice mug of cocoa?'

'No.'

He starts to cry again, a strange whimpering noise. 'Don't leave me,' he begs.

They sit on his bed for a long time, with one small light on in the room, talking to each other in quiet voices.

Tomorrow their guests arrive. They discuss giving up their bed to them and sleeping on a mattress in the sitting-room. The mattress is large and cumbersome and requires two people to carry it. Tony suggests they get it over with before they go to bed tonight.

All this in whispers. Both lapse into their own thoughts as Moth shifts and stirs.

'Carole, listen, I'm prepared to shuffle your folks around and do what I can but there's something I want you to do.'

'What is it?'

'Take a couple of hours off work and come to Selfridges to see Father Christmas with us. It's so important to him.'

'Oh, that. If I have the time, certainly. Some day next week, we'll have to see. Otherwise you and Johnny and Kerry can always . . .'

'Uh-uh, Carole, this isn't an "if". It's something you've got to do.'

'Now hold on, Tony. It's only a whim on his part, he'll be just as happy . . .'

'Damn you! It matters to him. You missed his school play, he was miserable. Don't look at me like that, he was.'

'Tony, if you knew what I'm trying to juggle.'

'But home has to figure somewhere, there has to be a balance, for Christ's sake.'

'Yes, but not in the middle of a working week. Or have you forgotten . . .'

She hears his intake of breath. She wishes she could take the words back. She's had a long day, and then coming in and. Then Moth's dream. She hasn't even had supper yet. Damn, damn, damn! Why can she be so diplomatic at work yet not with Tony? Now Tony will leave the room, and Moth is stirring, their raised voices have disturbed him; at any moment he'll start that nonsense again. And that is surely the end of any co-operation from Tony for the rest of the evening.

But Tony sits on, stroking his son's back through the bedclothes till Moth eventually relaxes and his breathing becomes even again.

'If you wanted to,' he says to Carole, 'you could adjust your time. It's two hours I'm talking about, not a day, not a week, it means a lot to your son. It would start Christmas off in the right spirit: for all of us. Will you?'

She looks at Tony. 'In return there's something I want to ask you. Have you ever had Alex up to the flat?'

'No.'

'I want you to promise me you never will. I don't want her here.'

'Christ, Carole!'

'Is it a deal?'

Moth is asleep again. They make their way back towards the kitchen.

'Shall we take the mattress in now, while we've still got some energy left?'

'I'd like an answer first.'

'The two things have got nothing to do with each other. And anyway, the second is much more complex.'

'Yes or no.'

'Don't push me, Carole. I'd like to think it over.'

'Is it so important then?'

'That isn't the point.'

'The point?'

'The point is . . . Come on, let's get that mattress shifted.'

Later, Tony went for a walk. It was snowing lightly.

*

But what about me? Was I too wishy-washy to count, stuck between the different but equally urgent needs of the two women and the simple, vociferously expressed needs of my children? I'm a mild-mannered man, except in a rage. But even I was steamed up. It was not that I had any pressing wish to have Alex back to the flat. For her own reasons she'd made it clear that she was reluctant. We were managing nicely as we were; except for Moth's occasional wingeing and that was always short-lived. I could envisage quite well never wanting, needing to have Alex back to the flat. But what I resented was having this small power of manoeuvre taken away from me. And in the face of the freedoms I have willingly given Carole!

No, the answer was no, the wishy-washiness had to stop. And now, at the advent of the Christmas period was as good a time as any.

For a while I didn't think at all. Just gave myself up to the bite of my progress through the falling snow. Then, enjoying being unfettered by the children and without thinking about it, I broke into a run. And the run became a pleasure so that I pushed on further and further, in the end running to the top of Highgate Hill and back.

The run was interesting. My body surprised me at how fit it was. How had this happened without me noticing? Where was the new energy coming from? As my breath came more and more easily, I felt that I wanted to break through the confines that have so restricted my life lately. As if the trap into which I had fallen was not something which would hold me indefinitely. There had to be a way to climb out. And I must find it. I must think.

After Christmas, get through Christmas. Let's have some family times. God, I hope they cough up their share of. Otherwise it's going to be tight. And with Moth wanting a new bike. Well we certainly can't give him that, now. After Christmas I'll have to. How to start? Got to somewhere. Look up Walter? No, not after this long time. What then? Can't see it straight now. It'll come. Start. Make a start. Stand up to her for one. And keep running. Right to the doorstep. Don't stop now.

*

'Carole?'

Carole is in bed but has waited up for him.

'That was a long walk.'

'Yes.'

He is still panting and tries to settle his breathing.

He sits on the bed to pull off his damp socks. 'Carole, listen, I asked you to do something for Moth. Something that isn't much, taken overall and considering how much of the parental responsibility you seem to duck. All right, that's the way we've arranged it for the moment. But still, I don't think this should be a matter of bargaining. I think – well, what would mean a lot is if you could see how important it is to Moth and just agree to take the time. And that's it.'

'I agree.'

'Ah.'

'Now will you agree not to have Alex back here?'

'Ah.'

He undresses slowly. 'So we're back where we started?'

'No, not quite.' She smiles at him. 'Please come to bed, I've been waiting for ages.'

'You're a nymphomaniac, did you know that?' he says, as he climbs between the sheets. 'How you can worry about something as silly as Alex coming back to the flat when you . . .'

'It's just because of that that I . . .'

'Anyway don't let's talk about it any more.'

And later, before they finally let sleep overcome them, 'Here's to a good visit.'

'And happy times,' murmurs Tony.

In his child's bed, his face in the subtle glow from the night-light, Moth sleeps more soundly, and near him Ellen in her cot is sprawled out on her tummy as if she is swimming through water.

Further up the hill towards Hampstead, Alex, Chris, Dan and Quentin are sitting on Alex's bed listening to Sting's latest album. Upstairs, Angelica sleeps soundly, not exactly snoring but making little grunts, while Jerry, awake beside her, debates whether or not to make the effort to get up and put on his dressing-gown and pad down to the basement to ask them to turn down the volume.

Further east, in Newington Green, Sarah and Nick, their arms entwined around one another, shift uneasily, attempting to get comfortable on their early Christmas present to each other: a two-day-old waterbed.

Christmas Eve. Nick and Sarah have been in separate rooms preparing stockings. Both now meet for sleep looking forward to the morning. They curl up on the waterbed; they already think it the most comfortable in the world and are persuading all their friends that it is the only way to sleep these days.

They are too tired to make love, perhaps they will on Christmas morning. For the moment they simply hug one another tight, delighted to be having their first Christmas together in their own home. Sarah, thinking about her parents, has a moment of guilt. She knows her mother will be missing her. Is she spoiling another's Christmas with her own selfishness, and yet? Then her mind passes on to thoughts of Carole. She tries to imagine her doing the children's stockings and finds it difficult. She has never seen them. Other people bring their children to the office, but not her. She wishes she would, just once. Her last murmured thought, 'I hope she enjoys the Christmas pud.' 'Who?' 'Carole, you toad.' Nick pulls her hair. And then with his fingers in it falls into a deep sleep.

But it is not that late. Up in Hampstead, Angelica, Jerry and Alex are still finishing off decorating the tree. A seven-foot one whose top branch nestles against the ceiling carrying the good angel on it, riding it more like a witch on a broomstick. Alex wants to cut the top branch but her mother is adamant. Angelica has fixed ideas about how everything must go. Alex looks at the tree; she would love to be free to decorate it her way. Her mother still uses the same decorations that her own mother did – those that haven't got broken by now. Most of them are so ugly, masses of silver and gold. Alex would go for simplicity. Real candles, brightly painted wooden toys and shapes. Things that were light and subtle and would glow in contrast to the deep green of the tree, not take over from it. One day. Meanwhile, she tries to not block the good feeling she knows her mother is trying to capture, a spirit of Christmas, at the eleventh hour.

This afternoon Jerry's mother has died. By chance he had been there, alone with her. When he arrived back at the house shortly before dinner he was grey with pain and grief. To make matters worse, she'd died calling for Jerry's first wife, Suzie. 'She's already there, where you're going, Mother,' he'd whispered. He didn't believe it though. Loss. On Christmas Eve he'd walked down the road and into the pub and this time sat there drinking a solitary brandy. Then home to Hampstead, which tonight, more than any other since he'd moved in, doesn't feel like home.

Both Alex and Angelica have dressed up for dinner. Angelica likes to make a big thing of Christmas Eve. She has cooked mushroom *vol au vent*, poached turbot, an old-fashioned cheesecake, one of her specialities. The two women have dressed up as gypsies. Angelica's whim. They are wearing the same exotic patterned material in mauves, pinks and blues.

The contrast. The inappropriateness. His mother dying in her little flat, the oddballs, the loners sitting over a solitary pint at the pub, many of them having nowhere to go back to, and then this. Jerry sits down at the table heavily and puts his hands over his eyes, shutting it out. His gesture inadvertently catches one of Angelica's favourite wine goblets. It rolls off the table and shatters on the floor.

'Oh no,' thinks Alex, 'now what kind of an evening are we in for?'

The atmosphere is sombre, the food difficult to get down. Jerry cannot help referring to that other Christmas Eve, that one a couple of years back when his poor mother . . .

'Stop it,' says Angelica. 'That's over now. It doesn't help.'

And Alex in her 'fool's get-up', thinks, never again will I try and please them. Really, what is the point? All right, she's dead. But she was old. She was ready to. It wasn't like my father. Jerry's just being self-indulgent. He wants to ruin our fun. I hate him. Two more whole days of this without any other company. I don't know if I can bear it.

Then Angelica, after the meal, after the mourning, cries out, 'Heavens, we haven't even decorated the tree yet! Come on gang, all hands on deck.' She goes to Jerry and kisses his hair, stroking it back from his forehead as if he were a child. Cradling the ball of his head in the palms of her hands against her tummy, she says to him softly, 'Do you want to watch, love, while we women do the work, or would you find it soothing to help? You choose.'

Gradually Alex watches her mother bring back her man's goodwill. She feels there is something gay and courageous in her mother's attempt to bring everybody's spirits up, and against her will she find herself melting. It is only fair. She too must. It is Christmas after all – whatever that might mean.

One-thirty a.m. on the Kentish Town Road. Johnny has just looked up at the clock on the wall and taken in that that is what the time is. He points it out to the others. All four of them on the floor around the coffee table, a couple of bottles of wine now emptied and goodness knows how many beer cans. The last of the smoked salmon sandwiches curls in its neat brown-bread squares. Date-stones and tangerine-skins making their own pattern in a blue bowl. From the stereo Tony's favourite jazz records. Carole is half asleep on the floor between Tony's legs but every now and again she jolts to life to join in the conversation. Thanks to the generosity of their visitors the kids' Christmas presents have been greatly augmented, and now two pillowcases, full of interesting lumps, are tied up and waiting for the next morning on the hearth by the gas fire.

'But it *is* the next morning, it's Christmas,' giggles Kerry, 'that's what you guys don't seem to realise. I've been trying to say Happy Christmas to you for at least the last hour.'

'Have you? Well you seem to have said a hell of a lot of other things too,' Tony teases.

'They do say I'm a chatterbox,' she laughs, 'but I've got to get to bed. Honestly, Johnny, come on. Do you realise we're in their sleeping space, we're keeping them up.'

'Don't you believe it, Kerry. We always go to sleep at this hour, don't we Carole? Carole?'

She does a pretend snore.

They laugh amiably.

That night on the uncomfortably thin mattress on the sitting-room floor Tony and Carole make love long and tenderly. They take one of the candles off the Christmas tree and leave it burning on the mantelpiece as they do so. The room smells of pine needles and beer and smoke. And candle wax. They cling together.

'It's a pleasant kind of chaos,' says Carole.

'Yes.'

'Hold me tight,' says Carole.

★

Boxing Day, mid-morning. Moth is sitting on the floor of his bedroom, piecing together the bits from a new railway set, gift of Johnny and Kerry. Ellen has been such a bother that he has to cry out, 'Oh please can someone control her?' But no one comes. He can hear the adults' voices in deep discussion. He listens. It is a safe kind of noise. Since his dream he has been scared of going to sleep and his nights have been more fitful. He has woken up frequently. His mother says that it is just the excitement of Christmas. He doesn't feel as excited as she says he does. Even going to see Father Christmas was a let-down. The queues were enormous. He hadn't remembered it like that from last time. They had to wait for ages.

Then, when it seemed like it would never ever happen and his legs were beginning to hurt from all the standing and he needed a drink so so badly, all of a sudden he could count the people ahead and there were only five and then it would be their turn.

He could see Father Christmas clearly. If he was a real magic person then there would be some sign. There wasn't; it was so disappointing.

'Hello little boy,' said Father Christmas, 'and are you a good boy?'

'Sometimes.'

'I see, and what would you like for Christmas?'

'Really, you mean if I had a proper wish?' It was getting exciting after all.

'Yes.'

'I don't know,' he whispered, suddenly sad because it wasn't toys he wanted, it was other different things too difficult to even think about.

He wondered what would happen since he hadn't answered Father Christmas properly. But Father Christmas put his hand in its red-cloaked sleeve into a large sack and brought out a present packed in pink-and-silver paper and said to him, 'Have this anyway, and I'm sure you'll have lots and lots more toys when the day comes,' and then he kissed Ellen on the cheek and waved them on, and then it was the next family's turn. Well that was that. He knew the truth then and confided it to Daddy on the bus going home.

It had seemed so important. And that was only . . . how many days ago? And now it is after Christmas and they've had such a lovely time with the games and the Christmas pudding and the crackers. And last night they'd put him to bed but when he'd said he couldn't sleep they'd let him stay up, just him with the grown-ups, it felt very important. Eventually he'd fallen asleep on Auntie Kerry's lap.

Now this morning she has said to him at breakfast, 'You could do with some country air, Moth, how would you like to come to the Lake District with Johnny and me?'

'Just me?'

'Well it could be, or we could take Ellen along too.'

'Me come too, me come too.'

'Would you like her to come, Moth?'

Moth looked from his mother to his father.

Carole said, 'It would be an adventure, Moth, and very kind of your auntie and uncle to invite you.'

'But what about school?'

'You'll be back before then.'

He'd looked again wide-eyed at his mother to see what she was thinking, but couldn't tell.

'What do you say, Moth? Kerry wants to know.'

In Newington Green, Nick and Sarah are packing up the car.

'Don't forget wellies,' she shouts to Nick, whose head is under the bonnet, checking the oil, 'country walks and all that.'

'Already in.'

'Do you think of everything?'

'No, you do.'

'Thinking of which . . .'

'Hang on a sec. Can it wait till we're on the way?'
'It can wait.'

'Well, what was it?'
'Nick, I wondered, you know your parents' cottage in Wales, well, whether we could offer it to Carole and her husband for a little holiday. After all it's not used much in the winter and . . .'
'Don't you ever stop thinking about her? For God's sake, it's Boxing Day, we've had a super time, we're on the way to your folks for lunch and . . . oh fuck!'
'I'm sorry,' she says, putting her arm round him, 'really it doesn't matter. Come on, you're right, we have had a lovely time. Don't get in a bad mood now. You're not jealous, are you?'
'Of a woman!'

Hampstead. Noon. Angelica's sister and family have come round for croissants and coffee and an exchange of presents and have just left. Angelica and Jerry sink back on the two comfortable armchairs. Alex hovers at the door. A conversation has started up about their projected trip to see Alex's grandparents in the Midlands. They are her father's parents and she's fond of them. It will be better than Christmas; still, she will be the only young person. She insists on being back for New Year's Eve. This doesn't fit in with Jerry and Angelica's plans.
'I can't talk to you if you're directly behind my head,' says Angelica. 'Sit down and discuss it with us.'
Alex reluctantly comes over and sits on the sofa. 'I could always get a train back, I suppose. But it's expensive. Would you go halves? It's you who wants me to be there.'
'You want to see your grandparents,' says Jerry.
Keep out of it, Alex thinks, but doesn't say. 'Well Mum, would you?'
There is a ring at the doorbell.
'Alex, darling, it's Chris.'
She is delighted to see him. It has only been a couple of days but shut up with her lot has seemed like forever. She hugs him extravagantly. Which gives Angelica an idea. 'How about Chris coming up to Hereford with a couple of friends, for New Year? I'm sure Grandma wouldn't mind putting them up for a night. You can drive, can't you, Chris? Do you think your dad would let you borrow his car?'
'The van maybe but . . .'
'Mum, don't you think it's up to us? In the first place, Chris might not even want to come. I might not want him to.'

'Well, do you?'

They look at each other, nonplussed by Angelica's force, not able to communicate the more subtle signals of their relationship.

'Yeah, I could probably make it,' says Chris, fired by the hug Alex has given him. 'Hey, Alex, I've got a present for you.'

'I've one for you, too.'

She ushers him downstairs, already regretting that she hadn't done so the moment he'd arrived.

On the M1, two hours clear of London, Alex, in the back of Jerry's Volkswagen, is feeling acutely depressed. How many more days of this? In the front Jerry and Angelica are talking to each other. She blocks them out and her thoughts return for, it seems, the hundredth time, to Tony. She wonders what he is doing right at this moment. She tries to imagine him at the flat with Carole and the children, and fails. She wonders how he and the kids have enjoyed Christmas.

Into this, Angelica's loud voice cuts.

'Tell me something about that man on the Heath with his children, Alex. Are you still seeing anything of him?'

How could she have done that?

'How do you know about him?' She instantly regrets this.

'Jerry saw you on the Heath with them.'

'Did you, Jerry?'

Jerry is concentrating on the driving, the road is windy, the visibility bad. He thinks it impulsive of Angelica to jump in like that and would have liked the conversation to have been handled with more forethought. But too late.

'Yes, I did.'

'When was that?'

'Some time ago. Really Alex, it's not important.'

What has he seen? What has he passed on to her mother? She is unnerved and more unhappy than ever, and her quiet, tight, 'It's my business what I do,' is not convincing, not even to herself.

'We'd like you to share, the good as well as the bad,' pushes on Angelica.

'It is good. I just help him with his children, that's all.'

'Fine, then I'm pleased for you.'

'Then can we not talk about it any more,' Alex says.

Carole and Tony stand with an arm around each other waving their children goodbye. The children's faces peer out of the rear window of the Renault 5 which Johnny and Kerry have hired for their tour of the Lake

District. Parents and children wave at one another until they are finally out of sight. Moth goes on waving a while longer.

Late morning. The whole rest of the day stretching ahead. 'What do you want to do with it?' Tony asks Carole.

Carole sighs, she cannot help but look guilty. And yet I have a right to do what I need to do. 'I was thinking of popping in to the office.' She tries to make it sound light; it doesn't come out that way. 'Just for a couple of hours.'

'Carole, not today. It's so rare that we get a chance. I was thinking that we might . . .'

She stops him, she puts her hand over his mouth and, though she hugs him at the same time, it doesn't feel good. 'I'm sorry, Tony, I've already made arrangements.'

'What arrangements?'

'To meet someone there.'

'You didn't tell me, you never mentioned that you were planning to go in today.'

Feeling guilty, she sounds crisper than she intends. 'I've mentioned it now.'

'Carole, I can't believe. Just on the one . . . just immediately.'

Stop this. What is the point of getting steamed up about it? Repeating the same pattern. Better not say anything more. I am not going to beg her this time. No bloody point anyway.

'Well there you go, that's the Christmas holiday over,' he says, making his way back upstairs into the flat.

Half an hour later she leaves. Tony wanders around the flat. It seems strangely empty without the children. Recently crowded to the seams and with all that has gone on during the last few days, it is desperately in need of a clean. Well I'll be buggered if I'm doing that, he thinks, nevertheless idly picking up cereal bowls, ashtrays and the odd beer can. He mooches around in the kitchen washing up, with the radio on full-blast.

I too could get down to work. But if you haven't got anything you have to do it's different. I haven't got the discipline. The discography? Who are you kidding, you know it's a dead duck. Such a long time and so difficult to get the leads. He tries to imagine what it would be like to be needed again in the outside world. To have a role to play. Then find one, make one. Yes but.

He even misses the children. Their needs are simple, immediate. It is something, some kind of buffer between him and. Alex has said about children's needs that. The first time he's thought about her since before Christmas. Now his mind dwells there. The photographs, that is something he could do. Up to the loft, get out the equipment.

'We'll need to set off for Nick's place sometime after lunch,' Sarah tells her parents.

'On the move again,' echoes Nick.

'We'll be sorry to see you go, darlings, we've loved having you. Make it longer next time.'

'We will at that,' promises Nick.

December 31st. Lunchtime. Carole is eating at the Savoy with the redoubtable writer whose excessive output of bestsellers has done much to keep A&P afloat over its leanest years. When she is in London she only likes to eat at the Savoy and A&P accepts that it is one of the prices it must pay. It has taken Carole weeks to set up this appointment, and all the way she has had to tread carefully so as not to be seen to be stepping on Lee's toes. Even now she has to go carefully.

Carole has been feeling more relaxed over Christmas. She has eaten well and put on a few pounds. But now back with the stresses of work she is already losing her appetite. Or is it work? She seems to be developing a phobia about that girl Tony is seeing. Of course it is quite ridiculous, she tells herself, even irrational. She tries to put it out of her mind but finds it more and more difficult.

She identifies with the original caveman. You make a home. You hunt, you fish, you gather. At home your woman is waiting for you. After committing acts of bravery and subtlety you return to her arms. She nurtures and feeds you. You replenish yourself. Then you are ready for a second trip, and a third, secure in the belief that inside the cave your woman and food will be safe. You don't want any other man muscling in whilst you are out performing heroic deeds.

Increasingly Carole feels on not quite such secure ground at home. What is Tony thinking about that he is holding back? Has she gone too far in getting things too much her way?

The latest stab has been the photos. She has asked Tony not to bring Alex to the flat. Now the bathroom has become a darkroom and the girl's photos are everywhere. Innocent photos, the gulls, the Heath, yet it seems to Carole a terrible intrusion. She wants to ask Tony to take them down, put them away. She even wants to tear them up. She tells herself she must not give in to this level of weakness. Meanwhile she wonders more and more what the girl looks like. She waits for hints from Moth, at the same time despising herself for it. She wonders, is she beginning to show her age?; she looks more critically in the mirror.

Now sitting opposite the huge mound of woman writer, who is saying to her querulously, 'Carole, darling, you're just picking at your food. Put a few forkfuls in your mouth or you'll make me feel even more of a pig than usual.' Her laugh is loud, raucous, it floats out over the softly carpeted space of the smart dining-room, attracting attention. Waiters hover behind the table, eager to be of service.

'Now as to that terrible young man . . .'

Carole finds herself building up Lee's character, trying to defend him, racking her brains to think of qualities he might possess which would appeal to this great lady. But at the same time, and she has to be careful here, trying to hit the right balance, to imply that Lee would not be the only one involved. There will be a broader spectrum, that is the joy of a new situation. (She has only just thought of this as she talks but finds it a good tactic.) A broad spectrum, so that instead of the old way of being close – and she knows how much that has meant to each of the outgoing editors' writers – it will now be a more open, flexible situation, so that if there are, for example, any disagreements with Lee it won't be the end of the world because there will be others involved too.

'Who?'

She holds her breath and takes a few risks.

Tony, in Kentish Town, finished his lunch (a cheese-and-pickle sandwich and a cup of one of the cheaper brands of instant coffee) some time ago. He is sitting at the kitchen table with a copy of the magazine *Records* in front of him, flicking through the pages. He has got used to the children being away, to the quiet of the flat. His mind returns more frequently to what has happened in the past, how he has been swept along by events, and to how he can find some way to be more in charge of events now. This whole question, for example, of looking for work. Glancing through the job adverts is enough to give him the willies. Imagine his *curriculum vitae* . . . Recent employment? How is he going to get round that? The thought of being called for an interview, assuming he could ever get that far, turns him cold. Yet he must be good for something, someone must want his knowledge. What he knows about selling, he knows. You can't take that away from someone. And as to the jazz scene, there can't be that many people in London who know as much. There is his pal old Walter Anderson, of course; the conversations they used to have. I wonder how he's faring in this new tide. Bet he's laughing now. We always knew. Give him a ring. Why not? Because it would be bloody awkward, that's why not.

He could try a different skill. Take up a craft. Lots of people retrain, why not him? There's the carpentry. Cut it out, Tony, it's unrealistic. You're never going to make enough money even to pay for someone to look after the kids. I've got to get back. And, thinking of Carole, I've got to be on top again, or at least a breadwinner too. Maybe it's not the only way but in this society it's one way to earn respect and I've got to right the balance. For my own sake, and for the kids as they grow up. I don't want them to think I'm a failure like we did at home of him. A man needs to work. A woman too, for that matter. And one of the worst things being done in this society of ours is having that right taken away. I'll always say Maggie has a lot to answer for. He glances at the early edition of the evening paper, which he's already read from cover to cover, and thinks again of Walter Anderson, wondering whether after all this time he should phone him.

In the atmosphere of Alex's grandparents' house even Angelica and Jerry have quietened down. The weather has cleared, they've been on long walks, her grandfather has played the piano in the evenings. Jerry has settled to finish a paper and Alex has taken out the notes from her project and begun to do the first calculations on the results. Though her mood remains far from even, she has worked to not let it show at the blackest moments, now she is with people she is genuinely fond of.

What she is thinking about as she toys with her project papers on her bed in a quiet hour after tea and before she goes to help prepare the supper, is that Tony and the kids have become a kind of outlet for her, which she won't exactly say she is addicted to, but without which she keeps getting this awful feeling that she is floundering, being sucked up in things that she doesn't want to be sucked into.

Nick and Sarah have just said goodbye to Nick's parents and are on their way back to London to a large New Year's Eve party. They are in high spirits. They've had a great few days with Nick's family and siblings but are now pleased to be alone. A few miles from the house, Nick draws into a lay-by, stops the car and takes Sarah in his arms.

'That separate room bit was a strain,' she says.

'Glad you thought so too.' He moves his hand lower.

'Let's find a wood, or something. I don't think I can wait for the waterbed.'

Not exactly a wood but a copse of trees on open land, it would have to do.

Dressed again and back in the car, Sarah and Nick sit close, she with her hand on his lap as he drives.

'What does that husband of Carole's do?'

'I don't exactly know. He used to be something in the music business, but he's not working now, he's at home looking after the kids.'

'What's he like?'

'I've never met him. He must have something if Carole's married to him. Why do you want to know?' She looks at him swiftly and then back out of the front windscreen again. There's that look in his eyes that I'm beginning to know. He's got to be leading up to something. She feels tense, unaccountably excited. She tickles his ribs.

'Well?'

He takes her hand and moves it so that it's round his waist, driving with one hand and holding the other over hers.

'I was thinking, we might choose a few days when the cottage is free and take Carole and her husband – I suppose the kids too – up there with us. What do you think?'

Sarah tries to imagine asking Carole. It's one thing offering her the place but another if they are going too. And of course she hasn't even come over to Sarah's to make the stuffing; that would have been a start. And then she is ten years older. But then again so is Nick, and Nick and she, from the odd meeting they've had in the office, seem to get on pretty well. And he is so confident. It doesn't even occur to him that Carole mightn't want to.

'Why are you suggesting this?'

'Because I sometimes get the feeling – I can't imagine from where – that it's something you'd like.' He smiles at her, a great beam of affection.

'And you like?'

'I like very much.' He nibbles her ear.

Perhaps then. Perhaps she might have the courage to. Who knows?

Alex's friends have been cooped up in the car for hours. Now, tumbling out onto the drive, they are noisy, excitable and gauche, in for a good evening. They hope Alex has put together some excellent grub; for their part they have brought some powerful grass, from a new source. Dave has also brought his enormous stereo which he carries blaring into the house. 'Turn it down,' Alex urges. On the other hand she half hopes it will mask or make difficult for her grandparents to catch half of what the newcomers are saying.

The 'grub' should be good: *moules marinière* in a wine sauce followed by a pasta dish Alex has made a few times. But the *moules* are something new. She's spent ages scrubbing them and is proud of the aromas issuing from the kitchen. She takes Chris off to see them cooking in their pot. They have a quick cuddle. By the time they leave the kitchen the others appear to be talking in a more civilised way with Alex's grandmother, and Alex begins to relax.

Alex's grandparents are already dressed in their evening clothes waiting for Jerry and Angelica; the four are going out to a party. But where is Angelica? 'She's not anywhere near ready,' Jerry apologises. 'She claims she lost track of time, but personally I think she dropped off to sleep. Anyway, she suggests we go on ahead, she'll follow in our car.'

Half an hour later Angelica sweeps down the stairs and into the kitchen just as Alex and her friends are lighting up their first joint.

'Can I join you? Do you mind?' For all the world implying that she would far rather be there, slumming it with the young people, than off with the oldies.

'Mother, the others are waiting for you!'

But Chris, Dave and Pru are happy for her to be there. Angelica sits down at the kitchen table and plunges straight in. She wants to know what they think about sex, about drugs, about the state of the world, the state of their souls. Not on New Year's Eve, prays Alex, please not. Now Angelica is asking her friends whether in the present climate they think that half a ton of condoms is a good present for a mother to give to her son – as has actually happened, she assures them, in at least one family she knows. Alex's mind reels, she tries to shut herself off from all of this.

Much later, slightly tipsy, slightly high, Angelica backs the car precariously out of the driveway. They hear jerks and squeaks of brakes and start to laugh. 'Your mother's a real character, Alex.'

Alex turns back to the mussels. Then – is it because she becomes too serious in response, or because they are ungrateful toads, on top of which, the pot and drink is a powerful mix? – when they eventually sit down in the formal dignity of the grandparents' dining-room the boys decide the atmosphere needs a little puncturing.

Dave starts to goad Chris, becoming sillier and sillier, real Boys' Own stuff with the girls looking on more and more helplessly, until they are smoking and eating and telling stories, laughing till they fall off their chairs and lie on the floor waving their legs in the air. The more the girls try to pull them together, the more hopeless it becomes. Eventually they roll off the floor and into the sitting-room and turn on the television.

'Hey, you can't do that,' Pru tries valiantly, 'not on New Year's Eve.'

'A whole wonderful morning in bed.' Sarah hugs Nick tight.

'Then tomorrow, back to the rat-race.'

Tony fingers his sister-in-law's postcard. They are enjoying themselves hugely, she has written, and plan to extend their trip by a few days. '*The children are fine and haven't cried for you once. Thank you so much for lending them to us.'*

The flat contains only his presence. Carole and he spent New Year's Eve watching TV, going to bed before the midnight hour struck. Carole left at the crack of dawn for the office, despite it's being a Bank Holiday. But he feels less at a loose end now than when the children had first gone. He has got hold of his old friend Walter Anderson's new business address, one of the huge modern structures down in Docklands, and left a message on his answerphone. He's been back to the employment agency, he's spent a couple of mornings at the library, hours listening to his favourite records, partly with the idea of picking half a dozen to sell in order to raise some cash. He's booked an appointment with Camden Social Services Department, though God knows what that will produce.

Carole thinks he's become secretive. She wonders if it is because he loves and misses Alex. She wonders if they write to one another. When she is with him she finds herself watching for signs and hates herself. Work is an antidote. And for all her recent problems with Lee, it is an area of her life she finds so much easier.

Still, the photos of the gulls have disappeared, the photographic equipment put away. Thank God that is the end of that. But why should he no longer want to tell her what he does in the day? It could be because he does nothing. But she doesn't think so. That isn't the sense she has when she comes home. She has a sense of new energy but an energy from which she is excluded. Well, the longer the kids are away the less excuse he has to see Alex. And again she thinks – with an irrational spurt of anger, so that the pencil with which she is making notes on a manuscript goes zigzagging across the page, making an ugly black line – God damn it, hasn't that girl better things to do with her time, why should she . . . And at that moment alone in the office on New Year's morning she feels a stab of pain. It is in her chest, or is it her lungs? At first it is too powerful, too stunning to locate. It crumples her so that she clings to herself as she doubles over the desk. What if, what if, here alone? She reaches for the phone and lets her hand lie there on the receiver. She tries to breathe. Concentrate on your breathing. Don't think of the pain, accept it. Go with it.

It passes. How many minutes? She can't tell.

He will not share with her because he feels the need to do whatever has to be done for himself. To take control of his life. If he shares too much at this point, if he lets her in too much, he will . . . no, he can't exactly articulate what it is. But her energy is so much more confident than his. How it swamps him. She would make suggestions, she would criticise, she would, probably without meaning to, put him down so that his confidence would again ebb. No, this time he must keep his own council. Afterwards, maybe. That's why he needs his own money, and has decided to sell more records. He puts away the postcard and goes into the sitting-room and settles down to make the difficult but necessary selection. Just one more time he will listen to each of them.

Chris wakes up with a hangover. He goes out into Alex's grandparents' garden and picks two solitary snowdrops (which Alex then said was a bloody stupid thing to do) and brings them to her with a solemn look on his face. 'I'm sorry about last night, Alex, Dave is too, you've got to forgive us. We didn't mean any harm, honestly.'

You're so immature, she fights back from saying to him. And thinks of Tony.

Later in the morning when they ask her if she'd like to travel back with them instead of hanging on for her parents, she decides to go.

Oh get me back to London, soon, soonest.

Winter and Spring

JANUARY 2nd. Alex makes her way across the Heath in the rain. They will be huddled in Mel's if anywhere at all, the children will inevitably feel cooped up and fretful. Maybe, knowing that, Tony will decide not to come. She wouldn't blame him. What a bummer of a day! She cannot be bothered to wear the hood of her jacket up. The raindrops trickle down her neck. Her long legs stride out, there is no one walking faster over the Heath.

By the time she reaches the brow of the hill and looks down on the sweep of ponds and the tennis courts at the far corner, her spirits have lifted. She is back in her own territory, breathing more freely. She hasn't even unpacked yet, the flat is a mess, there is no food, she has not felt like doing much this morning; but now normality hits. She is back, back.

They won't be there today, she thinks, longing for the little family in Mel's cafe. No, they won't come but so what? The bloody rain will stop in a day or two. We'll get back into our routine. Her mind shifts to other things, her mocks in only ten days, the need to get her project sorted out and handed in at the same time. All seems more possible as she strides towards Mel's.

They aren't there. It's the kids I miss, she tells herself. She wants to feel their arms around her, the warm breath of Ellen's face against her own, to laugh and be distracted by the stories of Moth's Christmas. Thinking these thoughts she exchanges a few words with Mel and sits down at a table with a cup of frothy coffee.

Shortly afterwards, Tony – Tony without the children – walks through the door. Then it hits her so forcibly that it is like a long expulsion of air being drawn from her, that it is Tony she's missed, Tony she's wanted to see, but has not let herself recognise it. Tony's steadiness, his certainty after Chris's childishness. Realising how much she wants him to walk up to her and put his arms around her brings tears to her eyes.

He has reached the table now and sees. 'What's the matter?' he asks.

'Nothing.'

He looks at her cup of coffee. 'I'll just get myself a cup, hang on.'

It gives her time to compose herself. 'Where are the children?'

'In the Lake District.'

'The Lake District!'

'Yes, Carole's brother and sister-in-law took a shine to them, offered to take them off for a few days. You know, it's the first time they've been away from us.'

'How does it feel?' She immediately regrets the question, it seems too personal.

'Strange. I thought I'd better come anyway, I couldn't just leave you in the lurch. And since you won't give me your phone number . . .' He smiles at her.

'It's . . .' Then she stops herself. Why change things now? Did you miss me? she wants to ask. She is more ill at ease than he, and drinks her coffee slowly.

The one who has had the better Christmas is in the stronger position. Tony tells her anecdotes about the terrible visit to Selfridges, about other outings, about the kids' presents, and observations of Moth's that he imagines will make her laugh.

But she is unusually quiet. Hanging her head, sipping her coffee though there is almost nothing left in the cup. He asks her about her Christmas, to which he receives a monosyllabic reply. He looks at her and wonders. 'Damn,' he says suddenly, 'I forgot to bring you the prints from your photos. I've blown up two or three and they've come out well. Did you take any over Christmas?'

She shakes her head. 'But I did do some work, you know, to kill time; I started analysing the results of my project. It's quite interesting,' she says with her half laugh, not sure whether he'll be interested. Without the children there is suddenly so much space to fill up.

He orders two more coffees and gets her to talk. Gradually her face becomes more animated. 'It's putting it all together, drawing the conclusions from all that stuff that bothers me.'

'Surely your teacher will help?'

'Nope. She's not allowed to. You're just meant to work it out for yourself. They give you someone else's project from another year, to go by.'

'Seems hard. I bet people do get help.'

'They probably mostly do. Angelica is dying to get her hands on it, it's right up her street. But she'd take over completely if I let her. No, I can manage.'

'What are you doing tomorrow?'

'Don't know. Why?'

She is back the next day in the early afternoon, carrying a pile of papers in a Budgen's carrier bag. The day is clear, the sun is shining; as she walks over the Heath she can feel its warmth on her neck and through her coat penetrating deep into her. Her step is light and springy. The new trainers she wears exaggerate this sensation. Though sad to have to be inside the fuggy cafe when she would prefer to be under the sky, she is pleased to be meeting Tony, just the two of them, very pleased.

She has not eaten any lunch, she is physically excited though she fights it back. At the top of the hill she collides with a kite. She laughs out aloud, delighting the owner. He is about to apologise but, seeing her laughter, laughs with her. He says something. She doesn't catch what it is, but gives him a gorgeous smile as if she has heard and agreed, and he, turning back to his kite-flying, feels the world this sunny afternoon is a happy place.

She hears the sound of reggae on someone's transistor and has an urge to dance to the beat as she makes her way down the hill. The sun soft, honeyed, is reflecting off the ponds and the trees. Everywhere birds are calling to one another. January, early January, yet she hears someone saying, 'Spring is in the air.' Yes, that is what it is; it is almost a spring day. She imagines longer afternoons, more hours of light, she imagines feeling warmer, coming on the Heath again with arms bare, wearing summer shorts. Soon, soon. I am coming out of hibernation, we all are. Maybe it will be a beautiful early spring, maybe.

She looks at the trees, wishing she had her camera. So many new branches, such proliferation. The sap, oh the sap. Everything sprouting, pushing upwards, the earth active once more. In the gardens the first spring bulbs are already green shoots. Not long till they begin to open. Oh I so much prefer summer, and by the summer all this stuff'll be over and I'll be able to do what I like. Though what, what? And he's going to help me, and it will make a difference.

*

When I went to Mel's it was pissing down with rain. I planned to take her the pictures. They'd been hanging around in my jacket pocket for days. But then because of the rain I grabbed my raincoat and forgot to transfer them. There were no children. Just us. At first she looked disconcerted. I wondered if she minded. Her face was blotchy, not beautiful. She was sitting there alone talking to Mel when I walked in.

'No kids?'

They're like a passport. 'I didn't know if I'd be welcome without them. But then I decided to risk it.' It didn't work, she didn't laugh. Just looked at me stonily, her face red in unexpected places, her throat, the sides of her nose, around her ears. Her eyes were mud-coloured, you couldn't tell what the hell was going on.

'Had a good Christmas?'

Some kind of noise. 'Yes? No?'

'S'okay,' she shrugged. Then for an awful second I thought she was going to burst into tears.

The colours changed, the red rearranging itself in other areas. 'I've missed you,' she said. 'Really, I've missed you a lot.'

I went to get a cup of coffee. The hand in my pocket that jingled the too few coins was not entirely steady. Could Carole be right? Surely not. Girls of that age. Girls with those kind of looks don't . . . not about someone like myself. Surely? Careful, anyway. You don't want to. You're a responsible man.

I took the coffee back to the table and slipping into my seat said to her – not making anything heavy out of it – 'I've missed you too. I've even missed the kids, occasionally.'

Where are they, by the way? I expect Carole's still on holiday and is taking her turn for once. Then why is he here, because? It does have some advantage not giving him my phone number. I don't know what this funny feeling is. Is this love? It would be love, I reckon, if I stopped noticing his awful clothes. Some consolation. It's not love. Oh Christ and yet I feel like saying a whole manner of crazy things to him like, I want to cook you *moules marinière*. I want to take off to the sea with you, Cornwall, Devon, some place like that. And go for long walks with the children. Without. Yes, without, and take lots of photos and be us like we are when we're being personal, when we're really relaxed with one another. I want you to put your arms round me and say not just the idiot things that Chris says but – oh fuck off Alex, stop being such a stupid little moo. You don't want any of those things. You want, you need; needs, says damned Angelica, are dangerous. Imagine Angelica and Tony meeting and . . .

'I've developed your photos and blown some of them up. Meant to bring them today, but in the rain . . .'

'So you remembered. I mean, you had time. I didn't think.' I keep feeling that I'm blushing but just my ears, it's crazy. It wasn't like this when the children were about. Or is it just that Christmas was so terrible? God I'm pleased he's here.

She was in such a strange mood, in the rain in Mel's. Everything she said was like a secret and yet she wasn't saying much. Sometimes I felt she had no idea how to relate to me but then who am I to talk, I seem to have related solely to Carole and the kids for years. Sometimes Alex treats me like a simpleton, a doddering idiot, often, though she doesn't realise it, like someone from the wrong side of the tracks. I saw her skirting carefully, with that promiscuous consciousness that Hampsteady youth seem to have, the liberal wishy-washies trying so hard not to step on anyone's toes. I half suspect it pleases her that I'm not someone who would fit comfortably into her mother's drawing-room. The seedier the stories I tell her of my present life, it has struck me before, the better she likes them.

Well there wasn't much that was seedy about our Christmas and the ordinary stories of our domesticity interested her not one little bit. Not today. The sense I had was of someone totally distracted. As if the small flame on her wick was being puffed at by breezes from all directions.

'How did your revision go?' Hating to sound like a school teacher.

'I did some,' she said. Her smile was challenging. No, I couldn't read it. I had a sense now that any moment she would get up and go. Of an explosion that would not take place near me. Yet as if she was saying, 'Help me.' But I didn't know how the hell to help her.

★

In the first week of January Tony and Alex meet daily in Mel's cafe, in the early afternoon when it is even more empty than usual. The two sit at their habitual table (third from the door, away from the draughts but still with plenty of natural light) poring over Alex's one hundred and fifty questionnaires.

When he says that about my project, that he will help me with the results, it's good of him, really kind. I tell him of course how piss awful they are at school and how they won't give you any help and say you have to work it out for yourself. He says, can't Angelica help? But Angelica – give her that material for half a second, I explain, and you'd see it in the newspapers the following week. 'But do you know about figures and things?' He reckons he knows enough. Then I think; he'll see what a fool I am. Then on the other hand I'll find out what a fool he is. And this will be over, whatever 'this' is.

Neither of us are fools. And the kids are away until the weekend.

It was fun to see her confidence grow as the days proceeded. At first she kept saying, 'No, I can't express it, *you* do it.' But by Thursday she took the pencil out of my hand and started to write herself. We sat on in Mel's for hours. She's an angel, that woman, not to mind. We ended up eating poached eggs on toast.

'Just deserts,' said Alex.

'For who, her or us?'

'Oh, I hadn't thought of that,' she giggled.

With the kids not being around, money was going less quickly this week, and I was able to offer to pay.

'We ought to go Dutch,' she said.

'Why?'

'Because that's the kind of relationship it is.'

'And what exactly do you mean by that?'

Her ears were fiery red. 'Anyway, I believe in going Dutch.'

'That was an afterthought if ever I heard one. I'd like to pay this once.'

'Why?'

'Because it would give me pleasure.'

'Thanks.' She clinked her mug of tea against mine.

'It's been good for me,' I told her, 'I've enjoyed it. It's reminded me that I can concentrate on bookwork if the need arises. I was worried that I might have lost the knack.'

'Were you awfully bored?'

'What do you think?'

'Tomorrow?'

'Yes, tomorrow.'

'When do the kids come back?'

'Saturday. You'll be okay now, won't you? Tomorrow I was thinking . . .' Hold on. You can't share too much with her that you don't share with Carole. Leave it. What you do tomorrow is your business. But why is it so much easier with her, when she's only eighteen, for Christ's sake? Because she's eighteen. Because she doesn't hassle me. Careful Tony, you've got to be careful. Keep on the right line of. A good thing that the kids are coming back.

'I never thought I'd say this but I'm beginning to miss the little devils, now, you know.'

'Me too.' Half true. I do. It's just that. Tuesdays Fridays, Tuesdays Fridays. Oh why is everything so unsimple, so unstraightforward? Why can't.

'Shall I then, shall I then see you on Tuesday, as usual?'

'Fine.'

*

The world has changed again. They are trapped back in the most icy of weathers. Where is spring? A false start, laugh the people on the Heath. Many don't mind, for on the ponds a rare event is taking place. People are skating, dressed up in brightly coloured scarves and mufflers. Looking down on the ponds from the top of Parliament Hill, the scene looks like something out of a Dutch or Flemish painting.

Alex has been watching the ice with interest, the way it half covers the ponds, creating a glass surface broken by occasional liquid pools of water. She watches the dogs trying to swim, the antics of birds and ducks, the children looking dolefully at the notices which say, '*DANGER! This ice is dangerous.*'

By halfway through the week the ice completely covers the ponds. The weather is so cold the breath is nipped, the cheeks sting. Ten below: who's heard of such a thing in London?

Alex is pleased at how much revision she's put in. Still, who can sit in one room all day? She needs to go out for milk, bread, new biros etc. She also wants to wander to the edge of the Heath, as far as the first pond.

She opens the window to let one of the cats in and is struck by the freezing quality of the air. It feels like the preparation you put on burns. With the cat on her lap she fingers through a book. Then shuts it and jumps up, surprising the cat, flings on her coat, the old navy one with the hood, the warmest she has, and leaves the house, banging the gate behind her.

It is noon. There must be fifty people at least on the trio of ponds. She looks for the sign with 'DANGER' on it; it has been turned around, whether by the authorities or by one of the skaters she doesn't know. But so many people on the ice, it must be safe.

Again in the afternoon she leaves the basement. This time making less noise as she shuts the door behind her. She is eager, she walks fast.

The kids were eager to see Alex. It was Moth's second day back at school and I had no trouble, despite the cold, herding them onto the bus and over the fields.

Moth runs ahead at first but then as he spots Alex he dashes back and grabs hold of me.

'What's she got in her hands?' he asks.

'I can't make it out either, we'll have to wait and see.'

But he keeps stopping on our way up, to peer at her.

'Come along, Moth, this is getting boring.'

'Lex, Lex,' says Ellen seeing her.

'That's right, love, you still remember her name then?'

It seems the most natural thing in the world to hug Alex. Ellen goes forward for a hug too. Moth hangs back.

It's skates she's carrying. A pair for each of us. She's rediscovered them in the loft at home, apparently. Moth suddenly starts shouting at the top of his lungs that he isn't going to skate, no one can make him. I feel ashamed of my son. The way Alex kneels down gently and says to him, 'What's all the fuss, Moth? No one's going to make you do anything you don't want to do. I'd thought it might be fun because before Christmas we talked about it and you seemed keen – that's all.'

He turns away from her.

'Moth, don't be so rude to Alex, especially after she's gone to a lot of trouble.'

'I won't, I won't,' he screams, loud enough for the entire Heath to hear, 'no one's going to make me skate.'

'Stop that noise this instant! Look, I'm sorry,' I say to her. 'Not much of a welcome for you. We could skate anyway. Moth could watch. It's years since I've been on ice.'

There's me and him and then there's me and him and the kids. What's got into Moth, is it something I've done?

'Let me go first,' I tell them, 'just to get my skate legs, and check that it really is safe, then I'll come back for you, Alex.'

'Me too, me want to come.'

'Well, we'll see, Ellen.'

'We've got to take her too,' says Alex, 'are you sure you'll be okay, Moth?'

'Sure you don't want to change your mind? I'd hold your hand, you'd be safe with me.' He shakes his head vigorously. 'Okay then, but listen, Moth, you'll stay here like a good boy, you won't move away?'

Moth looks deep into Alex's eyes, a look she can't interpret, then says, 'I'll stay here.'

Alex feels awkward on the ice for the first few minutes. She falls down and does her funny little laugh. With Ellen on his shoulders Tony can't, as he would like, bend down to help Alex up. Soon, however, she is on her feet and striking out more confidently into the middle of the pond. Tony catches her up. They begin to skate together, fitting their steps into the same rhythm. Ellen grabs Alex's hair. 'Here, be careful you little monkey,' Tony says to her, 'you'll topple us all over if you do that.'

'Want to go with Alex.'

'I don't know if I'm strong enough to take you like that.'

'Want to.' She struggles on her father's shoulders so Tony swings her down, and around and around, causing gales of laughter. Alex looks up to check that Moth is still where he said he'd be and catches the boy's serious eyes looking down on them.

'I've an idea, we could skate with Ellen between us, swinging her along. Would you like that, Ellen?' She would. Everywhere around there is laughter and excited voices, the air is crisp and exhilarating and in their lungs it feels like prisms of many colours.

Skating fast with Alex was a great antidote to most things.

'You're bloody good,' I told her.

'A bit out of practice, but it used to be a family sport. Mum and Dad and I every Saturday at Queen's Gate. I loved it. How about you?'

'Before my adopted father lost all his dough he was generous about things like this. Any sport, you just had to name it and he'd pay up.'

'Sounds super.'

'For a year or two, yes.'

'This too will change,' she chants.

'Surely your mother must have some new ones since Christmas?'

'You know, I think she's getting stuck in a rut. Probably the weather. But did I tell you she's writing a novel? It's bound to be terrible. There's even a chapter about her yoga class, apparently!'

'Carole's giving up yoga.'

'Why is that?'

'She says she's got too much work and can't make the time at the moment.'

'It must be frightfully boring. Yoga. I like fast things.'

'I bet you do. Race me to the other side of the pond.'

'With Ellen between us?'

'I'll put her back on my shoulders.'

'Let me have a word with Moth first.'

'He's all right.'

'That's the trouble, he's not all right.'

'Don't fret about him, Alex.'

'Just hang on a moment.'

She skates to the side, they talk, then she fishes out her camera and hands it to him.

'How many did you say he could take? He'll waste the entire film if you let him.'

'Only a few. My exams start the day after tomorrow by the way. Wish me luck.'

'I do wish you luck, I've even got a card for you somewhere.'

'You have?'

'I'll give it to you later.'
'Now I'll race you.'

*

Sarah watches Carole's every move, waiting for the right moment. Today she will find the courage to ask her about Wales. Nick and she have already quarrelled about it. 'Why make such a big deal? She can always say no if it doesn't suit. Why go on and on about it? You sound quite childish.' 'Childish,' Sarah flashed angrily. Does it seem that way to her boyfriend? She told him she didn't want any help in the kitchen, and cooked the supper in a storming rage. But deep down she knew that he was jealous. And it *is* crazy, why take him so much for granted and get so uptight over Carole? By the time supper was ready she was prepared to allow, 'I probably am making a big fuss over nothing.'

Still, today at work, she feels as nervous as ever. She can't bear it either that Carole might say no, or that she will think it a cheek. Yet today for sure she has to do it.

Today when Lee asks Carole to lunch with him she accepts, even though it means making a phone call to put off an old friend. But the relationship between herself and Lee is at an important transitional stage. Much rests in the balance. Somehow she has won him to her side, without giving in too much herself. Lee is beginning to confide in her. He has been unnerved by the B.B. incident and grateful to Carole for pulling the situation around. She feels she is gaining respect in his eyes although she can't quite take seriously his, 'You're really part of the backbone of this firm, they ought to make you a partner. Me first, of course. Then you. If we both stay long enough. I'll have to see to it myself for both of us.' She just laughs, not taking it seriously. What she does wonder over is his 'If we both stay long enough.' The very use of the words implies – surely not, he's only been with them for a matter of months, he couldn't already be thinking. Or could he?

He could. He's had another offer, 'The kind you would be a damned fool to turn down,' he confides over lunch. 'But this is in confidence, Carole, I rely on you – I can, can't I?' 'You can,' she sighs. It seems to her too many people at work say just that. 'What do you think I should do?' he wants to know. 'Seriously Carole, I respect your judgement, more than anyone else's here.' She looks at him thoughtfully. At the same time thinking how tough and overcooked the liver is. She has chosen a hot meal because Tony is finally meeting up with Walter tonight and there'll be no supper at home.

The children are going to Seth's house, something Tony's arranged himself.

When he'd told her that he was planning to meet up with Walter she'd been amazed. After all these years! She'd looked at him, trying to assess. Then he'd surprised her further. 'I need some new clothes. After all this time I'm not sure if I know where . . . I wondered . . . On Saturday would you come with me?'

'Clothes. Christ, Tony! Our overdraft . . .'

'Oh, don't worry about that, I've got the cash.'

Then he'd told her about selling the records. She felt angry, she knew how much they meant to him. And why hadn't he discussed it with her? But Tony would hear none of this. 'It's done now.'

'But why?'

Yes, she would go with him on Saturday, they would all go. But is it to do with Alex, is it really because he wants . . .? She has meanwhile lost the thread of what Lee's been saying. He talks so much anyway you need only listen to one sentence in three. Still, now that he's told her why her advice means so much to him, he is waiting to hear what she will say. Should he go, what kind of question is that? There is the moral prerogative. Should someone take on a high-powered job, be empowered with a great deal of responsibility, then leave it so soon, letting down colleagues, staff, authors? There is that kind of 'should', she supposes, but doubts that that is what he is referring to, except in passing. Should he for his own good, would it bode well for him, would there be any negative effects on his career, people thinking the worse of him for moving so soon? How would people assess him, is this what he wants to know?

What will she say, what should she say? If she has influence, which she tends to doubt, but you can never be too sure, then how will she use it? For a start, it is worth considering whether she wants him to go now, when he is turning out to be not quite such an enemy as she'd first thought. And who would come in his place? Someone better, worse? Then again, thinking of the firm, how good is he? On this she decides it's too early to tell, though she suspects that the kind of mistakes he has already made he will go on making. He is too self-satisfied and, despite the fact that he might be clever, she will never like him. But she could on the other hand work with him. So what will she say?

On the bus later. Only a ten-minute wait this evening. She hates it when the afternoon disappears like that. Being so late back. Not her style. Then all the appointments being squashed up one after the other. And so many calls that she is not able to get back to, and unfinished niggly things, and people coming and going with endless questions . . . had she? . . . would she?

She'd felt a headache coming on at the exact moment, in the loo – it was the kind of afternoon where there was hardly time to change a tampax – when she'd wondered if Tony was really meeting Walter after all. What if? No, impossible. He wouldn't. Then when Sarah brought in her tea, the milk was sour and she had been short with her. Not really short but Sarah was so sensitive. She tries so hard, almost too hard. And knowing this Carole shouldn't have. Such a small thing, but Sarah takes it so seriously. She'll have to develop a thicker skin when she works for other people, that's my only criticism of her. I told her that. Not in an unfriendly way. Before she left. She appeared to be standing around waiting for me to say something. Perhaps she was still thinking about the tea. She seemed washed out. Hope she's not going down with something. Hope this headache isn't the beginning of a bug we've both caught. Can't afford to be ill this month. 'Why not get off on time this evening?' I told her. 'Don't hang around for me. Doing anything nice?'

'Nothing particular.'

'Just going to cuddle up with that gorgeous man of yours, eh?'

'Carole . . . ?'

'Hang on a minute, Sarah, why does the phone always go the moment anyone starts to talk to me?'

When I'd finished talking to Jimmy Batesman, she'd gone.

The bus seems to take for ever through Camden Town. Why is there so much traffic tonight? It moves in fits and starts. Great lurches forward. The smell of sweat and a day's cigarette-smoking makes her feel sick. Her headache pounds. How good it will be to get home and have the flat to herself.

She puts the key in the door with relief. No one to need anything of her for a while.

Alex has finally got through to Chris. His phone has been engaged for hours, she claims.

'Well what's so important, anyway?'

'I was going to tell you about how today's exams went but it doesn't matter, forget it.'

'Listen, Al, my parents are away tomorrow night, I was thinking . . .'

'That is all you think about,' she grumbles.

She can hear him sighing, a huge theatrical sigh down the phone. 'Chris, tomorrow my exams will be over. If the ice holds what about having a skating party? Pru, Dave, all of us, we'll get as many people as we can.'

'You and your ideas.'

'Okay then?'

'I suppose.'

Alex's face is flushed, so that the bone structure in its perfect symmetry is highlighted. She looks young, so young, as if nothing has touched her yet . . . her almond eyes – Carole peers at them but cannot tell their colour – look up at Tony over Ellen's head as if what he is saying to her is of the utmost importance. She is wearing a blue padded jacket and jeans so skin-tight that every contour of her long shapely legs is apparent. Because the photo is taken in movement, her hair, dark marvellous hair, masses out around her and some of its dark strands brush across her husband's face. My mate. Mine.

What is happening to us? She looks again at Alex's legs in their tight jeans and then again at the way Tony is looking at her. No, at the way they are looking at each other over Ellen's head. She feels like a peeping Tom seeing something she shouldn't know about, something she doesn't want to know about. Forgetting that cameras lie, to her in that minute the camera says it all.

In pain she clutches her ribs, for that stabbing pain is starting again. Soon she is doubled over on the floor.

As the minutes go by she feels more and more scared. With her foot she pulls the phone towards her.

Tony sits in the Arches wine bar opposite Waterloo Bridge. He is wearing a new jacket, broad-shouldered, and black trousers, new shirt, new shoes: the results of a Saturday's shopping expedition. Across from him is his old buddy Walter Anderson. He had anticipated being envious when he saw his old friend again. He had schooled himself to try to take it without bitterness, bitterness because they had been part of each other's fate, and wasn't it just the luck of the draw that it had worked for the one, not the other?

The surprise is that he finds himself drinking a far-too-cold glass of Côtes du Rhone with a man whom he can hardly recognise as his old, cheerful, pleasure-loving pal. A couple of months previously, Walter tells him, his wife upped and left, taking the kids with her, leaving the most elliptical of notes.

'But didn't you see this coming?'

'I had no idea,' says Walter, bursting into a long tortured monologue about his wife's faults, her viciousness, her ungratefulness after all he had done. 'No one can imagine', he says, 'what it is like to come home to an empty house after years of a noisy happy family. The loneliness, oh the loneliness . . .'

He is like a large shabby dog, self-obsessed. Drinking heavily, not noticing that Tony is not. Forget the clothes, Tony reflects, if I'd turned up in my bathing trunks he probably wouldn't have raised an eyebrow, the way he is. At first Walter appears uninterested in anything Tony has to say, just muttering, 'Why did you phone, it must be for something, that's one of the prices of being successful. What do you want?'

He gets himself a quiche and salad, because he is going on to a concert at the Festival Hall – 'One way to drown my sorrows.' He stuffs food and drink into his mouth, more drink than food. He gazes at his fork, empty or full, then gazes at Tony from under his beetle-bushy eyebrows. A big man always. Now filled out. Middle aged. Unhappy. Then another long monologue, which in its strange way isn't at all personal, as if Walter is talking to himself. Tony imagines that if he hadn't been there Walter with meagre encouragement would have told the whole thing to a passing waitress.

But he tries to console, 'I feel for you. I, too . . .'

'You can't imagine it,' says Walter, jabbing his fork into the air.

Looking at the other, Tony thinks, Christ, other lives. Of all the things I expected to be feeling, it certainly wasn't sorry for him, the old fucker.

But just at that moment a girl comes up to them and kisses Walter. His daughter? No, his children aren't that age surely? She sits down beside him on the bench. How old can she be? Not much older than. Christ!

Walter is getting up, looking at his watch. 'Look, can I leave you to settle up?' He lays a couple of notes on the table. 'Got to be going. Sorry it's been such a rush. Nice to see you. Must do it again. Was it for anything in particular?'

Tony just shakes his head. 'Enjoy the concert.'

Lonely, my foot!

By the time Carole hears the thud of feet and the noise of the children talking to Tony outside the door, she has regained some kind of equilibrium. The pain has left her feeling washed out and the shock of the photos has made her tearful. So that when, deciding to nurture herself, she'd gone into the kitchen to heat up what was left of yesterday's fresh noodles, and then found that someone had eaten the remains of the sauce, she'd cried. Ridiculous. Only for a minute. Struggling to get a grip on herself, she grated some cheese, and melted butter with garlic. She turned on the radio and made herself concentrate on the panel game. But when it was over she could not stomach the play that followed.

She is calmer now. Reason tells her that if Tony left the photos about for her to see, then either he wants to hurt her pretty badly (and with everything she knows about her man this doesn't ring true) or the whole thing has got to be more innocent than it looks. Otherwise surely, and with Moth and Ellen being involved, no, it was impossible. Besides, in bed he wasn't any different to the way he'd always been. More distant perhaps. And he'd had that patch when he hadn't wanted. But now he seemed just as keen as ever. Surely. I'm sure he hasn't. Yet. But she's out to get him. I'm sure of that too. And somehow I've got to. Think, Carole, think, this is a time for using your head.

'Hello, all of you,' says Carole from the sofa. The children are tired and whiny and Tony doesn't look in her direction but says, 'Carole, Ellen needs a bath. She fell in a puddle, she's in a terrible state.'

'I can see that,' Carole tells Tony, at the same time thinking, why does he tell me his daughter needs a bath, just because I'm here why must I always be expected to take over?

And he, looking at her as she sits on the sofa, is pissed off and dejected, a complete dead-end that meeting with Walter was, and the kids fought the whole way home and Seth's mother looked at him reprovingly, implying she didn't mind doing him a favour but Ellen had become so tired. 'Couldn't Carole have picked them up on the way back from work?'

'I expect she's only just got back herself.'

'I see.'

'Thanks anyway, Joanna, you must let us do you a favour sometime.' And then that look she gave him (or was he just imagining it this evening?) implying, 'Tell me another.' It embarrassed him. And now here is Carole sitting back on the sofa enjoying herself and of course it wouldn't have occurred to her to go and pick up the kids, no, they are his department unless she is absolutely forced. Christ, he is exhausted, the pavements so hard, he seems to have been walking for hours. And she just sitting back on the sofa and. Why doesn't she jump to her feet and. Why does he have to ask her to?

Both parents eventually do their bit and the two children are finally put to bed, Ellen tearful, Moth awkward and demanding. When Tony pops back to their room minutes later, he finds them fast asleep in the positions in which they'd first hit the pillows. He stands looking at them, thinking about Walter and the sordid story he'd told. Thinking what it would be like if Carole had done that to him.

At least we do have them, he tells himself, at least we're a family. He goes back into the living-room.

'How did your day go?'

'Mediocre.'

'Aren't you going to ask me about my meeting with Walter?'

'Tell me.'

So he tells her.

Carole has never liked Walter's wife. Tony neither. They reminisce about earlier meetings, about their own predictions, which Tony has forgotten but Carole hasn't. Now they are drawn closer, the couple that has worked against the couple that hasn't.

This is going better than I expected, it's important not to let him see how tensed up I am, Carole thinks.

While at the fridge for a beer, Tony calls out to Carole to ask whether he should bring her one too.

She'd prefer tea, she says.

He puts on the kettle.

She is watching the nine o'clock news when he returns. He speaks over it, hanging on to the sense of communication that was between them before he left the room. The voice on the air is talking about the government's latest plans for privatising electricity. Parkinson's name comes up. Carole turns off the television. Jabs of jealousy and pain return. When Tony says, 'Of course there wasn't a chance in hell of talking to Walter about what I'd intended to talk to him about, Carole, I just found myself . . .'

She responds, 'No doubt that's what Parkinson once said, "I just found myself."'

'What are you talking about?'

'It doesn't matter. For heaven's sake, Tony, why don't you take control of your own life. If you wanted to talk about something to Walter, why didn't you get it together and *do so*? Oh, I'm sorry, really I'm sorry, I didn't mean to shout at you.'

She despises me, Tony thinks. Probably has for ages. Now we have it out in the open.

On the bus the following morning Carole's thoughts go this way and that. How did I let that happen? I thought I wasn't going to show any emotion. What happened to all your brilliant control, Carole? Trouble is I can't get the damn thing out of my mind. It's bound to come up. Yes but over side issues, that's worse, the coward's way. What am I going to do? Maybe I should confront him, show him how angry I am. He doesn't like my anger usually. But this isn't 'usually'. And what if I risk it, and lose?

'Morning, Sarah, you're early.'

Now or never, just ask her straight out. 'Yes I am. Nick dropped me off. Carole, Nick . . . Nick and I wondered . . . it's just an idea . . . and probably a very silly one . . . but we just wondered if you'd like to . . . you and your husband and the children . . . come to Nick's cottage in Wales for a weekend?'

'When?'

'The weekend after next, or the one after that.'

'Yes.'

'You will? You could do with . . . with some country air?'

'We could. It's a lovely idea, Sarah, and comes absolutely at the right time. How very good of you and Nick to have thought of it. But you're sure we won't be in the way? The children can be extremely noisy.'

'It'll be fine, there's plenty of countryside to run about in. I'll tell Nick yes, then?'

'Yes.'

What does she mean, just the right time? That's not the point. The point is. Oh God, she said yes.

On the lake that evening twenty or more of Alex's friends have gathered. There is a full moon. The ice sparkles. It isn't at all cold when you get going.

Pru had come to Alex's basement flat earlier and Alex showed her her old felt skating-skirt. It still fitted. Pru dared her to wear it. 'Just for a laugh. Go on, why not?'

'You've got to be joking. They'll all take the piss out of me.'

'They won't. Not if we do it properly, the full fifties gear.'

Alex puts most of her hair up in a beehive and then, compromising, lets a few strands trail down. She wears a fifties-style red angora sweater she's picked up at a jumble sale, red tights and very red lipstick. The skirt is black, short and full, with moons and stars around the hem.

'They'll all laugh,' she says again, but less convinced. She knows she is looking great.

Pru in green and orange is only slightly less spectacular. The two girls walk to the pond together. Alex carries her jacket. She isn't going to put it on. It would spoil the effect.

'I've done it,' Sarah flings at Nick as he comes through the door, 'and she said yes.'

'Good for you.'

'Aren't you pleased?'

'Of course I am.'

The two girls are skating alone on the pond. Everyone is cheering them. Taped music from the transistors blares across the Heath. When they stop, others scramble onto the pond, laughing and tripping.

'You're looking great tonight, like something out of a movie. Cool,' says Chris.

'Skate with me.' She takes his hand. He is less steady than her, but she helps him and soon he is going along as fast as she. He is looking good tonight himself. 'I can see all of the green of your eyes,' she tells him. 'They're like cat's eyes.'

'Come back home, afterwards.'

'Perhaps.'

'Please.'

'Ask me again later.'

It gets later and later. Many of the crowd have finished exams today and all these, like Alex, are stirred with a kind of post-exam fever. They lie on blankets on the cold ground, snuggled together for warmth. Intermittently, in pairs or alone, they skate. Alex skates more than anyone. She likes her image tonight. It is weird and exciting; tonight she feels she has power.

When she is skating alone Pru comes up and whispers in her ear, 'Chris is really keen on you, you know. I think he's in love, he's acting really strange, telling everyone that . . .'

'Oh fuck off,' says Alex, laughing.

'. . . that you're in love with a much older guy and that's why you won't . . . I don't know . . . a guy you meet occasionally. He says he's going to fight a duel with him here on the Heath, at dawn. Something like that. Of course, he's pissed,' she adds quickly, seeing the look on Alex's face.

'He's out of his mind.'

'But is it true, any of it, I mean, about – '

'No, it isn't.'

Pru skates off.

Dave comes onto the pond.

'Pru's over there,' she tells him. 'You must have just missed one another. Where's Chris?'

'Dunno, he's gone for a walk. To look at the moon or something. You're something tonight, Alex, that's a great get-up.'

'Thanks.'

'Skate with me.'

'Okay.'

He takes her hand. Then she sees Chris staring at her from the edge of the pond and waves to him to join them. The three skate together.

Another threesome. Don't think about it. Tony, what are you doing now, anyway? Are you asleep? Why don't you walk onto the Heath and surprise this lot? Though I don't know what I'd do if you did. But I'd like you to see me like this. Different somehow. The card made me laugh out aloud, by the way. It was a kind of good luck charm, you caring. Our jokes – I can't have jokes like that with them. On Tuesday, next Tuesday. And maybe Moth and I will be friends again. I wonder what was wrong with him.

Later still, maybe a full hour later, they are lying on the rugs. Goodness knows what time it is. Chris reaches over towards Alex. 'Put on your jacket, or you'll catch your fucking death.'

'I'm not cold.'

'Let me see.' He touches her neck, her throat. Then slips his hand below her jumper. She lets him pull her close.

'What are we doing here, when we could be at home?' he whispers.

Even later. The others have left, but Chris and Alex, plus one of the blankets and one of the transistors, remain, uncertainty hanging between them until finally she says, 'Okay then. But you'll have to wear a condom.'

'I haven't got a condom, for Christ's sake. Besides, I hate those things.'

'It's the only way.'

'Who says?'

'Nowadays.'

'Alex, you're behaving like some fucking virgin. I bet last year with Guy, you didn't make him . . .'

'It was different then.'

'And he's the kind who *would* give you Aids, according to all accounts.'

'What do you mean?'

'Didn't you know? He's bi.'

'You're just saying that to get at me. Oh let's stop squabbling. It's crazy. I suddenly feel all – shivery. Can't we just go back to your place and cuddle up together and then tomorrow if you do get some condoms, I promise.'

'What really turns me on is the way you're so fucking keen,' he grumbles.

Let it all be different from this. It's not meant to be like this. Surely, surely?

*

Jerry has not slept well. Has woken a half-dozen times, trying to get comfortable, and failing. Nothing is less in his thoughts than the ice on the ponds. If he looks out of the window what he sees is the dull, strange light with its sense of oppression, of things closing in.

As he is about to leave the house, he hears Alex's light footsteps coming up from the basement. She appears in an orange dressing-gown – in which she looks as if she's been sleeping – the strength of the colour of the robe making the pallor of her face all the more noticeable. There are dark hollows under her eyes and perspiration on her forehead.

'Lovely, you look terrible.'

'Where's Mum?' She is hanging on to the bannister, as if she can hardly manage to remain standing.

'Upstairs.' He makes a sound as if he is going to say something else, then changes his mind.

But Alex has lived with her mother long enough to know what he is about to say. She lets out a sigh which is also a sob. 'I've never felt as bad as this. Will you ask her to come and see me when she's finished writing?'

'Of course. Would you like me to call the doctor?'

'No, I'll be okay. I'm going back to bed.'

'Surely I can do something for you? What about a hot water bottle? Or a nice drink?'

'Nothing honestly. Tell Mum.' Then she is gone.

Jerry stands motionless staring out of the kitchen window. He would like to comfort but what can he do? He writes a note for Angelica and leaves it on the kitchen table then, picking up his briefcase, leaves the house.

It is much later when he returns home. Apron around her waist, mouth sticky from something deliciously sweet-sour and garlicky she's been tasting, Angelica comes to kiss him. She is in vibrant spirits, pours him a glass of wine, tells him the meal will be ready in fifteen minutes; he is in for a treat, taste the artichoke soup, it's a marvel. He sits at the kitchen table and looks at her with affection.

'Is the book finished then?'

'Not quite. But it's going well. Soon. God, Jerry, what a weight off my back it'll be.'

'And mine.'

'No doubt. You poor darling. You stayed out of the house especially to give me peace, didn't you? No, I know you, don't deny it. Didn't you?'

'Maybe. You got the note about Alex, incidentally?'

'Yes, indeed. She's gone and caught pneumonia, skating till all hours of the night on the ponds.' She sighs, raising her eyes, as if to say, what will I do with her?

'Have you called Tomlinson?'

'Yes. Meanwhile, I'm feeding her aspirin to get the temperature down.'

'I must say she looked pathetic this morning. Is she okay alone down there?'

'Since she won't consider coming up to the spare room, what can we do? She mumbled something about Chris coming round to see her later.'

'He'll be a fat lot of use!'

When Chris comes round Alex is asleep. He bangs and bangs on her door but she doesn't hear him. Swearing, he retreats up the wrought-iron staircase, then hovers outside Angelica's door. He could ask them to let him go down through the house. Trouble is, he is carrying a bunch of chrysanthemums and doesn't want Alex's parents to see them and get the idea that he is going soft. He rubs one shoe against the other on the doorstep, deliberating.

When eventually he rings and Jerry answers he puts the flowers behind his back but knows that Jerry sees them anyway.

Alex's parents, their very house, make him feel awkward. 'Just come to see her,' he half swallows, beetling sideways across the hall and down the stairs to the basement as quickly as possible. He does not even bother to give a courtesy knock but goes straight in.

Alex is in a deep but restless sleep. Relieved to get rid of the flowers he chucks them in the sink, forgetting to put them in water. Then he sits down in the only halfway comfortable chair and picks up one of her magazines. For ages, it seems, he remains there watching her. Alex's mother has rigged up two extra heaters and the room is suffocatingly hot. Alex in her sleep fights with her duvet; he cannot tell whether she wishes to push it off or not. She calls out, but the words are indistinct, something about Mel, or it could be hell. Jesus, she's delirious, he thinks, suddenly scared, wondering whether to beat a hasty retreat.

About an hour after Chris has got there Alex opens her eyes and looks at him. For a moment she doesn't seem to recognise him. It gives him an odd sensation.

Then. 'Chris,' she mumbles.

'Hi, Alex.' He thinks of going to the sink and presenting her with the flowers but is too embarrassed; it would look desperately uncool.

'Well I bought the condoms,' he says, and laughs.

She looks at him; her eyes tell him that she too thinks it's funny.

He comes and sits on her bed. 'One way of getting out of it.'

She doesn't have the energy to answer.

'At least you got your exams over first.'

'I feel so awful,' she says, and starts to cry.

Before, when she'd cried, he'd said, 'Piss off, I hate tears,' but now he says tenderly, touching her face, 'What a mess. Is there anything I can do?'

'Turn off the heaters,' she mumbles, 'and some lime, just some lime juice.'

Chris turns off one of the heaters. Then he pours her a glass of lime juice from the jug Angelica has made her. She tries to sit up but is unsteady. He props her up with one arm and helps the glass towards her mouth.

'What a bloody mess,' he says again.

She looks at him. Though she is sitting it seems to him that she is already asleep again. He puts the glass beside the bed and lays her back down.

Over the following forty-eight hours Alex wrestles in and out of sleep, in and out of bad dreams. Occasionally she is aware of other presences: her mother, Chris, Doctor Tomlinson. But the person she would most like to come and see her doesn't even know she is ill.

Monday morning, she sits up in bed, thoughtfully, eating part of the bowl of cereal that Angelica has brought down. Looking out of the window, she realises that the ice has melted. She gingerly gets out of bed and pads around the corner to her kitchen area, with the bowl in her hand. She sees the dead chrysanthemums in the sink. She feels tears spring to her eyes but tells herself crossly it is only the aftermath of her illness.

'Mother, who brought me the flowers?' (I can always hope, can't I, even if I know it's impossible.)

'I've no idea, darling, why, where are they?'

'In my kitchen, dead. You might at least have put them in water.'

'If I'd seen them of course I would have done. But I haven't been into your kitchen.' Pause. 'You know what they say, don't you? Bad temper is the first sign that you're getting better. See you this evening, my love. If you want anything before, Jerry will be about.'

Alex's excursion to the kitchen has been enough for her for the moment. She is pleased to be back in bed and fights the sensation of temporary dizziness. Who brought the flowers? Chris? He'd never spend his money like that. Perhaps he did. But whether he did or not, I can't. I know that now. It's got to feel right and it doesn't.

She lies in bed, dizziness gone now, trying to think how she will put it to Chris, hating the thought of any kind of confrontation. But all the time her mind keeps slipping. I was wrong all the time then. You can be in love with someone and think their clothes are awful. It doesn't take that away. I thought it would. Love. I want to shout it from the top of the house. Except I'm too weak to get out of this fucking bed. 'Course he'll never love me in that way. Still I can love him, can't I? Nobody can stop me doing that. I just don't have to let on. I just have to . . . get to the Heath tomorrow. I've got to, or he'll think I let him down.

★

I was flicking through the pages of *Music Maker* when the phone rang.

Having this kind of literature around again was still a novelty. It's only when the money dries up that you realise what a luxury magazines are. I kept on buying them when I still believed I'd get another job. But as time went by there seemed less and less point. But now there was still extra cash around – for a few more weeks – and I had a lot of catching up to do.

I was reading this article about ILI and before it came to the point I'd made the connection myself. Of course. They were beginning to seriously reissue from the Brooklyn Bridge Catalogue. After all, 'Penny Lane' was the second in the same month, and I knew then that it was no coincidence. I was dwelling on this, trying to get it into my old mind what it meant, how everything comes in cycles how . . . when the phone rang.

I picked it up. 'Tony Davis here.

'Hello Walter. No, you're not disturbing anything in particular. What can I do for you?

'I see.

'That's okay, mate.

'Who did you say? Sears? Yes, I remember him. Why?

'I don't really think so.

'It's just . . . well breakfast is an awkward time, with the children and that. And I doubt whether after all this time . . .

'Did he? Well send my regards back to him, mate. And if you're ever feeling too lonely you're always welcome to come over here for a meal – if it's not too far off your map.'

I could hear that laugh, the old bitter laugh, before I put down the phone, and didn't like it in myself. There is power in saying no. Besides, what the hell would I do with the kids if I had said yes to breakfast? On the other hand, having put the phone down I half regretted it. Might have been interesting to talk about this latest move of ILI.

The phone rarely goes in the flat. But today it seemed to be ringing all the bloody time. I picked it up again and spoke into the receiver through mouthfuls of egg-and-tomato sandwich.

'Carole?

'Listen, if you've got something to ask me, why don't you do it when you're here? We do live together, you know. Or is even that becoming difficult for you to remember?

'I know I haven't been exactly forthcoming these last few days. But sometimes you're so unhelpful. God, you've got a sharp tongue when you want. Doesn't it ever occur to you that a person might be offended. Listen, Carole, this isn't the kind of conversation to have on the phone. If you want to talk about it, why don't you wait till this evening?

'I see. And she wants to know today?

'Well, if you want to know the truth, I don't particularly feel like going away anywhere with you at the moment. I've got better things to do.

'No, I don't think I'd enjoy the fresh air. I get quite enough, thank you. Why don't you go, though?

'Then tell her, no.'

It's hard enough to keep believing in yourself in the circumstances I find myself in, and I certainly don't need Carole pitching in and making me feel a good deal worse, especially at the moment.

I said to her when she came home that night, 'Christ, can't we just get a little ordinary support from one another?'

'I feel the same way.'

'We must have different ideas about what support is.'

'We must.'

'Look, Carole, what I'm wrestling with is far from easy. Surely you . . .'

But she had left the room.

I looked up at the photos that Alex had taken of us skating (which had been on the mantelpiece for the last couple of days since I'd developed them) and particularly the one that Moth had managed to take of Alex, Ellen and myself: it was a damned good frame, more luck than judgement, but wasn't he just proud of it; and for the first time, looking at them in the tense silence of the flat, I longed to be with her tomorrow.

I hadn't seen her for a week. I looked at the picture of her for some time. I wondered how her exams had gone. Then it occurred to me with shock that it was actually becoming easier to be interested in hearing about her school work than about Carole's board meetings.

*

On Tuesday Jerry has an afternoon appointment with a neighbour whose house he is renovating. He has popped home and is in the kitchen making himself something for lunch when he hears Alex's steps, coming up from the basement.

'How are you feeling, lovely?'

'Better, thanks. On the mend now.' A light laugh.

'Is there anything I can get you? Here, would you like to share some of this tuna salad? There's easily enough for two.'

'No thanks. I couldn't eat anything, really.'

'Drink?'

'I've got some drink downstairs. Jerry . . .?'

'Mmm?'

She pulls the dressing-gown cord tighter into her waist, presses the sole of her bare left foot onto the cork of the kitchen floor and swirls it around a number of times as if she is stubbing out a cigarette, then comes and sits at the kitchen table opposite him.

'Listen, lovely, if you don't want to eat any of this I hope you don't mind if I begin? I'm ravenous.'

'No, go ahead.'

He helps himself to a mixture of tuna with celery and red bean salad.

'Jerry, listen, I've got a favour to ask you. I wouldn't normally, I just . . . Well there isn't anyone else.'

Alex, who has resisted many overtures. He looks at her warily.

'Fire away. You know I'll do what I can.'

There is a pause, then she says very fast, 'Will you go to the Heath this afternoon, at half-past three, and meet . . . this friend of mine. I'll tell you where. And just give him a message from me?'

He doesn't respond immediately so she goes on, 'We arranged to meet. And I don't want to let him down. Or the children.'

'Can't you phone him?'

'I've no idea of his telephone number.'

'The telephone directory?'

'There are pages of people with his surname. I don't even know his address. It sounds strange, but it's the truth. Please. Please, Jerry?'

Jerry has finished the tuna and, preoccupied, helps himself to more. He looks outside. The sun is palely shining. He notices for the first time catkins on one of the trees in the garden. It does seem much milder. He *could* stroll onto the Heath. On the other hand he feels an aversion to being complicit with Alex in whatever is going on between herself and this unsavoury character. Then again, since she has asked, if he now refuses would the door be shut again between them, whereas if he accepts might it be the beginning of bringing about some more reasonable communication? Yet it sticks in his gut. Really, it does. Seeking that chap out.

What would Angelica do? He would like to have been able to discuss it with her before making a decision. What do parents do in these circumstances? It's easier with your own flesh and blood. Or is it? Thinking about his friends and some of the trouble they'd had with their kids, he wonders if one can generalise.

What the hell, yes or no, it's probably about equal. But I'll do it anyway, no point agonising.

He walks slowly. He hasn't been out of the house for a couple of weeks except to get into his car. He feels stiff. Over the bridge and through the wooded area, he then comes out onto open ground and pauses to look up at the hill, where only a couple of kites are flying. There is very little breeze. He undoes the top couple of buttons on his jacket and looks up to the top of the hill, again considering. Then he continues at a measured pace.

Three-quarters of the way up he sees the man and the children.

He is expecting someone older, shabbier. In fact, if it hadn't been for the children he might almost have wondered if it was the same man. Tony is dressed in black jeans and a polo-necked sweater, over which he wears an old army coat that looks well on his tall, slim figure. His mop of very black hair, caught in the breeze that resides permanently at the top of this hill, even when there is none elsewhere, looks youthful and vigorous. His eyes, changing shades of blue, are deep and potent in this light. There is no moustache or trace of stubble on his chin this time.

But Jerry is far from reassured by all this. Younger and more attractive, another woman's husband – the two children, one in each hand to make the point perfectly clear – the man appears more of a threat to poor vulnerable Alex. Anger shakes Jerry, deep-rooted, even frightening.

Tony, and the children too, are looking impatiently down the hill, down the very path up which Jerry climbs unregarded, already about seven minutes late. Impatience the older man observes in the younger one's face. And, worse, eagerness.

God almighty, what . . . what . . . Jerry can't think of a word to express his indignation.

Now, on a level with Tony and near enough to talk, he finds he's breathless. So he starts by putting out his hand towards the other. Then says slowly and deliberately, 'I'm Alex's . . .' (Oh what the hell, now is not the moment to be squeamish about the facts) 'step-father.'

Moth looks on, fascinated, his eyes huge as fists. Does Alex have a father too? And what is that other funny word? Meanwhile, in an unconscious act Tony draws the children close to him.

'Tony Davis,' he says, acknowledging the other's hand. They shake on it ceremoniously.

'She's ill. Caught a chill and developed a high temperature over the weekend. Beginning to improve now, though still too poorly and weak . . . to help you look after your children,' Jerry says with measured evenness.

Tony's blue eyes lose the depth that Jerry has noted with irritation as being an attractive feature. Now that they are paler, less density in their colour, he looks less effectual.

Of course, Tony can't help but feel humiliated. How must his friendship with Alex look to the other man?

'Never mind,' he says gruffly, gathering up the children again and turning away. Then back again, 'Tell her to take care of herself.' He strides off with huge, angry strides, Ellen uncomfortable in his arms, Moth running to keep up.

Meanwhile, Jerry makes his way home. The meeting was briefer than he'd anticipated, for this he is glad. The man is after Alex, he is sure of that. A man with those kind of looks, with time on his hands and no proper job, of course in the end it would come to that. And Alex, eighteen to the other's thirty-six, say – almost twenty years between them, she wouldn't stand a chance.

But can anything be done? How much influence can you have when a girl of eighteen has already determined on a course of action? Not much, not with this one anyway. Yet can you stop wanting to? They should warn her, that at least they owe her.

So Jerry resolves to say as much to Angelica. With the end of her novel now in sight he recognises that she is hardly at her wisest, certainly far from her calmest. And he does have the thought, shall I wait till the book is out of the way? But then recalling Tony's potent maleness, he convinces himself that there are some things that simply won't brook waiting for.

*

Was I just het up? Of course, the look in the eye, on the face, whatever you like, of Alex's step-father compounded feelings that were running deep at the time. And yes, my steps were fast and angry, at least I have that, my physical fitness, my own comparative youthfulness. That middle-aged flabby desk-bound figure of a man, the way he looked at me with such contempt left my blood running hot with anger. He's the kind that divides men into those who work, those who have a place in the scheme of things, and the others, those not worth considering. Yes, I could see exactly what he thought of my relationship with Alex. How dare he make it smutty by his very inference? How dare he treat me like that? Or her.

'Walter, this is Tony. Listen. There's been a bit of a change in arrangements here. I think that breakfast would be possible after all. Is it still on, mate?'

When Carole came home I had to spill it to her. She'd just have to hang on at home and look after the children one morning for a couple of hours. And that was an end to it. But I doubted it would be. God, was I steamed up. We both were. And there were bound to be misunderstandings and confusion of intent. When I saw her come in I thought, yes, I know that look, she's got the old bit between her teeth again. But I held on hard to my own anger. I'm not good at it usually. Can't tell why. Sometimes I think it is the result of my adopted father's rages and seeing the effect they had on Caroline. Usually nowadays at the first or second whiff of it from Carole I capitulate, I find it too uncomfortable to live with. This time, however, I held on, held it in place. I told myself, you're going to need a dose of this stuff to get you through the next weeks; it's better than depression and lapsing back in front of the television, any day.

'That wasn't a very pleasant phone call,' she said as she took off her coat.

Moth danced forward, 'Mummy, Alex is very ill.'

'Is she, love? And how was your day?'

But of course she wasn't listening to Moth's involved answer.

At about the time that Carole gets home, unusually early for her, for she has a purpose and a strategy, Nick and Sarah meet at the Festival Hall intending to have a light supper and then move on to an exhibition of Surrealist Art at the Hayward.

'Oh Nick, you just won't believe this.'

'It can only be one thing.'

'Why?' She finds herself blushing defensively.

'Because . . .' His eyes tell her the rest of the sentence.

'. . . I'm so boringly one-track minded?' The blush is deepening.

They find a table.

'So she's not coming after all this?'

'It's not her. You see, Nick, she wants to tremendously. She told me so straight out. And I believe her. But he doesn't want to apparently. They had a terrible row, I heard some of it on the phone.'

'It's not the end of the world, is it? *Is* it?'

He looks at her quizzically, telling her with his eyes to cheer up, to let it go. He's had a full and pressured couple of days, and there will be more to follow. This is the only evening this week they will have just to themselves and he has been looking forward to it as an oasis of calm and intimate pleasure. Who are these people? How have you let them gain such importance? he thinks of saying, but she looks so dejected the words stick in his throat.

'Come on, let's leave our things here while we go and choose something to eat.' He pulls her up. He puts her hand in his and pats it. So much emotion in that hand. Such a sad hand tonight. He takes it to his lips and kisses the hollow between thumb and first finger.

'Buck up, do.'

The children were bathed when Carole came in. I'd made a point of having them fed and ready for bed lately. Carole read them a story. I wandered back into the kitchen and stood contemplating a cauliflower but was not in any mood to start our supper.

'They want you to give them their goodnight kiss,' she comes through and says.

'Carole, let's run wild and stand ourselves an Indian take-away.'

'I thought we might go out.'

'Out?'

'Yes, just an idea I had. Why don't you say goodnight to the kids whilst I pop down the corridor and see if Jenny will babysit.'

'She's bound to be busy at the last minute like this.'

'She'll be in, doing her homework. It's her A-level year, remember?'

By now both kids are shouting, 'Daddeee.'

'Why don't you . . .?'

I start off out of the kitchen towards their room. 'I suppose you might as well try,' I tell her.

The mention of A-levels reminds me. Alex. Oh please don't let her have got that pneumonia till after she finished her exams. After all the work she's put in. It wouldn't be fair. *She needs this chance.*

Carole returns.

'Any luck?'

'It's fine with her, she'll be round in a few minutes.'

'But why this big deal about going out? It's not like us.'

'It should be like us.'

'I must say I could do with it tonight. It's just what I feel like.'

'I'll take you to a restaurant in Camden Town that I went to with that writer, Tudor Balfour. You remember him, he was the one who made such a hit with his book on "situational morality".'

'I'm taking *you* out tonight. And I thought we'd walk down to the Kelly Street Tandoori.'

'But Tony, why?'

'Don't I have a right to take my own wife out sometimes, damn it?'

'Okay, okay.'

But what with? He must still have cash over from his records. Or has he been selling more? Whatever, if he feels better about it that way, let him.

I'll ask her later. Of course I could ask her now. Jenny won't be over for some minutes yet. There'd probably be time. Then we could go out and enjoy ourselves without this hanging over me. But then there are bound to be repercussions. We might as well make the most of the evening, now we are going to all this expense. It's no big deal. Only one fucking morning.

And yet it stayed with me as we ordered and waited and drank beer and nibbled our poppadoms. And I thought, when the time comes I'll tell her straight, tell her like I expect it. That must be the way.

'Stay,' says Sarah. 'Don't move off me yet. I like it like this.' She closes her hands across the small of his back and hugs him hard.

'Feeling better now?' he asks.

'Much better. You're right, I'm making much too big a thing about it. From now on I'm going to be philosophical.'

Nick gives a snort of laughter.

'You just watch.'

I lie in bed as far away from Carole as possible, thinking about what had taken place between us. Flipped by the extent of her jealousy. I'd simply no idea. Those old photos. 'How could you put them up on the mantelpiece like that, how could you be so hurtful?' 'But you never said, why didn't you say then? I can't understand you at all, Carole. I can hardly believe what you're telling me. Of course I wasn't trying to hurt you. I never thought, not for a moment. Don't cry. Not tonight. There's too much going on. I can't help you, I'm drained. I can't. Carole, woman, don't, not you as well. Here, do you want a handkerchief? Carole, are you listening? . . . No. No. No. That is something I can't do Carole. Listen, of course I don't want to hurt you but this is unreasonable. It's not equitable, it's . . . too much. Carole there's no *need* to give her up. Besides, what about her? I can't just drop the girl like that with no explanation, we're friends, she's become reliant on me. I mean for some emotional support through her exams and that. No, I don't think of her feelings more than yours. Yes, well normally if something was that important to you you know I'd do it, but this time . . . I just . . . can't. Not like that. It doesn't make sense, Carole. Yes, I know, but your jealousy's not enough. Please stop crying, please.'

Fuck it, fuck it. Where do we go from here?

It was only when we got home – she had eaten hardly any of the food and I had eaten too much – that I remembered that the surprise of her outbursts had taken away all thoughts of the business breakfast with Walter. And now how could I mention it? Wait, wait is the answer. What a nightmare all this is.

'How's my old warrior?'

'Don't call me that.'

It was the following evening. At least she smiled with the old spark in her eyes as she said it.

'How was work?'
'Hectic. Nothing new.'
'Carole, I'm sorry about last night.'
'Me too.'
'How did you sleep?'
'Badly.'
'I thought so. Look, I really am sorry.'
'Tony, listen, I didn't get to sleep till after five. And then at seven I had to be up. Then this afternoon I fell asleep in the board meeting. And I'm beginning to feel the strain. I've been worrying for weeks now. Please can you understand? It's affecting my work. And there isn't any right or wrong in it. I'm just a jealous person I believe. Please. Tony, please give her up.'
'We can't go through all that again. I've told you my side. And I'm not likely to change my mind. It doesn't mean I don't love you, of course I do. But asking this is way over the top. When have I interfered with the way you spend your time, at Frankfurt, or when you make those trips to New York, or all your intimate lunches and dinners, and what about those runs in Hyde Park? You *say* it's business. But I have to trust you, don't you see?'
Moth and Ellen had been preoccupied with something in their room. Now I could hear them running down the corridor, so I said to Carole quickly, 'Don't let's go over it all again, not tonight. Let's give ourselves a rest.'

For a few days, on the surface, a kind of uneasy domestic equilibrium reigned. I felt waves of excessive tenderness towards her. For she was a warrior (something I needed a stronger dose of myself). I began to think about sexual jealousy and to wonder about Carole's. This little chink in her armour moved me deeply. It was certainly a part of her I hadn't known existed; I felt I must respect it, however unlikely its cause.
Both of us treated the other with care. Both made small but significant gestures of affection, something which had lapsed lately. It was in this atmosphere that Carole told me more about her present problems at work than she had for some time. And I brought up the Walter breakfast and was more forthcoming about what lay behind it.
'It would make such a difference', she said, 'if you could get back into work.'
We had just made love with new tenderness and were lying close together, two halves making one, unwilling to break apart.
'Would it, to us?'
'To you primarily. But to us, I suppose it must. We'd have more to share. We'd have more the same kind of life – that's what it comes to.'
'We could afford more.'

She lay still, thinking. 'We haven't managed badly, Tony, all in all. There are bound to be strains. Lots of other people would have broken up.'

'Are you saying you stuck by me?'

'No, that's not what I'm saying. Don't be so prickly.'

'Listen, Carole, wanting work and getting it are two different things, you know that. And I don't want you to . . . how can I explain it? I've got to go about this my own way, can you understand?'

I felt that there might be other ways in which I could reassure her that I loved her, and that would prevent the Alex thing from coming to a head. Sharing with her was one way, and giving in about the unimportant things like this weekend of hers in Wales. I could hardly remember why I'd said no to it in the first place. And she for her part agreed to look after the kids while I saw Walter. In some ways, I couldn't help thinking, things were going better than they had done for a long time.

Breakfast with Walter and Ed Sears at the Savoy of all places. 'They do the best breakfasts,' Walter had said to me over the phone. I certainly couldn't find fault with what we ate. I tried to make myself enjoy the treat of a kipper (God, it must be years since I've eaten kipper for breakfast: took me right back to walking holidays with Carole before the kids were born) and not to let myself feel all the old inadequacies. Ed wanted to meet up with me – tell me another! It was hard to get him to address one straight word to me, you could tell from the start he thought I was a loser. I got round to wondering if I still had that smell on me, the way he acted.

Walter was trying to do me a good turn in his own way, but the other sure as hell didn't want to know. So I sat listening to a whole lot of chat about a world I'd been out of for so long that all the moves were different now.

When Walter picked up the tab and we took leave of one another, I made off for the Gents, then headed out onto the street. Was I pleased to be able to look up at the sky and be by myself! What am I doing this for? I started to walk, it has always given me pleasure to stride forward at a brisk pace, and I walked faster and faster. Mid-morning, so many people in Piccadilly, I had to weave my way in and out; I thought, I know what I'll do, I'll just keep on walking right back to Kentish Town. Until I remembered the time.

It was that very night that Carole had her next outburst. We'd had a peaceful run of days. I was caught totally off guard. We were watching telly. I didn't have much to say to her, it was hard enough to keep my own end up or to imagine where to go next. I'd been looking through my old address book, thinking of other leads, wondering. But it was difficult not to believe it was going to be much of the same. A few days before, I'd seen a job advertised for a manager of a video shop in Camden Town. A small outfit, hardly exciting, not my choice; still it could be something. I had sent off for particulars and they'd been there on my return, having come in the morning's post. I'd taken out the application sheet. But they all asked the same bloody thing, didn't they: work experience. Whatever your past record, who is going to take you on after seven years off the track? It wasn't worth the ink to fill it in.

So, as I say, I was pleased that the telly was covering whatever we were thinking about; it was a play, Armchair Theatre, or something, the kind that absorbs Carole totally, and my mind was half on other things, when suddenly she said to me, 'Have you seen her?'

'Who?'

'You know very well.'

'Alex is ill, Carole, I told you that. I haven't seen her.'

Then, I don't know how it happened, she just went for me. She said the most extraordinary things, she tried to fight me. I think she wanted to attack me, she kept saying, 'I hate you, I hate you,' and saying the most terrible things about Alex, using language I never knew she had in her vocabulary. I don't know whether I was more shocked or scared, or what I was. I tried to fend her off. I thought, this is crazy. I absolutely don't believe this is happening. Not with Carole. What can you hang on to in human nature? Oh, please don't let Moth wake up, he'll be so scared. I was pretty unnerved myself. Then she calmed down and cried and at first she would not let me hold her but eventually she did. And then she apologised and said she didn't know what had got into her. And I said, 'Phew!' and then we both kind of laughed gingerly, we were sitting on the floor by this time between the armchair and the coffee table with the coffee table virtually on top of us. And she said, 'Phew, yes.' And then I stroked her some more and then we went to bed. She didn't want me to make love to her and I was just as happy not to. And then I went to sleep and dreamt that I was in a horribly dangerous situation and was fighting my way out and it was pretty obvious where that one came from.

When she woke up I had already been awake for some time and I looked at her out of one eye without wanting her to be aware that I was looking at her. I had an odd feeling inside, a kind of churning feeling, like was it going to be normal between us or was she going to start again. She dressed briskly. I watched her put her make-up on, comb her hair, give herself the once-over in the mirror. She always looked good going off to work; she looked good now in her plum-coloured skirt, black tights, black long sweater. Briefcase in hand, she came over and kissed me on the forehead and said, 'I'm going in early. I won't wake the children. You'll do their breakfast, won't you? About last night, I don't know what came over me.

Probably just some strange left-over from childhood. But don't worry. I'm fine now.'

'Good,' I said, 'I mean good that you're fine; you certainly worried me.'

Then it occurred to me. 'Carole, it's Saturday, are you really going in to the office?'

'I must.'

'What about the shopping, do you want me to . . .?'

'If you can, otherwise I'll do it this afternoon.'

'No, it's okay. Can you leave some money? I don't think there's enough.'

This was one of the rare occasions where she actually handed me money. I wouldn't put out my hand. The notes fluttered down onto the duvet.

*

Carole's next outburst takes place in Hyde Park on Sunday, on a family outing. Her idea: 'Let's go to Hyde Park like in the old days.' Moth hasn't wanted to but has been persuaded. Ellen is more keen, the promise of feeding the ducks still sufficient lure. Though it is cold in the morning, by the afternoon a watery sun has come out. And there they are, the two children putting out their hands to feed a large number of ducks and pigeons, when all of a sudden this feeling comes over her. She looks at Tony. She feels inconsolably miserable. The tears dash to her eyes. In another moment, she won't be able to stop herself, it's so strong. She turns away, struggles with herself, and as the tears flow, starts to run.

'Where Mummy go, where Mummy go?'

'Carole,' Tony calls after her as he pursues her retreating figure with his eyes, wondering what is happening. Then something about her stance, the set of her shoulders, her arms, sends a draught of cold wind blowing right through him. He knows why she's going.

'Mummy's just, just gone to the Ladies. She'll be all right, she'll be back in a minute.'

'But what's wrong with Mummy?' Moth is now anxious.

'Nothing's wrong with Mummy, nothing at all.'

And Carole running, the tears flowing freely, cries inside herself, all these years I've soldiered on my own, being the breadwinner, coping, making decisions, and now it's too much, it really is, that he can just. I can't. Bear it.

'I can't cope with it,' she tells Barbara Moffitt, one of her closest publishing friends, over lunch the following week.

'So let's have it then, what's happened to the insufferable Lee?'

'You know, that's completely receded into the background. I don't think I care any more whether he stays or goes, or what he does. No, what I can't cope with is Tony.'

'Problems on the home front?'

'You can say that again.'

'Another woman?'

'Sort of thing.'

'Well frankly, darling, the hours he spends by himself, it's bound to happen.'

'Why?'

'He's got the emotional space for it, he's got the time. All those bored housewives in Clapham, it's the same sort of thing.'

'I suppose. But Tony. He's such a. I always thought I could rely on Tony.'

'He's a man, isn't he?'

'He's a good man. I don't know how to explain it, but there has always been, well, trust between us—and now . . .'

'Mmm?'

'Now it's different.'

'You're going to have to live with it. You're a sensible woman. Just keep your cool. Be nice to him but let him know you're hurt too. It'll pass.'

'But that's just the trouble. I'm *not* being sensible. And I can't make love with him. It makes me feel . . . I wish I could explain to you what it makes me feel.'

'How do you know he's having an affair with this woman, whoever she is?'

'Actually, I don't think he is sleeping with her, yet. But he's in love with her. He's gone and fallen in love with her, Barbara, and that's far worse.'

'Come on, Carole, tell me another.'

Nick to Sarah. 'Don't tell me she's coming. This is becoming ridiculous.'

'She's coming. They're coming. The weekend after next. Oh God, we can make that weekend, can't we Nick?'

★

Early February. Not as cold now, but oh how dull and grey. One day after another with little to distinguish them. Few people walk on the Heath for pleasure. Only a steady trickle of regulars, those who walk their dogs, or jog. Or those who are driven out into the air because they are not natural house-dwellers and feel more comfortable under the sky whatever the weather.

Alex is of this sort, but even she finds the Heath depressing. For the sky has closed in over it like a lid. The grey is impenetrable. The new shoots on the trees are difficult to pick out. Only the mud seems real, from persistent rain – and the litter, which makes sights she normally enjoys ugly.

She is thinner than before, and paler. The way her ribs stick out of her flesh alarms her. There are dark shadows round her eyes. She walks with difficulty. As she climbs the hill she has to concentrate on her breathing to keep going at all. She does not expect them to be at the top, or at the bottom near the tennis courts, or by the ponds. It is Friday; she looked for them on Tuesday and on Wednesday. Now she tells herself they have given up on her.

She is wearing white tracksuit bottoms, which look too roomy over her thin legs, a thick white sweater borrowed from Angelica, wellington boots, her old blue jacket, which is warmer than the one she has been given as a Christmas present, and a long orange scarf. A blue beret perched on her head covers most of her hair. She wants to hide its lankness; she hasn't had the energy to wash it this week.

That she is in her mother's sweater is not without significance. For they have spent time together, just the two of them in Devon while she's been recuperating.

Reaching a bench at the top of the hill, she sits down. There is no breeze, there are no kites flying. The vista is shrouded in mist. She is irresolute, a strange kind of tension inside her. They will not come. On the other hand she doesn't want to go back to the basement so soon. She's still bedevilled by a hacking cough in her chest, which erupts for hours during the night and fitfully during the day. However, she went to school today, Jerry having given her a lift, and discovered that the results of her mocks are better than she expected. 'Course, it doesn't matter, isn't really important, she thinks, the cough threatening to erupt so that she wraps her arms round her ribcage in an unsuccessful effort to stop it, it leaves her chest and makes a strange uneasy noise as it disappears into the mist and down the hill – yet it is something, passing the exams, being on course. She would like to tell Tony.

Cursing her cough, she gets up. Jumpy. Thinking she hears the footsteps of someone approaching from behind, but turning round, sees no one. She contemplates the ponds. If she walks down to them it will mean climbing up again. Not today. Takes too much energy.

So, keeping more or less on the flat, she sets off in the direction of Kenwood, passing the very place where Moth was first surrounded with his mushrooms, passing the tree itself under which they grew. Now into the thicketed outskirts of the grounds of Kenwood. There are few people around. In the distance occasionally the dark shape of a dog and its owner. No man with two noisy children. If I keep going then I'll be completely out of sight of the dog-walkers. Turn back, turn back. No, can't, it can't happen to me. Why be scared? This cough will keep anyone away, surely; it's hardly a turn-on.

Now in the narrow path leading to Kenwood she tells herself there is no turning back. She walks quickly, her heart uncomfortably pressing against her ribcage, in some odd way liking it too in that it directs her fear and discomfort rather than leaving the jumpiness vague and amorphous.

There are still leaves lying on these paths, sodden and uninteresting. They squelch against her boots. A spray of muddy water from a puddle leaves marks on her white sweatsuit trousers. She curses, and coughs. Walk faster, almost out of this bit.

She's relieved when she sees the imposing calm exterior of the white house ahead. I'd like to sit down, got to sit down. Why did I come this far? Got to get all the way back. Hell! She visualises lying horizontal in her bed and feels that is the only place in the world she would like to be. But can't face that path again, not quite yet.

She puts her hand in the pocket of her jacket and feels around. Enough money for a cup of tea and a sandwich or something. Did I have lunch? Probably not. They could be there. Silly thought. They wouldn't come this far without me. Oh fuck, it doesn't matter, it really *doesn't matter*. How can Angelica claim that he's a kind of surrogate father to me, I don't understand how she could be so off the track? She's got it all wrong and at least I told her so, shouted it at her, and I had to shout bloody hard over the roar of the waves that day, 'You've got it all fucking wrong, you don't understand me, so kindly leave it alone, will you?'

'I understand you far better than you think.'

'Well you don't know this, you don't know the first thing about it. He's not a father to me. It's more like I'm a mother to them. But it's not important, it's only just. Oh why make such a meal out of everything?'

'Because we care for you.'

'Then if you care, stay out of my fucking life!'

But they looked at each other, mother and daughter, and Alex felt defeated because she knew that she was pleased that Angelica had brought her away, and even as she said it she wanted to slip her arm through her mother's and lean on her as they walked back to the farmhouse, and have her meals brought to her until she felt better and threw this horrible illness off completely.

There had been another day, a worse one, just before they'd returned to London. Angelica had woken up with the bit between her teeth. It seemed to Alex that it was as if she was determined to prise Alex open. And it was raining, there was nowhere to go. They were the only guests in the farmhouse. They sat around in the lounge, just the two of them, drinking cups of sweet synthetic coffee.

'You're mourning your father,' said Angelica.

'Oh don't be silly, Mum.'

Angelica tried to take Alex's hand. 'Darling, it's perfectly natural, don't think I don't miss him myself, often, and think about him. However happy I am with Jerry doesn't make up for that.'

Alex's face clamped tight shut, her look saying, I don't want to hear, it's got nothing to do with me, keep your intimate revelations for someone else.

'Perhaps we didn't mourn enough,' pushed on Angelica. 'Together, I mean. What do you think? Do you think we should have rocked in each other's arms with grief, like some do? I was too frightened of falling apart, you see.'

Alex found her breath coming faster and faster. This was unbearable. She looked at the shut door swiftly, envisaging escape. But said to her mother with a hard flip little laugh, sounding much colder than she felt, 'You're hardly suggesting that we make up for it now, are you?'

It was meant to be a joke, meant to defuse her mother. But Angelica replied, refusing to let go of Alex's hand, 'That is just what I'm suggesting, yes. I think you – we – should really try and let your grief out. With me. Here. I'm here for you.'

Alex looked at her mother, hating her, hating the tears that were beginning to well in her eyes. Hating everything about it. She wasn't going to cry, she was going to resist. This time she did, leaving the lounge and running to the room they shared, and even locking the door. But Angelica sat on in the lounge. It was only half-past eleven. They had a whole day ahead. At some point she could see that her daughter would let go, could not keep it up. And letting it all go, all that pent-up anger and misery, wasn't that what the textbooks recommended? Hopefully, afterwards, she'd feel better. With luck it would release her from her strange fascination with this man, Tony. Hopefully, if she mourned her own father properly, completely, something would be shifted.

But the effect of all that emotion with Angelica has been to blow Alex more open than ever.

At Kenwood she stares into the dregs of her tea-cup and pushes around on her plate the second half of a tomato sandwich that she doesn't have the appetite to eat. At least with the warm tea her cough seems to have temporarily subsided. Better make a move, no point in hanging on here.

With the onset of late afternoon the grey is less impenetrable. Alex stops at the lake, watching the leaves of the water lilies, wishing for the first time in weeks that she had her camera. The last photos she'd taken were – oh God, every thought seems to lead to him. Is this what it's like? Is this what it's really like? Now, which way? Out of Kenwood and back alongside the women's pond? Might as well, it's all the same. What a piss-awful stupid way to spend the afternoon, bed, bed where are you, lovely bed can't you just come and carry me back?

By the time she reaches the first path which will take her away from the side of the ponds and up towards Parliament Hill, that thought is paramount. She has stopped even looking or hoping for Tony and the kids. Now she is coughing again, the cough winding her so that she is left breathless and with an acute pain in her chest. Her legs seem to be made of a feathery substance no longer sufficient to the task of holding her up. She can hear Angelica say, how foolish of you, Alex. She's just got to get home.

Then, in the misty translucent light, she stops in her tracks.

I had to keep stopping, see. I wasn't looking. I was staring into the hollows, the voids, the valleys, ravines, that revealed themselves as the fog or mist or whatever it was, lifted, thinking of my bed, visualising it, wanting it so much. Everything hurt but I had to go on. Had to. Then all of a sudden I became aware that what I was looking at was them. They were way down the bottom and I wasn't making it up. They were playing ball, he and Moth and Ellen. They were miles and miles away. Moth was happy, I could tell it from here, from the way he was throwing his arms about, from the sounds I could hear, or could I hear them? Tony was running in between the kids for the ball. Oh God, he doesn't need me. He's forgotten me. Oh God, oh God. He. And yet surely. Surely. *It's downhill all the way* – isn't that something he says to Moth? *Your legs will carry you.* I try. Although I know it's in the opposite direction to going home, it's crazy, I'll never get back. But get to him. Then somehow. But now they've stopped, he's gathering the kids to him, he's setting off. I want to shout out. There's nothing in my lungs but water. They'll be out of sight in one more minute. The stupid mist envelops them. I can't believe it. Oh, what am I going to do?

*

Friday, three-thirty, a dull day at the end of the second week in February.

Tony walking towards Moth's school with Ellen in the push-chair, feels he is treading a tightrope between the volatile home situation and the daily rejections and despair brought on by the job situation. He has not seen Alex for some weeks. She must be better, back on those strong legs of hers, back at school. He hasn't exactly been avoiding her, he has just extended in his mind the time of her absence. Although he has told Carole he intends to see her – and does, looks forward to it – at the same time the scenes are a screw turning in his navel, drawing the flesh tight as it does so, and if he can put it off, just for another week or so.

Problem is to get above this bloody weather. Spring seems interminably far away. Just as he thinks this, it starts to drizzle and he curses. It'll probably piss down the entire time we're away.

Inside the school, Moth finds himself continually distracted. Every few minutes he looks at the big clock on the wall and watches the hands. They hardly seem to be going round at all, they are *so slow*. Oh the excitement of what lies ahead!

Moth is too excited, nothing but questions and answers, jumping, bumping into things, knocking things over, he's been like this all week, driving Carole and me quietly crazy as if we weren't going that way already. He's just too hyper for words. 'Have a word with his teacher,' says Carole. So I did. 'Just one of those naturally gifted children who needs to be kept occupied.' 'Naturally gifted, my foot. He needs his attention directed,' I said, 'he's all over the place.' 'What about hobbies?' 'You mean take up an instrument or something? I doubt if he'd have the patience.' 'No,' she said, 'I was thinking of drama, there's a woman in Islington . . .' 'Forget it,' I said.

Now he's on about it again as we start walking home, his talk is a jumble of, when is Mummy going to be home, and tell me again the name of the lady that's coming with her, and why is she coming with her and how far away is Wales and at the same time how this lady came to school and said she was looking for 'new talent' and how his teacher had said how he had 'lovely diction', and how he'd had to read a poem, the tiger one, you know that one Daddy surely and please please . . .

'Moth, stop this immediately, if you pull any more on my arm you'll pull it off. Just calm down. Or talk to Ellen. Anything.'

'But she's boring and besides she can't hear me with that rain-cover thing over her. Daddy, Daddy . . .'

'Just settle down, can't you?'

'But why aren't you excited, Daddy? Mummy is excited, I know she is, and she says there'll be ponies and cows and perhaps we can ride, the ponies I mean not the cows and . . .'

'Shut up, Moth.'

'Oh Daddy, you're such a spoil-sport, you're such . . . Who was that?'

'Where, what are you talking about?'

'That was Alex.'

'Where? Of course it wasn't.'

'Yes it was. Down that street. It was. Daddy?'

'Yes?'

'We mustn't see her. We must hide.'

'What are you talking about now? You're full of nonsense today, Moth. I hope you're not going to be like this all afternoon.'

'Like what?'

'Ants in your pants.'

'I haven't got ants in my pants,' Moth laughs and wriggles. 'She looked so funny.'

'Who did?'

'Alex. She looked like a ghost.'

'Moth, you're letting your imagination run away with you. Stop this.'

'Honest, Daddy.'

Alex feels like a ghost. She has come to Moth's school driven by forces greater than herself. Puffed by the winds and the rains. Puffed right off the Heath. She has to see him, to tell him. It would be all right when they were together. Everything would fall into place. He would not want to desert her, not when he saw her, not when she explained. If only she looked more attractive, if only the cough would go, if only her hair wasn't falling out, if only you couldn't see her ribcage, if only her legs didn't flap about in the extra space inside her trousers.

She thought it would be simple, just bumping into them at the school gate and saying. But somehow when she sees Tony, when she sees them all, she can't. Not yet. It just doesn't feel that easy to expose herself. Not in front of all the mothers, all the kids, Moth's friends.

She watches Tony set off with Moth jumping up and down beside him and little Ellen in her push-chair. She follows them, keeping her distance. You see it done all the time on the films. It ought to be easy. But it isn't. The drizzle turns to rain. It comes down in sheets.

'We'd better run the last bit,' says Tony to Moth. 'Here, hold my hand.'

'Daddy, it is Alex, I've seen her again.'

Tony looks around. In the pelting rain there is no sign of her.

Goose-pimples, oh no, not this afternoon. And yet joy, too. I want to see the girl. On such a grey day. Alex. And yet what the hell is she doing out here? 'Stay here,' I say, 'stay here with Ellen and don't move an inch.' I draw Moth and the push-chair out of the rain and in under the awning of the carpet showroom we are passing.

'Daddy, no Daddy, no don't . . .'

'Wait there, Moth. Do what you're told.'

I start to bound back along the street, checking in alleys and doorways. More intensely alive with every step. Surely. I run as far as Moth's vision would have carried, and further. There are hundreds of people huddled together trying to keep out of the rain. None of them Alex, or Alex's ghost.

Damn the boy, damn, he's dreamt it up. Again the unlikeliness, the incongruity, of Alex following us to Kentish Town High Street in the pissing rain strikes me. Why would she be following us in the first place? I slow down, I turn around. Then the skies open and within seconds the street is awash. With one wave the people on the pavement pull back against the buildings for protection. I hope Moth has the good sense to work out what has happened.

From inside the shop I see Tony against the window-pane. He doesn't seem to be doing anything. Just waiting. It is dark with rain, there are hundreds of people about. Inside and outside the shop. He's waiting for me. He's seen me, he's come back for me. He feels as I do. Then I know it is going to be all right. And at that moment my cough stops. I feel altogether steadier, it's going to be all right. I open the door of the shop.

'What are you doing?' says a passing man. 'You can't go out into it now.'

Can't I just.

Alex, Alex. It upsets me to see her, how thin she is, so pale, almost not there. A skinny, radiant presence. She simply steps or rather blows into my arms and her sad hair heavy with moisture warm against my chest. 'I thought you'd deserted me,' she says. Her vulnerability. The look she gives.

'I wouldn't do that.'

And yet you almost had, Tony, you almost had let her down. You didn't know how much it meant to her. You did really. As she slips her arm through mine and we walk back towards the children, braving the downpour as best we can, I keep looking at her, this light slip of a girl, and wondering how I could have ever thought of it.

Inside the flat. The four of us laughing as we flap around in sopping wet clothes, trying to get them off as quickly as we can but finding our hands too cold, too wet and cumbersome for the task of undoing buttons and clasps.

Then the children take Alex to see their room and their toys. I go into the kitchen to put on the kettle.

'Alex, do you like crumpets?' I shout down the corridor.
'You bet.'

There's no jam but the butter melts through the crumpets onto our fingers and the tea tastes wonderful.
'You know that first time, in the rain, I imagined having crumpets here.'
'That first time with the mushrooms?' Moth asks.
'No, after that.'
'Alex, have another one.'
'I couldn't manage any more.'
'You look as if you need to. What have you been doing with yourself? Tell me . . .'
'I've a lot to tell you.'
'Fire away. Start with your exams, I'm longing to know how they went.'
'Daddy, we've got to finish packing, don't forget that.'
'Soon, Moth. Listen, why don't you take Ellen into your room and help her choose the toys she wants to take.'
'What about me?'
'Make a pile of yours too.'

'I think we've just about covered everything,' says Sarah to Carole, in the offices of A&P.
'Five o'clock and yet I feel positively guilty to be leaving this early,' says Carole gaily.
'A lot of people leave the office every day at this time. You overdo it, Carole, though I know it's not my place to say so.'
'Some people might think you're just gunning for an easier life yourself.'
Sarah opens her mouth to say, 'Oh that's not true,' then realises Carole is teasing her. She laughs, still a little uncertainly.
'I'll just pop upstairs and have a quick word with Charles, then that's it. We'll be on our way. If anyone calls, say I've already left. I must say, Sarah, I'm looking forward to it. And the children are over the moon. I hope Nick knows what he's letting himself in for – you did say he liked children, didn't you?' Not waiting for an answer, she grabs a couple of files and leaves the office, heading for the stairs with a 'See you in a minute' to Sarah as she goes.
Sarah feels as excited as a schoolgirl, though she tells herself it's ridiculous. Also, suddenly horribly shy, she can't imagine what she will talk about on the bus to Kentish Town, let alone for the whole weekend. But afterwards it will be easy, there will be diversions, the children, Nick, Tony. She looks round the office, eyeing Carole's phone. She silently tells

it, if you ring I am really going to say that Carole's already gone, otherwise we'll never get away. Five o'clock. They still have plenty of time. Nick won't be picking them up from Carole's place till a quarter to seven. Still why is her heart pounding so? She wishes it wouldn't.

Alex, too, is wishing that her heartbeat was more regular. The way it feels inside makes it difficult for her to talk. She has told Tony about her exams and the intervening weeks, including the hideous trip to Devon with her mother. Though here she has skirted round the subject of what actually made it so awful. But there are other things, the central things that she wants to tell him, and these are impossibly difficult.

'I'll help you wash up,' she says. 'What was that Moth said about packing, where are you going?'

Tony tells her.

'Oh?' Alex carries the tea things into the kitchen. 'I've got to be going soon myself.' That makes what she wants to impart all the more urgent.

Tony starts to wash up.

She comes up behind him. And simply stands there. He can feel her presence a hair's breadth away.

'Why did you, why didn't you . . . keep coming to the Heath on our days so that when I was better . . . you wanted to stop, didn't you?'

Tony goes on washing up. He will not turn and look at her.

'Well?'

He cannot think what he should say. His instinct is to tell the truth. But somehow he is ashamed. Even more so after this hour or so of being together. To say the things that Carole suspects will do something to their relationship, push it into something it has never been; and once it has been stated, assertions or denials will make no difference at all. To even use those words with Alex feels such a mistake. It's a very beautiful friendship; and again as he thinks that he feels angry with Carole, that she cannot see it. Yet how to respond to Alex's questions?

'I had wondered whether – for both our sakes – we might find it easier.'

'What do you mean?'

'Well heavens, Alex, Jerry didn't exactly give me the feeling that . . .'

'Jerry! So that's the reason? I thought you were annoyed because I'd let you down.'

Now he is facing her. She looks so utterly doleful. He takes her in his arms, as gently as he can manage.

'There are things, lots of things.'

'You're my only real friend. Don't let me down, Tony.'

The 34 bus rattles its way through Camden Town. At the top, towards the front, sit Carole and Sarah. The bus is crowded and smoky. They can hear the conductor downstairs having an argument with a drunk. The argument rises and falls; meanwhile the bus remains stationary at the bus stop. Others overtake it. People on the top of the bus get restless. They sigh, some stamp their feet. Carole says to Sarah, 'You know, normally I get as impatient as the rest, but today, I don't know if you feel it too, the holiday spirit is already upon me.'

'Oh I do feel it,' assures Sarah, wishing she wasn't so tense, wishing she didn't keep making lists in her head and checking that she remembered which meals she was going to cook when.

'I just hope there won't be any leaks from the roof or any frozen pipes,' she says. 'No one's been down, you know, since Christmas.'

'Don't worry. We're going to have a wonderful time.'

At that moment the bus jolts forward.

Carole and Sarah get off the bus. 'Here, let me take one of the handles of the bag,' says Carole.

'No, really, you needn't.'

'But I'd like to. We've timed this perfectly.'

'Tuesday then, promise Tuesday,' says Alex at the door of the flat.

'Whoops! Bugger! Sarah, hold on.'

Hardly has Alex left than Nick arrives.

'I'm early,' he says.

'That's lucky because I'm running late. Do you want a cup of tea?'

'No thanks, really, don't bother. Can I give you a hand?'

'Do you happen to have any string on you?'

Everything is ship-shape and ready to go by the time they hear the women at the door.

'Christ! What's happened to you, Carole?'

'The heel came off her shoe; I think she's sprained her ankle.'

'I just need to go to the bathroom and wash off the blood.'

'Should we get you to the doctor?'

'No, Tony don't fuss, it's nothing. Why don't you all get in the car? I'll be with you in a moment.'

*

The journey was a long one. So much traffic heading out of London on a Friday night. Outside Oxford we stopped and ate the sandwiches and drank the coffee that Sarah had packed. The kids were still awake but drowsy and sometime later Ellen fell asleep on Sarah's lap while Moth slept lolled up against me, his head against my shoulder. In the front Carole made conversation with Nick.

We arrived sometime after seven. One couldn't get any sense of the place, that would have to wait till tomorrow. Nick and I carried the sleeping children upstairs and settled them on a mattress, with a duvet over them.

'Thanks, mate.'

'It's a pleasure. You sure Carole and you will be okay here? I'm sorry we couldn't give you a double bed.'

'Two singles will be fine.'

'How's your ankle?' I asked when the door was shut and Carole and I were alone.

'Fine. Which bed do you want?'

'Let's put them together.'

'We'll wake the children.'

'No we won't, they sleep through anything.'

I particularly wanted to have her in my arms. Even if we didn't make love. The thing with Alex bothered me deeply.

The cottage was sparse, even ordinary. But the view from the kitchen window down a narrow ravine with hardly another house in sight for miles and miles was magnificent. Besides, the sun was shining. We ate our breakfast fast. The house was freezing. It was sure to be warmer in than out. The cottage was on the edge of farmland and Sarah had been telling the kids about the animals. They were eager to go and make acquaintance themselves. Carole was still limping. We all felt that she should take it easy for a day. But Nick had a bee in his bonnet about his boat. 'Nothing like a winter sail. We can't let a day like this go by. There's even a south-westerly blowing.' I looked at Carole. In ideal circumstances she'd enjoy sailing too. It would be just the change of scenery she needed.

'Can't we wait till tomorrow?' I suggested.

'Who knows what tomorrow's conditions will be like. I doubt if they'll be as good, not at this time of the year. Come on, I vote for leaving women and kinder behind today. Sarah'll probably be quite relieved. Won't you? I'm always dragging her along against her will.'

'Carole?'

'You go,' she told me.

Midday. Carole sits on the sofa in the sitting-room which is now lit up by winter sunshine. She has a number of Saturday papers that Sarah has brought for her from the village shop and beside her lies a large tabby cat, on top of this month's *Cosmopolitan*. I hardly know what it's like any more, thinks Carole, to read simply for pleasure. Upstairs she has a couple of manuscripts but is too comfortable to get off the sofa; she tries not to allow herself to feel guilty. 'You owe yourself something,' Sarah has said. Too right. She idly strokes the cat's fur and against the background of his loud purring drifts off into a half sleep. Nothing to worry about, she tells herself. Maybe that jealousy thing has gone. I haven't had an attack for days now. Sarah's being an absolute lamb with the children.

I hadn't sailed for near-on twenty years. The sun shone fiercely for a winter day. The sea was choppy, the wind gave us a headstart but was inconsistent. As crew I was all fingers and thumbs at first. So Nick was both shouting instructions and then coming to my rescue. These modern boats have all sorts of new gadgets. As we jibbed I lost my footing and skidded across the deck, thankful for the reassurance of the life-jacket and convinced I was going to need it. As I mastered one technique so a second was required. 'Don't worry,' said Nick, 'it will all come back soon. Can you just . . .? No, not like that, like this.'

'There's a pub I know along the coast,' he said later. 'We can anchor up and lunch there. Now don't you think this is about the best way to spend a Saturday?'

Night. Nick and Sarah lie cuddled up under their striped duvet after good sex which has left them both extremely pleased with the world. 'I think today went really well,' says Sarah. 'Didn't you think the *crème brulée* that Carole made for supper was delicious? It completed the meal perfectly. I must say, I do think she's a good sport, helping with her ankle hurting and everything. I told her she didn't need to do anything. But I don't think she can bear to sit around. She's one of those types. It was interesting this evening hearing her talking about Australia. There's never time for conversations like that at work, of course. But what do you think, Nick, she's certainly someone who thinks for herself, isn't she?'

'She's all right. I've nothing against her,' Nick yawns. 'I just get the distinct feeling that people around here treat her with too much respect.'

'You mean me?'

'Yes. And Tony too. He seems to be too aware of her. Poor blighter can't even decide to come sailing without kowtowing to her.'

'Oh but that was only considerate. Did you have fun by the way? What's he like when you're alone with him?'

'He's a good sport. I think he enjoyed the sailing once he'd finally got the hang of the thing. I like him. I think he's just downtrodden.'

'You can hardly say it's Carole's fault that . . .'

'Darling, listen, don't let's argue about it. You have a blindspot when it comes to her. I'm tired now. We've brought them down here. I'm trying to do what I can. Let's go to sleep, please.'

'I hate you. You're a pig,' says Sarah, turning away from him in a flounce. Over her shoulder she says, 'You think you know everything. You think you're always right.'

'About this I know I'm right.'

'Oh piss off!'

'Sarah. Sarah?'

Moth up bright and early and sitting on his mother's bed has a hundred things to tell his trapped audience. 'Do be quiet and play with your toys, Moth,' she urges. But no, not this morning. He pulls at the bedclothes, he wants to tell her all about each animal on the farm that he has fallen in love with, he wants her to agree to come with him this morning and be introduced to Smokey and Beauty-Boy and Buttercup and all the others. He wants to tell her, oh he wants to tell her a hundred things that he never gets a chance to tell her in the week, about school, about how he and Seth have been chosen, at least he thinks Seth has been chosen too and on Friday . . . and please can he go to drama, please Mummy, and his thoughts are leaping away with him and what else yes, did Mummy know that Alex has changed into a ghost, no what he means is . . .

Tony knew it would come: he'd been sitting on a time-bomb.

'In the house, you actually had her in the flat, after you'd promised?'

'If you remember, I didn't exactly promise.'

'I can't believe I'm hearing this.'

Moth begins to cry, it is all so frightening. Tony tries to quieten him and over the din Carole swears, saying terrible words, terrible words about Alex, each one digging into Moth's heart, and terrible words too about Daddy, and Moth doesn't know what to do or where to look, he just wants to die. And Mummy is weeping now, Mummy, his own lovely, strong Mummy, that is the worst of all, he tries to go and comfort her, he wants to put his arms round her to make her stop but she pushes him away.

'Daddy, Daddy, oh Daddy do something,' he screams.

In the adjoining bedroom, Nick and Sarah pulling out of sleep wake up abruptly to the sound. 'Bloody children,' Nick moans, 'that really is the worst of them and at eight o'clock on a Sunday morning too!' But then it becomes clear that it isn't only Moth. Sarah, her arms around Nick, freezes as sounds continue to transcend the barriers of the bedroom walls, Carole's voice, high-pitched, shouting, then crying, then shouting again, Tony's, low, urgent, the wails of the children. 'What can be happening?' she says to Nick. 'It doesn't sound at all like Carole, she's usually so controlled. What can be the matter?'

Nine o'clock. In the kitchen are Sarah and Nick, Tony and the children. No appearance from Carole yet. Nick has made porridge. Moth will not eat a thing, Ellen tucks in, Tony tries to eat a few mouthfuls to give as much a semblance of normality as possible.

The weather is not as fine as yesterday. The clouds are banked in the sky to the west but there are patches of blue too. One of those days that could go either way.

'What do you lot fancy doing?' asks Nick.

'We're in your hands.'

'Sarah, why don't you take whoever wants to off for a walk to the river and I'll stay here with the lay-abouts and invalids?'

But Sarah is thinking that maybe Carole would like to have another woman to confide in. 'That's really nice of you,' she responds, 'but I'm happy to stay, honestly, and I'm sure Tony would prefer your company, wouldn't you Tony?'

We should never have come away, not with things as they are, thinks Tony. But somchow we've got to keep this thing going now that we're here.

'Really, we're happy to fit in with whatever,' he tells them.

'What about a spot of fishing?' Nick suggests. 'And Moth, I might find a rod for you, too, would you like that?'

Ellen mumbles something.

'What did she say?'

'The farmer told us we could come back and help collect the eggs,' says Moth. 'Anyway, I'm not coming fishing with you. I'm staying with Mummy.'

'You two men go fishing,' Sarah insists. 'There's no problem. I'll take the kids over to the farm later, perhaps Carole will come too. Off you go. Just promise to be back by twelve-thirty at the latest.'

'Okay, boss. Come on Tony, we've got our marching orders.'

Nick is delighted to be out of the house. Family life, eh, it's enough to put anyone off. 'You look as if you're letting things get you down too much,' he says to Tony. 'Mind you, I couldn't do it.'

'Do what?'

'Be with my kids all the time, however super they were.'

'I would probably have thought the same before they came along. Oh fuck, Nick, look I'm not going to be the best of companions this morning. Things are . . .'

'Getting on top of you.'

'You can say that again.'

'It would be stupid to pretend we didn't hear a bit of it this morning. But we're out in some of the most beautiful countryside in the world and whatever it is, don't let it pull you down. Pull in a salmon or two instead and you'll be a new person.'

'Yep.'

'Here we are. Now, if you can just help me get the stuff out of the boot.'

When Sarah appears in the guest bedroom with the Sunday papers and a breakfast tray, Carole has managed to pull herself together.

'You are wonderful,' she says. 'Really, you shouldn't have. I don't deserve it. I was about to get up.'

'Why shouldn't you spoil yourself? Take all the time you want, there's nothing to hurry for.'

'And the kids, I hope they're not in your way?'

'No, they're being as good as gold, we're having a great time.' Sarah wonders whether to mention that Moth hasn't eaten any breakfast, maybe that would lead in. No, better let it come from her.

Carole looks at the younger woman. 'It's you who's being so good. I can't remember when I was last brought a tray in bed.' It goes through her mind to say, jealousy is such a strange thing. The power of it. I've just behaved so irrationally. And involved Moth. I feel horribly guilty. God knows what effect it will have on him. The look on his little face. The sort of thing I'd have been so critical of if another parent had done it.

Sarah seeing her look is encouraged. She sits at the edge of the bed, but then, nervous, she hears herself saying brightly, 'It's roast beef and Yorkshire pudding for lunch.'

'Yorkshire pudding, how lovely!'

Damn, thinks Sarah, why do I play the polite hostess like this, why can't I relax and be myself. Meanwhile, having started on this tack, she goes on to say, 'I only hope it comes out okay. I'm not much of a cook. I'm sure you'd do it so much better. You just seem to be one of those people who are good at everything you touch.'

'But I'm not like that at all! Listen, Sarah . . .'

'Yes?'

Then Carole hesitates. She looks at Sarah's open trusting face. How good it would be today to have someone to talk things over with, someone to explain what it feels like to be her, someone to console her. But – is it Sarah's over-eagerness that restrains her, or just an old maxim: don't mix your personal life with work – it always goes wrong in the end? Coming in to the office every morning, Sarah knowing, I'm not sure. If possible I'll work this out myself. Give me strength to get through today. Get up, keep going, keep a semblance of calm. I'm all aches and pains today. Ankle, stomach, cramps. I'm an old woman. Curse you, Alex!

The fishing is going slowly. There is nothing like the yank of a salmon to cheer one up. Trouble is, there aren't any yanks. And as time passes, Nick, who is not the most patient of men, finds his own mood taking on the colour of the other's.

'It's a damn fool way to spend a morning when you think about it, especially when Sarah's back home preparing beef for lunch. Shall we call it a day?'

Tony is reluctant to go back, heaven knows what will greet him. 'Why don't we give it another half-hour,' he suggests, 'and then go if nothing's biting by then?'

But soon after this it begins to rain. First lightly, then more consistently. They are beginning to pack up their things when there is a sudden downpour. They decide to make a run for it.

'There's a short cut,' shouts Nick, 'here, through this field.'

One field, two fields, the third has barbed wire but they squeeze between it.

'Bloody hell, is that a bull? They've never kept a bull here before.'

'Always a first time,' says Tony. 'Better go back.'

'No, it'll be okay if we keep to the edge. Look, the stile's just over there. We're not wearing anything bright, are we? Anyway, it's probably a bullock, it doesn't look fierce.'

'It looks pretty fierce to me.'

'We'll be okay, follow me.'

But they aren't. It is fine for Tony, who is still by the barbed wire, but not so for Nick who has moved further into the field. 'Move!' Tony shouts. 'Just run for it, run back here.'

Nick takes off in another direction, the bull careering over the field towards him. Tony sprints around the field to where Nick is heading. Nick arrives only seconds before the bull.

'I can't get over,' cries Nick, starting to curse.

Tony tears at a branch of a tree. He throws it over the fence at the oncoming bull, who swerves.

Somehow Nick manages to get through the wire.

The two men look at one another. Then start to laugh. 'Who said that the fishing was too tame?' says Tony. He starts to laugh louder.

Drenched, back in the car, the two pass Nick's emergency half-sized bottle of Jameson's backwards and forwards.

In the cottage the women are putting the finishing touches to the lunch, Sarah with her eye on the clock. She watches the Yorkshire pudding rise in the oven and calculates that if the men don't arrive back soon even that will fall. The let-down feeling has been growing all morning. She has so much hoped that a camaraderie would develop between herself and Carole whilst they were away. She has imagined the conversations they would have, the jokes and fun as they shared domestic tasks. But none of this has happened. Carole is being pleasant, even helpful, despite her ankle, hobbling around laying the table, chopping parsley, heating serving bowls. Just keeping her distance. Sarah longs to change things but can't think how to. Expectations, she decides, it's better not to have any.

'Thanks again,' call out Tony and Carole as the door slams shut. Nick turns the key in the ignition and puts his foot on the accelerator. Sarah moves nearer to him on the front seat.

'Well?'

'Your Yorkshire pudding was a success.'

'That's not what I'm talking about.'

'Okay. I'd give it seven out of ten as a weekend; turned out far better than I expected. I like them. I like him a lot. Yes, all right, both of them. You know, Sarah, I think I might be able to put Tony in the way of a job. I've got an idea, he was telling me . . . Oh I won't go into it all now. What about you, did you enjoy yourself?'

'So-so. It seemed like a lot of work for very little.'

'Well what did you expect?' Then he takes his eye off the road and glances at her. 'I see.' He sighs. 'What am I going to do about you?'

'Take me to a witch-doctor and get it knocked out of me.'

'Won't I do instead?'

'You could try, I suppose.'

'Listen, here have I been standing on my head to give your friends a good time all weekend and now the woman talks about trying!'

His outrage amuses her, even cheers her. What was the point, anyway, of wanting something so much that you couldn't have? She wasn't going to any more. She strokes his arm momentarily through his thick sweater. 'By the sound of things, some parts of the weekend you thoroughly enjoyed.'

'It was bloody scary. And I didn't see you clucking round *me* with concern afterwards.'

'You were half pissed when you came in, remember? Anyway it sounds from Tony as if you got what you deserved. Go on, admit you enjoyed it.'

'Don't you push me into a corner when I'm driving, young woman.'

'When else?' she says airily. 'I can't wait to get home now.'

The steps up to their flat seem to take forever to Moth who has been asleep but has now woken up and is carrying a plastic bag of clothes in one hand and a couple of board games in the other. Ellen is being carried by Daddy. Mummy's ankle is better now but Daddy still says she'd better not carry the heavy case. She's all right again, she's his own strong rock-like Mummy. All day he's kept having to look at her to see if she is going to cry again but she's been smiling and talking to everyone like she is better now.

At one point, when they'd been packing up to come home, just he and she in the bedroom, he'd said to her, 'Are you better now, Mummy?'

'Yes, thank you, my little man.'

'I'm never going to like Alex any more, Mummy. She's horrid to make you cry.'

Mummy had put her hand through his hair the way she sometimes did to Daddy. 'There there, Moth, don't say any more about it.'

'Mummy, will you stop calling me Moth?'

'What would you like to be called?'

'Timothy.'

'I see.'

'How many more steps Mummy?'

'Just a few more, Moth, keep going,' Daddy answers.

'Daddy, don't call me Moth.'

'Why not?'

But Moth is too tired to explain.

Carole gets her key out of her bag and opens the door to the flat. 'Home,' she says, with relief.

'I liked the animals, let's live in the country,' says Moth.

'No more talking, bed now,' Carole tells him.

'Who will tuck me up?'

'We both will,' says Tony.

'How can you live with someone for years and years and then find them such an enigma?' Carole asks her husband.

'I don't know,' says Tony. 'I'm not an enigma really. Don't shut the door, I've got to go down for the second case.'

*

Alex has been awake for hours. A hurricane has blown through Britain in the early hours of the morning; the worst hit area, claims Capitol Radio, is the South Coast. There are reports of all manner of damage in Sussex, Essex, Kent. London has been hit badly too. Alex woke sometime in the early hours. The noise from outside was incredible and scary. It was pitch dark. No street lights. She reached for her bedside light and turned it on, to no effect. Here, what the hell . . .? For a moment she thought of some world disaster, nuclear war; it was so strange, so eerie, lying like that in the dark with the sound of the world gone crazy outside. The Virginia creeper flapped violently against the pane and then there was a terrific wrenching noise and part of it fell to the ground. The dustbins rolled down the street. She heard the copper beech groaning and wondered if it would fall on their house. She heard other noises; all the trees in the road seemed to be groaning and flapping like a mighty flock of birds. Further away on the Heath noises were indistinct. She lay with the duvet up around her face, coughing and listening.

There was no school, no transport, but after the electricity came on and she'd made herself an early breakfast she settled down to her school work. The central heating was roaring away – since her illness her mother had been extra solicitous and in the snug room she concentrated on her next Politics essay. She left the radio on, though, and listened to the intermittent bulletins. She wanted to go out, she wanted to see the damage. But this afternoon would be soon enough. She would make herself work first. It still surprised her that she could. How had it happened? She had got the bit between her teeth. Even her teachers noticed it and had started saying friendly, encouraging things. Now she had a different feeling, oh not that she liked the work any more than before but that she could do it and would. Somehow this was connected with Tony. It was all very curious.

At lunchtime Chris phoned for a chat. He was going out with Vicky Dawson now and apparently having more luck. But he wanted to know anyway how was she in the storm, had she woken up, had there been any damage to the house? His Dad was really pissed off, he told her, because their neighbours' tree had fallen through the roof of their garage and wrecked his car.

'Yes, hundreds of cars have been wrecked apparently.'

'What are you doing? You don't want to come and have a look at Hyde Park, do you? They say that's the worst.'

'No. But thanks for asking, Chris.'

'You're okay?'

'I'm fine.'

*

She wishes she was. She looks at herself searchingly in the mirror, an hour before she is due to meet Tony on the Heath. At least she's got him back, at least, at least. But what happened last week makes her insecure. She wants to bind him to her. So that he won't slip away. This is the first time she's thought that. She looks at herself critically. Why is her skin so blotchy, her eyes not bright and clear, her hair, oh her hair, she can't bear to think about her hair.

She dresses carefully, indecisive about which of two pairs of jeans to wear, changing pullovers a number of times, trying different hats and woollen caps. She makes up her eyes, but doesn't like the effect: they look large and woeful in her pale, drawn face. She rubs all the make-up off. Now she looks as if she's been in a fight. Oh nothing will do, she says to herself, it's a hopeless case. Alex you're a hopeless case, a nutcase. Ha!

With that she strides out with impatient steps onto the Heath.

The world outside her flat looks as if it's been engaged in a battle. She gets to the first upturned tree, the second overturned fence, and then runs back for her camera.

It is strange, this afternoon, this cool, still, windy afternoon in the aftermath of the storm. Of course it is painful, so many old trees, torn up by an unbelievably strong hand. Like a giant, or an army of them, has swept over the Heath. Making havoc. It's a sort of a *Lear* day. It makes her want to choke and cry. At the same time, and this is the awful thing about it, it is exhilarating. And judging by the number of people on the Heath, all like her, gawping, many others feel the same. The best free entertainment today in London! she says to herself, and laughs. As she clicks away on her camera she feels as if she's photographing the wounded in a battle. And yet it is exciting too, fascinating. It is like being way out at sea, remembering that you are so small, so infinitesimal, utterly insignificant.

She knows he'll feel the same. She can hardly wait. But the path through to the hill is blocked. She tries to climb between the trees but so many have tumbled together, making it impassable. She climbs back and takes a northerly detour, walking faster because of the time, hoping she'll be able to find a way through the wooded area and out into a clearing higher up.

There they are, Tony with Ellen, Moth way behind. She starts to run down the hill towards them. Then stops, cursing her cough. Her breath comes with difficulty, she doesn't want him to see her like this, to think of her as ill. So she waits, breathing in and out impatiently, then when the coughing has stopped she walks on rapidly towards them.

'Oh, Alex, there you are.'

She kisses Ellen on the cheek and looks at Tony. He wants to make some gesture, let her feel acknowledged. But what kind of a gesture? He touches her lightly on the elbow. 'Good to see you. What a storm! What a night!' They exchange stories.

'England's going crazy. I think I might leave, I might emigrate.'

'Really? This is a new one.'

Would he miss me, does he feel a pang? 'No, seriously, but I might go abroad for a year after my A's.'

'Sounds like a good idea.'

'Moth, what do you think of all this?'

But Moth will not be drawn today. He will not look up from the gravel.

Anything wrong? her eyes ask Tony. He indicates yes.

They start to follow the line of the ponds, on the way to Kenwood. Moth trails behind. He carries a football which every now and again he throws into the air and catches. Sometimes he goes on looking up at the sky for minutes afterwards. Alex tries to draw his attention to the debris all around. But if he notices he will not communicate as much to her. Ellen is on Tony's shoulders. Alex walks beside Tony quietly, stopping to comment on each new overturned tree. Sometimes she takes out her camera. Sometimes they join with huddles of others, all exclaiming in the same mix of dismay and amazement. It is a communal activity. Not for the first time Alex enjoys being shrouded like this in anonymity with Tony, as if they are together taking part in something greater. She is frightened to ask him what is wrong, almost doesn't want to know.

But eventually she can't help herself. 'Was the weekend . . .?'

'A mixed blessing.'

'Tell me just the good. I'm just up for the good today.' She laughs her funny apologetic laugh. She says it like a twenty-five-year-old but feels like a fifteen-year-old. He knows it. His hands, ungloved, are in the pockets of his army greatcoat to keep warm. She would like to take one out. To hold it tight.

'The good?' she says again.

In the car, with the windows wound up, himself and Nick after having been chased by the bull. The rain outside coming down in buckets. They are drenched and hot from the running, the edge of fear still with them, making them triumphant in their escape. It is the first moment that Tony has really relaxed with Nick. The thought has come to him, I've been so much with women, I've almost forgotten what it's like to be with someone of my own sex. Nick turns the car radio on by chance to some of the old Benny Goodman recordings, and the conversation gets around to music, as Nick's emergency bottle of whisky passes between them.

Nick is in advertising but because one or two of the firm's largest clients are record companies he has developed a considerable body of knowledge in an area that overlaps with Tony's interests. And Tony, loosened by the morning's excitement and the whisky, finds himself talking about what he would do if he was given his chance, if he was back in the record business now.

'I might be able to help, Tony.'

'Don't get carried away by this good stuff of yours.'

'No. I mean it.'

He hadn't asked for this, hadn't expected it. But – it could be the combination of booze, exhilaration and relief, it could be a lot of things – for the first time in years he had thought, there might just be a chance.

But the other. Of course Moth would have to tell Carole about Alex's visit. The two had only missed each other by minutes, after all. The little chap was bound to say something, Tony couldn't ask him not to. It was only a matter of when. That's what had made it so awful, particularly with other people around.

The good side, Alex wants to know. Again he touches her, just her shoulder. Strange, he is beginning to feel guilty to be with her, yet at the same time he wants to be closer, to feel the reality of her presence, to reassure himself that he is not about to forsake her.

He doesn't want to talk about the weekend, the good or the bad. He doesn't want to think of troubles – or even of hope. He wants rather to find a way to dip back into the magic of the curiously isolated world they've created. Yet it is becoming increasingly difficult to do so.

Moth, catching his ball, looks up at the endless sky across which there is a great commotion of cloud movement. The ball satisfactorily falls plum into his hands. He remains squinting up into the air so that the others move forward without him.

When Father Christmas had asked him what he wanted, he hadn't had a want that he could articulate. Now there is something, something gigantic that matters enormously. He wants to go to those acting classes. And it doesn't cost any money, his teacher has said yesterday, it is something called 'state aided', whatever that is. It isn't money that's stopping Daddy. Not like when he'd wanted to go to the circus or have a birthday party with everyone eating Big Macs, and a film show in their own home, and Daddy had said it cost way too much.

Lots of things cost too much money. Some people have more money than others, and that is the way it is. Sometimes Moth has squealed, 'It's not fair,' but then Daddy's put on his tight face and Mummy's looked annoyed and said, 'Stop it immediately, Moth.'

When the acting classes had first been suggested, he'd been sure it would cost a lot of money and others in the class – even if they didn't have good elocution – would get to go and he wouldn't be able to. But it didn't cost any money, so then, why couldn't he go?

He'd heard Daddy talking to Mummy about it in the night time. It would mean walking a long way after school and hanging around. And what was to be done with Ellen meanwhile? And it seemed quite the wrong time to take on a 'commitment' of this kind. What did that word mean? Mummy had said to Daddy, 'If you get work then we'll have to make other arrangements anyway and surely whoever collects Moth from school can . . .'

'I think we should leave it for now. Don't push me, Carole, I've a lot on my plate.'

'On your mind, you mean.'

'It's hardly number one priority, you must agree.'

Oh but it is, Moth wanted to burst into the room insisting. He waited to hear what Mummy would say. Surely she would see how important it was for him. But Mummy started to cry and Moth crept back into his room and lay on his bed shaking, thinking about the way she had cried in their bedroom in Wales. And he'd been telling her. And afterwards she. And he'd been so frightened.

Last night, there she was, crying again. It made him feel all funny inside, like butterflies, no not something as pretty, like moths perhaps – oh why oh why did they go on calling him that silly name? – were flapping their wings furiously inside him, so that all he could do was curl up in his bed with his knees to his chin and wait for it to pass.

He'd said to Daddy when Daddy had collected him from school today,

'Why must we see Alex, Daddy? We don't need her, she's horrid, she makes Mummy cry.'

'Of course she's not horrid, what kind of talk is that? Don't you want to see what the storm has done to the Heath?'

'But Daddy . . .'

'Moth, that's enough. I don't want to hear any more about it.'

'My name is Timothy.'

He'd flung it at his father, the best he could do. He could walk all the way in silence, except that it was so very boring and when Daddy talked to Ellen on the way it infuriated him so that he had to break the silence once or twice. He could sulk, he could turn his face away when Daddy came to kiss him. The trouble was he liked to talk and he liked to be kissed. And he couldn't stop Daddy from taking them on the Heath.

Now he sees that the others have moved ahead without him and starts to run to catch up, unable to tell from the back of their necks what they are saying, whether they are talking or laughing, whether they've forgotten him. He runs faster and faster. Then suddenly he picks up his ball and throws it very hard, very viciously, at Alex's head.

★

She came flying onto the Heath. Coughing and flying along. She was wearing a little woollen bonnet. As she ran the wind caught at it and pulled it off her head. She bent to catch it. Then ran with it in her hand. Ellen was on my shoulders, Moth lagging behind. After what we'd all been through, he didn't want to come. I felt sorry for the little chap, wishing he wasn't in the middle of this thing. Half wishing that I hadn't promised to come today. But when, all of a sudden, without any warning, he threw his football hard at her, I was furious. 'Moth, how dare you! Say you're sorry this instant.'

'I won't!'

'Christ, Moth,' Alex said, having drawn a few deep breaths, 'that wasn't very nice.'

I took him by the arm. 'You'll do as I say, you little . . .'

'Oh leave him alone, Tony, I don't mind. There was probably some reason. I forgive you,' she said to Moth. 'Do you forgive me?'

Always I'll think of her sweetness with the children. She didn't deserve. Ellen wanted a ride on Alex's shoulders, 'I don't think she's up to it,' I told her, but Alex insisted, 'I can try for a bit anyway.'

We were a motley collection of people that day. We walked mostly silently, in a strange mood. 'You're very quiet,' Alex comments to me.

'A lot's going on inside.'

'Will you lift Ellen down, I want to take some photos.'

I put Ellen on the ground. Other kids were climbing the fallen trees. Ellen ran between the torn branches that littered the ground, shaking the leaves, telling herself, 'Sad, sad.'

It was sad indeed. While Alex was photographing two oaks whose roots, with a huge shelf of earth attached, had been pulled clean of the ground, Moth crept up to me.

'It's like a battle,' he said. 'It's like a giants' army.'

'Did you talk about it in school?'

''Course we did.'

'Tomorrow you'll be able to tell them about the Heath.'

'Yes, but I want to go home now and watch telly.'

'Soon.'

Alex slipped the camera back in her jacket pocket. We walked on quietly. Time and time again our favourite routes were impassable.

It was a strange day. We were at sixes and sevens with ourselves. And when Moth next started on about going home, I said, 'Perhaps we've all had enough. You too, Alex, you look as if you still shouldn't be out for long.'

'Oh don't be so fatherly!'

'Whoever said that? You've never said that before.'

'I'm sorry. I'm all strung up. I'll see you Friday.' She touched my arm. 'Tony, I was wondering. I'd like to see you alone. Just us. This is' – her gesture indicated the children – 'difficult and I'd like to talk to you. Really, be with you once and . . . um . . . Oh hell, you know what I mean.' She looked deep into my eyes. 'You do know what I mean?'

'I don't know, Alex, at the moment things are so volatile, and with the kids . . .'

I wished she wouldn't cry. Both of them crying, it was too much. Alex's tears, God knows what it is, are irresistible. There's no way. 'All right, all right, I'll try, on Friday.'

'You promise?'

'I promise I'll try.'

Promises.

We're hardly in the door at home when the phone goes.

'I promised to be in touch,' says Nick. 'I think I might be able to set up that interview. But we should meet and talk first. How are you fixed for lunch next week?'

'Nick, I can't handle interviews. It's a dead duck if . . .'

'Got to go. I'll phone you back.'

*

In the following week the weather changes radically. At last, the first real warmth of spring. Within days, everywhere the hint of blossom fringes the trees. Oh, the fragrant smells as doors are opened and people breathe in the air, even London air, with long deep breaths!

Above Alex's basement flat Jerry and Angelica watch her comings and goings, trying to read the clues. They have been concerned that since her illness she has looked so washed out and now hope that this balmy spring weather will help to increase her energy level and bring back her buzzing prettiness. Still, they're reassured by her exam results, her regular trips to Swiss Cottage library, the recent purposefulness of her step as she leaves the house. The door bangs less, which, in Jerry's optimistic code, must mean something. 'Those days away with her,' he tells Angelica, 'seem to have helped, whatever you did.'

She smiles at him fondly. They are off to France in a couple of days' time. She is looking forward to it now that the novel is finally finished.

She feels pleased with herself. Her agent has said that it won't be a critical success, but will make masses of money. How satisfactory! Leave the critical success to others. And what with Alex seemingly getting herself more centred, life on the whole looks rosy. Now, to cap it all, here is the sun. Hardly any need to go away to France.

To Alex, the sun suggests all good things. She is sleeping better, coughing less. Her appetite has improved. This morning she has eaten two chunky slices of buttered toast with marmite, and drunk a glass and a half of orange juice, before setting off for school. She closes her front door carefully and lets out a soft 'ah' of delight as her body receives the impact of the sun's warm rays. She has washed her hair, now it bobs about on her shoulders, released from the headgear in which she has hidden it these last weeks. A neighbour standing in a front room, happening to notice her pass, the bouncing dark hair, the short skirt dancing below the line of her jacket, the zig-zag patterned tights, the swing of the arm carrying a bright pink carrier-bag full of books, lets out her own version of 'ah', remembering her own young womanhood, and is propelled into attacking the day's tasks with new vigour.

The refuse collectors whistle at Alex. She smiles at them. On the bus the driver jokes with her; he is one of the regulars, one of her favourites. She sits on a seat at the front. As the bus starts to move forward she notices a girl from her school running towards them. 'Do wait,' she says to the driver. 'One of your mates?' he wants to know. 'Sort of.' There are no more free seats. The girl stands close to Alex, holding on to the rail and chatting away. A man in a seat across the gangway tries to join in the conversation. Neither of them mind, they just keep going, every now and again including him; it is that sort of a day.

Outside the school Alex lets the other girl go in first. Hanging back, she takes one more look at the blue blue of the sky. Be there when I come out, she tells it, just like now; not a single cloud. Stay like that till Friday. Friday. Two more days. She pushes the heavy door open and climbs the stairs to her History class, feeling that she can tackle anything and everything.

Angelica and Jerry are leaving at the crack of dawn the following morning. Alex has cooked supper for them: leek and potato soup, followed by lamb chops with tomato wrapped in silver foil. And because Jerry has a sweet tooth, lemon syllabub to finish.

To be served by your daughter – her short skirt, Jerry notes with appreciation, swirling this way and that as she bustles round, collecting dishes, moving things from the oven to the table, refusing all help, 'No, you just sit still, I want to do it all for you tonight,' – is such a wonderfully satisfying feeling – at last wheels coming full turn – that it almost wouldn't have mattered what they ate. As it is, the food is excellent and Alex doesn't mind how many times they tell her so. She is all smiles, all amiability.

'And Jerry, there's something special for you for pudding.'

'Syllabub, wonderful!'

'It's still your favourite?'

'Of course it is, now, Alex, this is really quite lovely of you.'

There is in most parents a deep set desire to think well of their offspring, a robust optimism. Angelica, full of satisfaction for the world she has created, gets up from the table, goes round to where Alex is at the fridge carrying out the last syllabub, and embraces her.

'What was that all about?'

'This is such a treat, darling.'

'Mum, it's only a meal. Don't go over the top.'

'It's more than a meal, it's a symbol.'

'To good family relations.' Jerry toasts them with the last of the rosé.

'Well of course,' beams Angelica, with her arm still round her daughter. She picks up her glass. 'To your A-levels, my love, and your adulthood.'

'Oh Mum, you're embarrassing me. Why don't we leave all this stuff now, and eat our syllabub.'

'You know your mother, she likes a sense of occasion.'

'That reminds me, we ought to be drinking to your book, oughtn't we, Mum?'

'If you insist,' Angelica purrs, looking from one to the other.

'You know, Tony's wife is in publishing and he was saying . . .'

Too late, it has just come out the way things do. 'Specially when you've buzzed around cooking, and you've had a bit of rosé and you feel awkward with your parents, especially how things have been recently. Then you begin to relax. And this other thing is on your mind. And suddenly.

Now she is blushing, which makes it worse.

Angelica has to fight with herself. She and Jerry have been fairly convinced that. No, well that was obviously blind of them. 'You're still seeing him, then?' She tries to not make it sound like an attack.

'I'm a big girl now,' says Alex, regaining her composure, 'a grown-up, remember? Don't *worry*, Mum, everything's under control. We'll probably stop seeing each other soon. Very soon.'

Angelica is determined to be mollified. Why ruin such a good evening? So somehow the note of gaiety returns. Soon the three are laughing over family jokes and Alex is promising to look after the house while they're away and do all the chores her mother asks. She will be completely reliable, she promises. Angelica is pleased that she seems so co-operative.

'On any count,' she says to Jerry as they retrace their steps upstairs at the end of the evening, 'that is a blessing, there are definite improvements, wouldn't you say, and Rome wasn't built in a night.'

'In a day. Stop babbling, Angelica, and come upstairs. I don't know why it is but syllabub always makes me feel randy.'

And downstairs, Alex stacking the plates by the sink thinks, Friday, come on Friday. Of course I just said that about us not seeing one another. I had to. Lucky they didn't make a big thing of it. For a moment I thought, there goes the evening. But they were okay, really. I think they did enjoy the meal. And if I have my way. If the fates are on my side. Oh hurry up Friday. I don't think I can live through tomorrow.

Then it is Friday. Each day of the week has become increasingly warmer and today is in the mid-twenties. The sky is as consistent a blue as Alex could have hoped for. She dresses with care. None of her jeans look good on her now; in each the legs are too roomy. She opts for her new short skirt, her zig-zag cream tights, the same orange boots that she wore the first time she wandered over the Heath to meet Tony so unexpectedly. She doesn't need a jacket, a cream sweatshirt will do, the sleeves pushed up to the elbows of her thin arms. She examines her face in the mirror wishing there was more colour in it. She pinches her cheeks a number of times, then laughs at herself. It's hardly going to make a difference by this afternoon. Still hours to go.

In the mirror she looks at herself this way and that, profile, front view. She swishes her skirt (she loves the feel of it) and examines her legs critically. Is she sexy? It seems such a mystery to be sexy when you don't want to be, but then when you do. She's only going to have this one chance. If he kissed her, if he let himself. Oh, Tony. She has a vision of them tumbling onto the bracken on the Heath. He's got to feel the same as I, he's *got* to. It's just that he doesn't know it, that's what.

School is intolerably slow. Mrs Morrow's earnest nasal voice comes and goes from her consciousness. Into the pattern of the words Alex weaves her own. She thinks of phrases she might use, of replies Tony might make when all defences were down. She has never had such a longing to be hugged and held. And more. It can't be wrong, she thinks. That wife of his, she's got to be a cow, she doesn't even. Even I give the kids more attention than she does, Tony's always saying.

Jolting back into her immediate surroundings, she wonders what Mrs Morrow has been saying. There seems no connection now to the last paragraph in her notes. What the hell has happened? She looks over her neighbour's shoulder and tries to catch up on the lost passages. But on Mrs Morrow goes, getting further and further ahead, till it hardly seems worth bothering. She stops writing and, folding her arms, gives herself up to her private world.

Breaktime. A double session of Politics ahead. She wavers. No, impossible to go through with it. Might as well leave school now.

But what to do with so many hours still to kill? She goes to chat to Chris's Dad at the garage, then wanders slowly down Kentish Town Road looking in shop windows. When she gets to the end of the shops she makes her way back to a place near her school, where she often hangs out with her mates in the lunch break. No mates in there now, just lot of people having an early sandwich or bowl of soup. She can't eat a thing but orders a coffee, wondering if they'll complain. They don't. She sits there sipping it, thinking, I wish someone I know would appear; it would make time go faster. I don't mind, anyone will do, I don't want to think any more. Well, perhaps not exactly anyone.

The first familiar face to come through the door isn't one of the girls from her school but a boy who had been on the fringe of their group the year before.

'Jason, I thought you were meant to be in Leicester?'

'God, what a dump, what a d-u-m-p! Got to get away every now and again or you go insane. I mean it.'

'You remember Sophie, Sophie Baldwin, she's loving it, I'd thought . . .'

'Each to their own. Wasn't she doing dance? That might be different. I should never have left London. The teaching is okay but otherwise . . . Trouble with us Londoners is that we're spoilt. Anywhere seems tame afterwards – unless you opt for New York. What are your plans, by the way? I must say Alex, you're looking pretty dodgy. Anything wrong?'

'Dodgy, what do you mean?'

He's sat down opposite her at the table by now and peers closely into her face, then shakes his head. 'Been ill or something?'

'Yeah, but I'm better now.'

Silence.

'You know, I've got this friend in Leicester with Aids who's dying, I mean in the next few weeks. It's been horrific being around, watching. You can't believe it. I must say we're all going to have to be much more careful now. That kind of total freedom of last year in the sixth, all those parties and things, that's certainly something in the past.'

'Why did you say that, why did you say that about Aids?'

'I dunno. No reason. Christ, just because it's in my mind, because if you know someone . . .'

Her hands instinctively go to her ears, 'I don't want to hear.'

'Well, Alex, for fuck's sake, these are real things happening in the world, ducky, and some of us are not going to be alive in ten years. And if it's not you or me, just thank your lucky stars.'

'Jason, I've got to go now. I didn't realise the time, sorry. It was good to see you. We'll be in touch. I'll . . . Sorry, but I've really got to go.'

Outside the cafe Alex is shaking like a leaf. Clasping her arms round her body, cold even in the face of the sun, she sets off at a half run. As she runs here comes the cough. And with the cough her terrible fear, unable to be held back any more.

*

And now today has an entirely different consistency. It was one thing then suddenly. How could it all change like that, without any warning? When it's the height, the pinnacle, when only half an hour ago she was thinking. I can't take it in. Bloody cough, stop! stop! I could have . . . but then so could hundreds of people. It's a chance in a million. Chris did say about Guy. And what if it was true and it would explain why I'm not getting any better. He wasn't even bi then for heaven's sake. Was he? It was only a few times. You don't always. And somewhere into this, into the crack not taken up by thoughts for her own survival, poor friend of Jason's. That was terrible to rush off like that. When I'm better, when I feel stronger I'll make contact with him. When I've stopped coughing. Oh God, God, what now? Make it not true. Please.

Even if I have, these things sometimes take years, you don't necessarily. No, but I could never marry. I could never have children. Then if I can't. It'd be all over. You might as well commit suicide. I think I would rather than. No! No!

Quarter to two now. She is on the way to the Heath. And her thoughts fly to the time ahead with Tony. She tries to blot out everything that has happened since she went into the coffee bar. To go back in her mind to when she'd been at school. To simply – eliminate it. She tries to imagine again greeting Tony. The two of them, the sunny day, him liking her skirt, the way they would talk and joke, the way he would move towards her. The way he would. She could imagine his lips on hers. And what if they found an out-of-the-way spot and under a tree in the long grasses they lay down and. Well, would all that be ruined for ever then, her one chance because she would tell him? No, better blank it out. It's a chance in a million.

Two o'clock. She is entering Parliament Hill Field from Constantine Road, walking past the children's playground. There are children playing with their mothers. She grips the rails and looks at them hard, all their little faces. She looks at the mothers' faces. She has so much longed to have children. She has taken it for granted. She watches an elderly man swinging a little boy back and forth on the swings, back and forth. She thinks of all the times that she and Tony have swung Moth and Ellen on these swings over the last six months. She thinks of Tony, he'll be setting off towards her now along the path from the tennis courts. I can't do it. I can't risk—him. No, I just – love him too much for that. And love's got to be unselfish. That's what it's all about. He's. I can't do it, Tony, that's all there is to it, you've got to be okay, whatever happens.

Tony and Alex see each other at a distance, and wave. They walk towards one another. They are a long way apart. It takes time to traverse the necessary distance along the straight gravel path.

'Was it difficult?' she said. Her loveliness. Perhaps I've never seen her looking more lovely. More translucent. More ethereal.

'Getting away, I mean.'

'It was difficult. I had to lie to Seth's mum. Alex, you look stunning.'

'Do you like the tights?'

'I like all of it.'

'What shall we do?'

'What do you want to do?'

'It's funny having a choice. Not having to consider the children, I mean.'

'It was you who wanted to . . .'

'I know. I know, Tony.'

She seemed ill at ease. No doubt for different reasons we both felt far from comfortable.

'Will you take my hand?'

I think she must have heard my intake of breath, 'I don't know, Alex, whether it's wise.'

'Don't say anything, please. Let's just hold hands and walk awhile, please. Till I've – till I feel calmer.'

After last night's dreams, and not the first ones this week by any means, it was extraordinarily difficult to just walk beside her holding her hand. I willed my sex out of my body. I was so aware of all that had taken place at home recently. The tension that permeates the flat and affects the children, Moth particularly. The tight knot inside that's now a permanent response to the new unpredictability of Carole's moods, her anger. Her anger at me.

'Have you slept with her, yet?'

'There's no "yet" about it, Carole.'

'I bet you want to.' She had turned sideways in bed to look at me. 'I bet you want to.'

'Carole, you're behaving like a child. For God's sake, let it be!'

'You're the one behaving like a child, pretending you don't know what you're doing. Involving the children. Christ! I thought you were meant to be looking for work, not . . .'

'I am looking for work. I've got an interview coming up, and I'm terrified every time I think about it. Or don't you remember? The trouble with you, Carole, is that you don't think about anything but your own . . .'

'That's not fair!'

'Isn't it? No wonder I've been driven to someone else for companionship – and companionship is all it's been.'

'But that's the trouble. Even if it's true, it doesn't seem to make any difference.'

She turned away from me in the bed. I fell into a fitful sleep. And had such dreams. Making even me begin to wonder. In one of the dreams Alex said, 'I want to take you away from all this, to love you and look after you, to cook you *moules marinière*.' God knows why those. What I remember most particularly is not the words, the actions, but the sensation of enormous lightness, of hope, of fresh possibilities. But with my rational mind, as I walked beside her, I knew of course it was simply out of the question.

'Alex, love, we've walked around this pond three times.'

'Don't you like watching the trees reflected in the water?'

'Yes – in principle. Is that what you're looking at?'

'Remember when Angelica had that phase of saying, "This too will pass"?'

'I remember it well.'

'Oh.'

'Are you – where are you? You seem to be down in your little burrow, today.'

'I am, I suppose.'

'What do you think, shall we go over to Kenwood and get ourselves a cup of tea, and talk there?'

'Not Kenwood.'

'No? Where then?'

'You choose.'

'Right. The lilypond, with the Victorian viaduct bridge.'

'That's a great place,' she said. 'It's always been one of my favourites. You're telepathic, did you know that, Tony?'

Then if you're telepathic, Tony, read everything that's in my mind, so that I don't have to tell you. If I hold your hand, let it all come to you.

Carole, at home last night.

'Give Alex up. Do this one thing for me. In every marriage comes the time when something is demanded, and even if the other partner can't see it as equally important, that's the whole point – to take it from the other, on trust.'

'Sometimes it seems to me that you're always the one who gets your way. It didn't start out like that, but that's how it's become.'

'Basically I'm more successful and you resent it.'

'Oh, for Christ's sake . . .'

'Listen, I've done a hell of a lot of giving, or did at one time, and it didn't make any difference. I can't make up for the other.'

'I know.'

'Tony, I'm so bloody jealous.'

'I don't know what you want me to say. That side, the physical side of our marriage, isn't enough, Carole, don't you see? That's why I've been drawn to Alex. Sometimes I think you're hardly aware of my existence.'

Long pause.

'We've got to keep trying,' she said. 'I'm a sticker. And right or wrong, I believe in us. But with this between us, it's hopeless to even begin to. Tony, I beg you . . .'

Moth at school this morning. 'Moth, listen, you're going home with Seth after school.'

'Why Seth? I want to go with Adam.'

'No, Seth's mother has kindly offered. And it's more convenient with Ellen if . . .'

'I want to go with Adam. I don't like Seth any more.'

'You do, don't be such a pain.'

'Why aren't you coming to collect me? You said you'd come and talk about the drama lessons, you said . . .'

'Tomorrow.'

'Why, Daddy?'

'It's something special.'

'Is it something to do with Mummy's birthday?'

'Perhaps.'

'It is, isn't it, Daddy?'

Big eyes looking at me.

I'm not going to say anything till we sit down. Then I'm going to tell him, quite unemotional, just precise and to the point, keeping it to just a few words – I hate scenes, well, they're so messy, I never want to be like Angelica in that – that we should stop seeing each other, that it will be easier all round, for both of us – I'll tell him that then it'll feel better for him. I'll tell him I like Chris and he's jealous – no, he won't believe that's the reason. I'll just tell him it's not possible, that's what. And I won't say anything about the other, not to – worry him. I'll just shake hands and that. Or maybe. I've got to say goodbye to the kids. They'll wonder. Oh heck! Here we are, I wonder which way round the pond he'll go. I wonder what he's thinking. He's as quiet as I am today, 'course he is, he's got to be feeling something too, hasn't he? Well, I'll say it in just a minute.

'Alex, love, listen, there's something I want to say to you. It's hard but it's better to get it over with. I've got to let you go. We've got to stop seeing one another. You do know that, don't you?'

'Oh, and why would that be?' A brittle little voice.

'Because . . . because my family life, for what it's worth, is being destroyed by us seeing one another. It seems ridiculous, I know, but that's the way it is.'

'Why do you say, your family life "for what it's worth"? It must be worth a lot!'

'Alex, let's sit down. There's no point standing.'

'I'm not sure if I want to sit down with you. I think you're a jerk and a coward. I despise you. You don't even have the courage to stand up for. Oh, what's the point? Things are getting better for you – you don't need me any more. I get the point. And silly Alex to take so long. Forget it. We might as well shake hands on it here and now.'

'Alex, sit down.'

'No.'

'Alex, don't say those things, they're so terribly untrue. Come here.'

'No.'

There was a kind of scuffle. I couldn't tell what was happening, what we were feeling, only I knew I couldn't let her go like that. I was trying to get hold of her, to get through to her. 'You remember when I came after you at your school and apologised . . .'

'You never came after me.'

'I was kind of looking for you, in a vague sort of way. The point is, from the very first moment on the Heath I knew that I wanted to get to know you, be close to you. It's the strangest sensation. You'll never know what your friendship has meant to me.'

'Why don't we call it what it is?'

'All right then. But you're a schoolgirl . . .'

'Don't belittle me.'

'I'm not. I'm just saying that you've got your life ahead. It's not possible. And I'm married, Alex.'

She seemed to be beating me, her fists hard on my chest. I tried to hold them. 'For the third time, let's sit down. It's silly standing like this.' I pulled her down on a log. She started to cry onto my shoulder. All the while I was thinking, does she really despise me? I was aware of Carole saying, you're only drawn because she's young and you need someone to look up to you. Looking at her in her distress, thinking of Carole. What had I done? I stroked Alex's hair, praying for peace. Let this end now, let there be some calm way out.

'You know why I hate you so much?'

'I don't, no, Alex, but I probably deserve it.'

'I hate you because I was idiot enough to think you deserved a sacrifice. A huge one on my part. And you've just disillusioned me so much. It makes me want to laugh.'

'Well that would be better than crying.'

'I can't think why I ever bothered.'

'So what was the sacrifice?'

I told him very fast, very matter of fact, then, all what I'd been thinking, everything that happened. At first I kept thinking how angry I was with him. I told him in anger, it fired me along. All the words came out clipped, jerky. I wouldn't look at him. I told him what an ass I'd been about him. I said everything I could to hurt. And then I got to the bit about when I was in the coffee bar and Jason coming in and then I just kept right on talking, I told him every single thing. And then I was crying and crying and crying and I was holding onto him and he was like a log in the sea and he was all I had.

'I'm so shit-scared,' I said, 'you can't believe it, Tony.'

'I do believe it,' I told her. 'And can *you* believe that there are hundreds of people just as scared as you? But in this case – from what you've said – the chances are so remote.'

'I think if I had Aids I'd commit suicide.'

'I think you wouldn't. You've got too much "oomph" for that.'

'"Oomph!" You've got to be joking. Do you think I ought to have a test? I don't know if I'd have the courage. And there was I talking about you being a coward, ha!'

She got up from the log, and, moving away, took swipes at the long grass, her shoulders heaving.

The sound of his voice. The touch, the feel of his body against mine. Knowing I'll never have. His voice saying,

'Listen to me. I want to tell you something, Alex. Look at me. Come here. Come. Can you hear me through all that hair? If you won't look, nod, okay? There's nothing wrong with you. Trust me over this. You're run down, that's all. But you're getting better. Remember you told me how ill you were a few years ago. You recovered then. It'll be just the same now.'

'But . . .'

'The other is such a slender chance, from what you say. No one's ever told you that this boy you slept with, whatever his name is, has even got Aids. Have they?'

'No, but Chris said.'

'What?'

'That he didn't look well.'

'You can say that about hundreds of people. It's not like you to have these morbid thoughts, to get things so out of proportion.'

'It is.'

'No, I know you well now. There's just one bit of Alex, a silly old bit, Alex's pessimism.'

'How do you know that's all it is?'

'I do know. I recognise it. Probably because I'm pessimistic too. But you've been good for me, helped me to start enjoying all sorts of things again. And I hate to see you like this. I want to give you a good shake. Shake all this out of you.'

She turned to face me. Her eyes awash with such a giving of herself that I felt humbled.

'Go on, shake me hard.'

So I gripped her arms and started to shake her and she cried out, 'Maybe I am going to live and I should feel comforted but you're going to leave me, Tony. Like he did.'

'He?' Then I realised who she was talking about.

'Hold me tight,' she said, 'please.'

'Oh, Alex.'

'It's okay, I understand about the rest, I do truly. But just for now. Just while I get used to.'

She came into my arms. I began to stroke her hair, warm from the sun, wet from her crying. The fringe of her short skirt hovered around my trousers. I put my arms round her waist. The March sun beat down on our heads. Everywhere on the Heath were the signs of new growth, even around the recently slain and fallen trees. People passed by where we were standing, neither of us minded. Desire her? Yes, of course I did, as her body swayed with mine. Who could not have done? I don't know how long – I eased my grasp slightly and put my hands on her shoulders instead. I don't know how long we stood like that silently. I hoped my body would tell her some things, not others. Perhaps it was a vain hope. It was the best I could do.

Eventually we eased apart, and with our arms around each other's shoulders, started to walk over the hill towards the tennis courts. And I had a sense that resolution if not immediately here was at least in the air.

Before we parted Alex expressed to me that she would like to see the children once or twice more so as to 'round off our meetings in as natural a way as possible, and to give us all a chance to get used to the idea'.

'I see. You mean a kind of snail's approach.'

'You're insulting me. Don't you dare, Tony Davis.'

'That's better, that's more like the Alex I'm used to.'
'Which you're soon going to have to do without!'
'Believe me, I hardly know how I'm going to – and I'm not joking now.'
'Ah,' she said, the first hint of a smile. 'That's the only nice thing you've said today.'
And so we left it, at the tennis courts, agreeing to see one another the following week. And the bus didn't come, and the bus didn't come.

*

Carole is in the flat waiting for Tony and the children when they return from the Spaldings'. It is late. The kids have already been fed, they are excited and clamouring to tell their tales. Carole has decided to try to badger Tony less, try to let him work things out his way, have faith in him. So now, though messages run between them they are hidden ones, questions and answers unexpressed, unexplored, unresolved.
The two bath their children, sit on opposite beds reading bedside stories, walk back along the corridor together, conscious of their familiarity, the easy motions like a ritualised dance: safe territory, well worn, home territory. Yet Tony can't reassure Carole. Not tonight when he is so acutely conscious of Alex's wretchedness. And later, as Carole curls up on the sofa, and starts to work her way through a bulky manuscript, he appreciates it that she is able to give him this space when most he needs it.

The following days are quiet ones between them. Perhaps Tony should feel pleased with himself for having done 'the right thing', but he doesn't. He simply feels empty. Hollow. Though he knows he could have behaved in no different way, though he wouldn't have wished to, still he sometimes wonders whether he has been a coward.
Then at the end of the week he has his lunch with Nick, taking Ellen, who's as good as gold, with him. And Nick now comes clean about the job. It involves going to Japan to set up a jazz department in a large record store in downtown Tokyo, the latest outlet for an American BTN subsidiary.
'Tokyo, you must be out of your mind, Nick, I can't go there, what about the family?'
'It's only to set the outfit up. Six months, something like that. What they're looking for is someone to order the stock, and give the staff guidelines on selling jazz. Tony, with your knowledge you'd be ideally situated, it's a gift horse and I happen to know from my contact that they haven't got anyone inside who they want to send . . .'
'Who'll agree to go, you mean. Anyway, I don't know why we're talking about it, it's out of the question.'

Nick sighs. He drums his fingers on the table. 'It's no skin off my nose. I'm just trying to help you out. But the point is, Tony, it is an opportunity. I've mentioned you; they're interested. And if they like what you do, you'll be able to transfer back, you'll have your toe in the door again. Looked at like that, what's against it?'

'What's against it? Fucking hell, Nick, the children, Carole, everything!'

'But if it was your only chance?'

A long silence ensues.

I felt an overpowering sense of dismay. Even this, this small ray of hope for us, seemed now to be something else I must let go of.

They finish their meal. Nick calls for the bill and inwardly curses. He says again to himself, no skin off my nose. But he's tried to do Tony a favour. He'd thought, when they were out sailing, that there was a chance for this man, if only. He'd thought he'd seen a gleam of something. But it was his business. You can't make a man's life for him. Shame, though.

The sensation was strange. Of a rock being pushed by forceful waters. Life itself driving me: refusing this time to be denied.

'Wait a moment, wait a moment,' I said to Nick. 'Carole will go bananas of course, and what about the ch – ? Yes, but we'll manage, somehow. Nick, forget about the rest. You're on, mate. And if I do land this job I can tell you I'll be grateful to you for life.'

'Good man,' said Nick. 'For a moment I thought the worst of you. The point is, I've already set up a meeting, so apart from anything else I'd have felt something of a fool.'

'I've got to admit that after all this time the thought of an interview freaks me like nobody's business.'

'It's not a formal interview, you'll be fine. They'll want to see your c.v. of course. Did you remember to bring it for me to cast my eye over? And what about references? Will that Walter character you mentioned help you out?'

This was beginning to feel more real by the moment. But what to tell Carole, and is it better to wait? Everything seems so very iffy at present.

It was the waiting, the tension, the not asking, that Carole found so very hard.

★

Until at last, after a day in which Lee had told her that he was definitely leaving and had asked her to come too, and she had said that she would think it over, but knew she wouldn't. Then in the aftermath she had inadvertently spoken sharply to Sarah, Sarah who had been quite blameless, just a little irritating, it wasn't she, after all, who made Carole angry, but she was there, within reach. But it simply wouldn't do, Carole knew. And when Sarah popped her head round the door at the end of the afternoon, Carole had felt the need to apologise.

Now she enters the flat late, apologising for that too. 'But why apologise?' says Tony, 'there is absolutely nothing new in your being late.' She is late because she has been drinking with Sarah, and has opened up to her this evening more than ever before, not about Alex, but about a number of other matters relating to work and home. And Sarah too has become expansive. And a bottle of wine has been consumed. And now, tired and mellow from the wine, she comes home and says,

'But I intend to stop coming back late, that's what I want to tell you, that I plan to change, and I mean it, oh this time I do, only please tell me that you are going to bring the other to an end, I have been patient, I've tried to be patient.'

'I am,' says Tony.

'You are?'

He nods.

'You mean you have already, you strange man, and you've not told me, you've let me go on and on worrying?'

'No, wait a moment. Not that. But we've decided. It's just a matter of giving the thing a kind of resolution.'

'Sometimes there aren't any easy resolutions,' says Carole. 'Well while we're talking . . .'

'But we have decided. Soon.'

'How soon?'

He doesn't immediately respond so she says, 'It's my birthday in three days.'

'Yes, I hadn't forgotten. And it's the interview in two.'

'That's more important.'

He is surprised. 'You think so?'

'How could you imagine otherwise? I am selfish, Tony, but not that selfish.'

'Carole, has Sarah ever said anything more to you about this job? I mean anything from Nick?'

'What are you talking about?'

'Come to bed, old girl, I want to talk to you.'

'No "old girl",' she says, 'I'm only going to be thirty-four. But I suppose in comparison . . .'

'Don't, Carole. You must know how much you mean . . .'
'I don't like the sound of this,' she says, 'somehow it sounds worrying. Come on, let's get it over with.'

'You know it's funny,' Carole tells Tony later that night, 'when I was in the office this afternoon thinking about compromise, it was more a matter of coming home earlier, not working all hours and Saturdays, spending more time with you. And now if this job really comes through, you won't be here to spend any time with.'
'Only for six months.'
'If we're lucky.'
'You could ask your parents to come over and stay.'
'Mum would drive me bananas in no time at all.'
'Then we'd have to have an au pair.'
'An au pair, what a thought!'
'What was that beautiful word you used?'
'What are you talking about?'
'Compromise.'
'Oh I see,' she laughs. 'Tony Davis, I might have drunk a lot of wine but I'm certainly not too pissed to realise that you've won this round.'

And I remembered Alex's words, I'm not into winning, and was about to say them to Carole, but I couldn't.

'I can tell you this, anyway,' says Carole with her arms comfortably round Tony, 'Tokyo or whatever, I shall be gunning for you for that job.' Then, beginning to slip into sleep, 'You won't forget my birthday, promise?'
'It's very much in my mind, the children won't let me forget it for a moment.'
'Ah, that reminds me,' she's wide-awake again, 'talking of the kids, I thought of seeing Mrs Harrison about Moth's drama lessons. He does seem so keen. Somehow we'll accommodate it, like everything else, just as long as we're strong together. What do you say, Tony?'
'I say, go ahead.'

At five to midnight in Newington Green, Nick is turning off the television and stretching his arms to the ceiling. He calls through to the kitchen, 'What are you doing, Sarah?'
'I'm baking a cake,' she says.

'At this time of night? You're crazy, woman. I hope it's coffee, my favourite.'

'It's for Carole, it's her birthday in a couple of days' time.'

'I don't believe this!'

Sarah brushes the flour off her hands and comes through into the sitting-room. Nick has flopped back on to the sofa. She puts her arms around him from behind. 'Now you're not to be jealous. There has been something I've been waiting to tell you all evening, but you've been too preoccupied.'

'And how do you know I'm not now?'

'Listen, you and I are going to have to find something else to quarrel over. 'Cause it's gone.'

'What has?'

She kisses him long and hard. And he responds, so that it is moments later before he has the breath or the inclination to ask, 'What are you talking about?'

'My fixation with Carole. She's no longer my idol, I realised that tonight: she's just human, like the rest of us.'

'But you're still baking her a cake, at what, nearly midnight?'

'Yes, to celebrate how human she is. I'd do the same for anyone – even for you.'

'It's good to know how things stand. But after a kiss like that . . . let the bloody cake burn!'

Only two days later Tony is running onto the Heath and towards Alex with the news. She sees his big smile and knows that something, something; there can only be one thing.

And Tony, as he moves towards her, the children in tow, profoundly pleased, very much looking forward to telling her, nevertheless takes in that the roominess inside her jeans isn't quite as poignantly obvious, the watch on her arm no longer appears to flop quite as much round her wrist.

Alex doesn't at first know which way to turn, they are all clamouring at once. But the children simply must wait.

'Tony, tell me,' she says.

'Nonsense, of course I'm not wonderful,' Tony is saying to Alex, 'just a very ordinary man. Still I believe that without you, without knowing you perhaps, I wouldn't have had the oomph in me to do what I had to.'

'And so you've got it, you actually mean you've got a job and you're going away?'

'Oh lots and lots is happening,' cuts in Moth. 'I'm going to have drama lessons. They said I have beautiful diction.'

'Well done, Moth.'
'He wants to be called Timothy now.'
'Do you indeed?' She tousles his hair. 'And when do you start?'
'When is it, Daddy?'
'May 1st, I believe.'
'Is it after school, Timothy?'
'Yes, it's on Tuesdays and one other day, I've forgotten when.'
'Two and a half weeks' time,' she says to Tony, 'shall we see each other till then?'
'It does seem to make as natural a break as any.'
'And when do you go away?'
'June.'
Timothy looks at Alex, considering. 'Will you cry when you don't see us any more?'
'Oh lots and lots I expect.' But when Alex sees the concerned look on his face she takes him in her arms and says, 'No, Timothy, I won't cry, I promise. And you won't either. I think it's a marvellous thing about your acting, I really do.'
It makes him feel expansive. 'It's Mummy's birthday tomorrow,' he tells her, 'we've baked her a cake and I've made her a card at school. And we've bought her a plant, three lovely hyacinths. But she's going to be late, you see, because she's going to see the drama teacher, I don't know why.'
'You're a star, that's why.' She takes his hand. 'Come on, Ellen too, we'll run as fast as we can, till our legs can't run any more, we'll be kites.'
'We'll be one kite,' says Timothy. 'And Daddy will be the tail. Come on, Daddy.'
Tony catches Alex's arm and squeezes it. 'At least you're well enough to run, that's some improvement.'
'Oh,' she says, 'don't worry about me, please don't worry about me.'

The weather continues kind to them. To all of England. Such hot weather, it isn't even spring, it's more like summer. Day after day in the seventies. Alex wears a blue-and-white summer dress in a 1950s print. The children are in shorts. The Heath is packed, the heat bringing everyone out. People are sunbathing in all sorts of states of undress. Alex and Tony and the children enjoy the hot weather in other ways. They bring a frisbee, they have races, they find new trees to climb. Then they flop on the hot grass and eat apples. Still, of course they all get brown, without attempting to.
Tony lying in the warm grass notices the new colouring of Alex's cheeks and neck against the white-and-blue collar of her dress. Her cough appears to have stopped troubling her. Her clothes look less loose on her slim frame. Rather than remarking on these, he says,

'You've caught the sun today. A few more times like this and you'll be brown as a berry.'

'Being with you all gives me an excuse to be out.'

'You make it sound like walking the dog.'

She giggles. 'No, but seriously, when we stop I reckon I'll just work and work, you know flat out till the exams are over. It'll only be another five weeks till they begin. And in seven and a half . . . heaven . . . heaven.' She lies with her arms spread-eagled on the ground.

'Yes, but don't overdo that work thing.'

'Whoever thought that anyone would say that to me.'

She is talking like this, more easily than expected. As long as there are still more weeks. Put the other out of her mind.

Next time when Alex walks Tony and the children right down to their corner of the Heath, Timothy notices that there is a boy little older than him playing tennis. They stop to watch. 'Do you play tennis?' Alex asks Tony.

'It's another thing I haven't done for years.'

'Oh, but it will come back, do let's have a try. Timothy will be ball boy, won't you?'

'Me too,' insists Ellen.

'Yes, you too.'

'Alex, it costs to play. Besides you have to join or something. It's not worth it for one game.'

'We could play a couple of times, come on. Why not? I'll pay, then I might play with friends later.'

'You've persuaded me,' he says. Now, with the possibility of a future, it's not so hard to let her pay.

'How's this job thing going?' she asks as they sit on the bench later that week after a half-hour of tennis. Timothy is mucking around with Alex's racket and a ball, and Ellen is running all over the court.

'I mean, really, tell me everything. Go on, tell your pal Alex. After next week you won't have me to talk to, remember?'

He grunts.

She sits on the bench beside him in dirty white shorts that she hasn't used since last summer, that still have clinging to them the smell of sun oil and sandy beaches. Over them, hanging loose, she wears a new white T-shirt. All the exposed parts of her are quickly tanning.

How very much better she looks now, almost back to normal. But afterwards, will she. Try not to think about it. Trust.

'I've had a number of meetings,' he tells her. 'I've met a lot of different people within the firm. The MD, Leo Ross, is decent enough, though he's a bit of an eccentric and takes some getting used to.'

'I wouldn't have thought you'd have much difficulty. But the whole thing, it'll be an adjustment won't it, at first, I mean?'

'Of course it will. The first few months in Tokyo are likely to be bloody strange. Besides which, there are people I'm going to miss terribly,' he looks directly at her, 'you, the kids, Carole. It will also be a challenge. I've no secure work after that; they are only employing me for six months in the first instance, leaving their options open. The rest will depend upon how I perform out there. Dicey times, eh? But you know, for all that, I'm just pleased to be getting another chance.'

'I know,' she says, 'and I'm pleased for you. Of course I . . . I don't know what I'm going to do after my A-levels are over. I'd like to take a year off, work my way round the world perhaps and take photos as I go, you know, build up a portfolio. Definitely get out of London. Angelica came up with the idea that I could train to be a kind of ecological photographer. I'm not sure what she means exactly, though I've got the general idea. Anyway, it's a thought.'

'I'm glad,' he says, 'really glad. I'd hate to think.'

'Stop it. What will you do about the kids while you're away? You haven't said.'

'I don't know. I'm hoping Carole's parents will come over. If not, we'd have to get some kind of minder, I suppose.'

'Poor Moth and Ellen.'

'Now don't *you* start wringing my heart.'

'I don't know. Mum did always try to be there when I came home from school, I'll say that for her. It did make a difference.'

'And look what a wreck you are now!'

'I hope you're teasing me,' she says, jumping off the bench, and agreeing with Timothy that it is time they stopped talking and let him play a few shots with her, as they'd promised. But still, after a few minutes she comes back to the bench.

'You were teasing, weren't you?'

'Of course I was, Alex.' He gets up too so that she won't see the emotion in his face.

It is she who says to him as they part, 'Last week then, next week.'

*

Then all of a sudden it is their last meeting. She tries to be brave, but is nervous about it. She doesn't like endings, issues being made out of things, drama. For a while she thinks about just not turning up. Wouldn't that be the easiest way? But a coward's way too. No she'd go, see it through, chew gum and tell herself, so what? What do these people matter to her? At the beginning of last autumn she hadn't even known them, she'd just been walking on the Heath on a day not unlike today and he had said . . . But autumn, winter, spring: it seemed a whole lifetime somehow. And everything we start has to come to an end, has to have a cycle, so why, she wonders, is it so hard? After all, the leaves drop off the trees and I bet they don't flinch. No, but for a time you think something's going to go on for ever, it seems as if it is, that's the killer. But I never thought. But then why, why do I mind so?

'You okay?' he asks her.

'Yeah, of course, why?'

He shakes his head. She busies herself chatting to the children.

Carole has asked him, '*Will* you bring it to a close today?' and he has told her, 'I told you I will, Carole, and I will. It's agreed between us. Don't make a big deal out of it.' 'No, I won't,' she hugs him, 'I'll just be so relieved when you tell me it's over. And you won't offer to write to her or anything like that?' 'Carole, I've never written to her.' 'You don't know what it means to me that you're doing this.' 'Well I'm doing it.' 'I'll remember it always.' 'Dangerous promises,' he warns her. He is at the door of their bedroom, she is putting her tights on, sitting on the bed. He knows he has sounded cold, distant, in these exchanges, now he goes towards her, sits down on the bed next to her and hugs her.

'I love you, you silly mug. And you have got it out of proportion, that's what makes me angry. But there you are, if you're jealous, you're jealous. I've hated to see you the way you've been these last weeks. Nothing seems worth that. We've had our ups and downs but, we're married, it's got to mean something. I don't want you unhappy.'

'Thanks,' she says, 'thanks isn't enough, but you know what I mean. What can I do for you?'

'Nothing. Just don't get at me so much, don't make me feel you don't respect me.'

'But I do respect you. I know sometimes I sound impatient. Lately I have been *trying* not to.'

'I've noticed.'

'Christ, the time!'

He knows how she'll look when she comes through the door this evening, her pencilled eyebrows and those clear blue eyes asking the question, over the heads of the children, 'Well have you done it, have you really said goodbye?' It's not what you think, he's told her many times. But what is it? Alex has been a kind of extra something in his life, he won't call it love because it doesn't express what it is he feels. And yet.

'Alex, you've given me a lift, that's the best I can tell you. And how very much I appreciate it, do you understand?'

'A pick-up?'

'You know what I mean, a pick-me-up, if you like.'

She turns away, and chews on her gum frantically, holding back emotion. Then spits the gum out into her hand and shoves it into the pocket of her jeans. She takes his hand, why not? – everything is possible, she thinks, last time.

'Bloody sticky hand,' he grumbles. But he holds her tight and they swing them gently together, the children doing the talking for them.

Half an hour later, or thereabouts, they part. In bright sunlight. On a day when the Heath is crowded, full to bursting, when the fine weather suggests the possibility of a gorgeous English summer, when people are full of plans, full of hopes. Where the mating cries above their heads, in the trees, through the long grasses, yet to be mowed, are everywhere to be heard. When the Heath seems to be full of lovers, when everything is beginning, beginning, beginning, when a new tryst is made each moment.

She hugs them each in turn. Ellen first. ''Bye you funny little thing.' ''Bye,' says Ellen waving eagerly, oh how she loves to wave. There can never be enough people on the Heath for her to wave to. Her face is one big grin. ''Bye, 'bye, 'bye.'

Then Moth – whoops, Timothy. Their hug is a long one. 'Won't we ever see you again, ever ever?' He doesn't know what he feels, pleased or sad. Some things he is pleased about, that Daddy too now calls him Timothy, that he doesn't have those horrid fluttering things in his tummy, that Mummy doesn't cry any more. Besides, the Heath is getting boring, and next week is so exciting but if only he could remember how many more days there are till next week. He pulls out of Alex's embrace and looks at her judiciously. Then hugs her again. Goodbyes are funny things, you think that you'll miss someone. You don't know whether you will or won't. You could. 'I love you, Alex.'

'I love you too, very much.'

'You taught me about mushrooms,' he suddenly tells her.

'She taught you a lot of things.'

'But Alex,' he is all excited, 'I can't remember the name of those mushrooms?'

'*Agaricus* . . . *Agaricus* . . . damn! I seem to have forgotten too.'

'Was I very naughty? You ran after me, didn't you?'

'I did. We all did. You wouldn't do that kind of thing now, would you?'

'But I'm a big boy now.'

'Yes, you are.'

It is hard for Alex to look at Tony, am I a big girl? she wonders. She pulls her upper lip down over her teeth and bites it. She is tempted to turn round and hug him and move away fast, to get this next bit over as quickly as she can. Oh, goodbyes are hateful. And anyway, the last bit isn't what's important, it's all that's gone before. Suddenly she flings her arm around his neck. She feels the shock of the skin of his face, of his cheek against hers.

'Don't go losing them any more,' she says. Then she walks away.

The Heath is so green, thinks Jerry, freshly back from France. Now all the trees are in leaf, and each a different shade. This is the best time of the year, the best. Oh he is in happy spirits, he too is tanned, and a few pounds heavier in weight, thanks to the delicious French food. His shoulder is no longer troubling him, due to the French sun. But how good, and how rare, to come back and find the weather as hot here. Angelica is in the house unpacking, but he apparently was simply getting in the way. 'You know I think I'll take a walk,' he tells her. 'After so many hours in the car I could just do with stretching my legs, are you sure you wouldn't like to come with me? We could do all that when we come back.' 'No, you go off by yourself: I'm fine.' 'I'll miss you,' he tells her. They have barely been out of one another's sight in the ten days they have been away. She cocks her head and looks at him with affection. 'You old liar,' she says.

Carole, in her office, looks out at the trees in the square. Three large horse chestnuts. She sighs. Suddenly it seems terribly stuffy in the office. She looks at her watch. If she is lucky with the bus she might just arrive in time. Grabbing her bag, she leaves the building.

Alex walks fast. First in one direction, then another. Her progress, if anyone had been watching, would have been strange to see. She appears to be zig-zagging over the Heath. First in one direction, no she will not take that path, then back. Then starting off in a different direction, then yet another. She wears the white T-shirt she has played tennis in, tucked into her jeans. Folding her arms over her breasts she appears to be clutching her sides.

Tony walks slowly, clutching the hands of his two children, particularly slowly because Ellen insists on trotting beside him and will not be carried. What with that and Timothy's questions, 'How many days in a week, how many weeks in a year, how many months in a week . . . no . . . no I mean the other way round . . . tell me again, Daddy?' he has much to occupy himself with. Still, when they reach the ponds he turns round and looks back up the hill. It seems there has not been a day in which there have been so many people on the Heath. None of them she. He didn't really expect that she would still be there. Timothy is watching two children quarrelling over a toy boat. 'Can we stay here and play just for a little bit, Daddy?'

'Okay, then home. A bath and mushy eggs on toast. How does that sound to you?' he asks his children.

'Good,' says Timothy, already hopping round the pond to get nearer to the children with their boat.

Again Tony shades his eyes, as eight months before, from the same spot his son had done, and looks up the hill. But only for a second, then turns back. He starts to make Pooh-sticks for Ellen. I wonder if one day, in another life, under pressure, working all hours of the day and night at other people's beck and call when for so long in my funny way at least I've been my own master, when the kids can make their own supper and aren't interested in Pooh-sticks and only want to know things I can no longer teach them, if I'll look back on the days of endless slow walks, and even of mushy eggs, with nostalgia. I'll certainly think about you, with nostalgia, he says in the direction of the hill. But it had to come to an end. You do understand, don't you, Alex?

'Alex! Lovey. *Alex!*'

'Oh God, Jerry, it's you, I'm sorry, I didn't at first.'

'We thought you'd be at home to greet us, with a meal ready and . . .'

'I thought it was tomorrow, didn't you say the twenty-eighth?'

'No, the twenty-seventh.'

'Oh.'

'What is it? Do you want to sit down? You look – '

He signals the nearby bench and then his eyes travel back to her face. She keeps her head down so that he shall not look at her so searchingly, but follows him towards the bench.

'I don't want to pry. I'm . . .'

'You're not. It's okay, Jerry. I've just said goodbye to Tony and the kids, we're not going to see each other any more.' She continues to look down so that their eyes should not make contact.

'Alex. Alex.' He, a man of many words, is without any that he finds adequate. Instead he sits there with her, keeping her company.

Out of nowhere a wind blows up. The branches of the trees, with their new green leaves, are tossed this way and that. White blossom is blown in their direction. She swings her legs gently and watches the blossom fall on her trainers. In the grass nearby two young squirrels are surprised to find themselves submerged in it.

'I don't want to go back, not for a while,' she says, 'but you go ahead.'

'I'll stay here with you if you'd like. Would you like?'

'I wouldn't like. But I don't want to sound rude.' She even touches his arm, feeling stronger than she has yet in relation to him. 'I hope you understand. I just want to be alone.'

Tony with the children has come level with the tennis courts.

'We seem to have been an awfully long time. I think we'll hop on a bus, Timothy.'

'We might have to wait.'

'If the wait is too long, then we'll walk. We'll see what happens, okay?'

'Okay, Daddy.'

But what is this? Timothy's little ears are scarlet with disbelief.

'Daddy, look, look, look.'

Now Tony sees. Pulling the children with him, he starts to walk faster. All of a sudden they are running, they towards her, she towards them.